# A Favor For A Fiend

## Charm City Darkness
### Book 2

# Kelly A. Harmon

Pole to Pole Publishing
Baltimore

## Other Stories by Kelly A. Harmon

# A FAVOR FOR A FIEND

ISBN-13:  978-1-941559-02-4
ISBN-10:  1-941559-02-6

*For Mom,*
*Who indulged my passion for books—*
*And Dad,*
*Who agreed with her.*

*I love you guys!*

# A Favor
## For
# A Fiend

# CHAPTER 1

THE BUS PULLED TO THE CURB IN FRONT OF Baltimore City Community College with a squeal of hydraulic brakes and the odor of diesel exhaust. Assumpta Mary-Margaret O'Connor cleared the Plexiglas shelter, felt the brief, delicate touch of November snowflakes on her head and shoulders, making her long auburn curls droop, then climbed aboard wearily, dropped her quarters into the fare box, and headed to the back of the bus. She brushed her wispy bangs off her forehead, and held her voluminous purse more tightly to her as she swept past the other passengers.

*Thank God no one sat in the back row.* She hated having to sit anywhere else. From the rear, she could see all the comings and goings.

And she could be reasonably circumspect when—*if,* she thought, correcting herself—*if* Jak ever decided to visit her again. She squeezed her eyes tightly closed, willing away the tears, realizing that he probably wouldn't. She'd done her good deed, helped him to escape the bonds of Hell where he'd been unrightfully trapped, and he had moved on as he said he must. She knew she shouldn't feel so abandoned, or so hopeful that he might come back to her. It had been six weeks since she'd seen him, after all. And his last visit had only been in a dream.

But *if* he did return, she'd be prepared, sitting in the back of the bus. She didn't need people thinking she was crazy. Because when she talked to the dead, it looked as if she talked to herself—and that looked a little bit nuts. People could think what they wanted—they'd do as they pleased anyway—she just didn't need the guys in the white coats chasing her down to take her to her own private, padded room.

Maybe all those crazy people *weren't* crazy, she thought. Maybe they chatted with the dead, too.

She sighed heavily, letting out a pent-up breath as if she'd been storing it all day, then breathed in deeply, trying to relax. She regretted it. The back of the bus smelled like urine with high notes of vomit. No relaxing here, but at least she was on her way home: the home she was going to have to move out of soon.

*I'll move out next week*, she thought. *I refuse to take advantage of Greg any longer.*

Her back itched, right between her shoulder blades, the exact location of her demon mark: the booby prize for helping Jak out of Hell. She twisted her arm up behind herself to scratch it. The mark had never bothered her before. *Why now?*

The itch grew worse, the muscles near the mark tightening.

"Greg won't mind if you stay," said a voice beside her.

She flinched. The bus hadn't stopped again, so this guy had *materialized*, not walked on board. *Just what I need*, she thought, *another damn demon.* She couldn't stop the gallop of her heart if she wanted to. A sheen of sweat broke out on her brow.

The demon's blue eyes twinkled, letting her know he knew much more about the situation than she did, and he enjoyed it. His blond hair look sun-dyed and windswept, as if he'd just come off the beach, but his nose had been broken more than once, giving him a rakish rather than boyish appearance.

He'd be attractive if she thought she could trust him. But he already knew more about her than she liked—or he'd read her mind. She didn't care for either scenario.

She detected the faintest whiff of sulfur. Then she sneezed.

"Who are you?" she asked, pulling a tissue from her purse, but keeping an eye on the creature.

"Friend of Jak's. *Dan.*" He held out his hand.

Assumpta ignored it.

"Oh, really?" Jak never mentioned anyone named Dan. "How'd you meet?" She gave him a look that said, *I don't believe a word of your bull.*

The smile in his eyes dimmed. "We were introduced by a mutual... *acquaintance.*" He put the hand he'd previously held out to her on her knee. She slapped it away, but her hand went right through his and struck her own thigh. Still, she felt the warmth of his palm as it traveled up her knee to her hip.

"Jak!" She wondered if calling for him in desperation might bring him around.

A few passengers from the front of the bus looked in her direction, then turned away. *Uh-oh, white coat time,* she thought.

"Jak can't come right now," Dan said in a soft voice, leaning toward her ear. "He's busy."

*No, he's just not allowed to come anymore,* Assumpta thought. That's what he'd told her the last time she'd seen him in person. But he'd left her with that tiny bit of hope that she might see him again. Why had he been so cruel?

"I can't imagine why you're here," Assumpta said, sliding over one seat. She pressed into the wall of the bus, trying to get as far away as possible. Dan slid along with her, trapping her in the corner seat.

"Please leave," she said.

He looked down at her lap, his hand on her thigh, and chuckled. His hand smoothed down to her knee again and fingered the edge of her hunter-green tartan skirt. *Thank God for thick woolen stockings,* she thought.

"I'm not leaving until I get a little taste of what Jak's been getting."

He leaned into her, curling his fingers under the edge of her skirt, pushing it higher. His lips touched her neck, hot and burning. She could smell the sulfur more strongly now, enveloping him like a cheap cologne. The mark on her back fluttered wildly.

Assumpta twisted away. Pushing was useless. Her hands went right through him.

His hands searched for the buttons to release the skirt, fingers fumbling at the closure. She wondered what the other passengers on the bus were seeing. Did they see Dan, or just her flailing around like a crazy person just as she feared?

"Ahhhh!" he screamed suddenly, pulling his hand from her waist. A terrible, burnt-flesh odor filled the air. "You bitch!"

He shook his hand as if to cool it, pulling away from her entirely.

*Thank you, Grandma*, she thought. Dan must have touched the religious medals she kept pinned to the hem of her skirt—medals that had originally belonged to her grandmother. Nearly all of them had been blessed at one point or another. She knew from firsthand experience that demons could not touch blessed things.

The bus stopped, making its familiar wheeze of breaks and exhaust. Assumpta catapulted from the seat, torpedoed through Dan, and jumped out the rear exit of the bus. She took off running, slinging the long handle of her purse over her head so she wouldn't lose it as she ran.

Snow fell harder now, and a breeze pushed the snowflakes across the sidewalk in front of her. The cottony whiteness seemed to insulate the city, muffling the road noise from Cold Spring Lane.

Assumpta sprinted down Kenwood, passing the topiary trees and high, wrought-iron fences that signaled she was closer to Greg's apartment than she thought. She turned left at the corner and saw the familiar covered portico.

"Where do you think you're going?" Dan materialized right next to her, running beside her at her pace. Still, she ran.

He showed her his burned hand; a spherical shape blackened his palm. She didn't stop, but continued running toward the apartment.

He shoved his hand in her face. Inky, vein-like tendrils, dark and bold, radiated out from the center, blackening his skin. "Do you see this?" She jerked away, lost her footing and stumbled, but caught herself on a lamppost and kept running.

"I'll get you for this, just as soon as I take care of it."

And then he was gone—and so was the itch on her back.

She slowed to a quick walk, breathing heavily. Despite the falling snow, she felt hot under her corduroy coat. When she reached the apartment a few minutes later, Assumpta typed the code into the keypad by the front door and let herself in, heading toward the elevator.

*Good Lord, what had she gotten herself into now?*

The elevator dropped her off in front of Greg's door. *Her door*, but not for much longer.

She unlocked the deadbolt and stepped into the marble foyer, still holding the doorknob in her hand. Entering the apartment alone had given her the willies ever since she'd been attacked by demons right here in the doorway. She looked around, seeing nothing amiss: ashes in the marble fireplace, pillows stacked neatly on the leather couches, tiny herbal wreaths still hanging in all the windows to ward off demons.

With a sigh of relief, she closed the door behind her and locked it, then knelt to the threshold with her bottle of blessed oil and salt. She poured a little on a rag, then swiped it across the floor where she'd passed. Then she checked the other rooms in the apartment to make certain all the windows were closed and still wreathed.

Finally, she felt secure enough to relax.

She headed to her bedroom, pulling her pendulum from her purse and tossing it on the nightstand. She bent to untie her leather ankle boots, then kicked them under the bed.

She needed answers, and she needed them fast.

But first, she needed to look at her demon mark.

Six weeks ago when Jak had come to her in her dreams to warn her she had one, he couldn't tell her what it did. Now, she had an unsettling feeling she knew.

# Chapter 2

A**SSUMPTA'S PRIVATE BATH CONNECTED TO THE** bedroom via a pocket door next to the closet. With a flick of her wrist, she slammed the door aside, then stripped off her dark green turtleneck and turned her back to the large vanity mirror.

Over her shoulder, she inspected her demon mark, a supernatural scar she had acquired when she helped Jak flee the bonds of his Hellish prison. The mark looked like a finely drawn tattoo in brown ink—about the size of a quarter—of an upside-down cross surrounded by a circle. It you didn't scrutinize it, it looked exactly like cross-hairs viewed through a rifle scope.

The skin around it looked red and inflamed.

*Was that due to Dan's visit?*

Her back had itched just prior to his appearing. Did the mark act like a beacon? Why was her skin so red? And did the mark look darker? The lines thicker? Was the skin on the inside of the circle just a tad bit darker than it used to be?

*Oh, that's just what I need,* she thought, *a demonic skin condition that changes with each infernal encounter.* She thought she might be sick.

"Jak!" She waited a minute for him to appear, hoping he would come this time. When he didn't, gooseflesh prickled her skin and she felt a sudden chill.

"Where the hell could he be?" she muttered.

Assumpta stepped back into the bedroom and pulled up the hem of her skirt. Safety-pinned underneath, where no one could see, were a wad of seventeen religious medals: several versions of the Miraculous Medal depicting Mary, two Sacred Heart medals showing Christ, one of Saint Jude, and another of Saint Michael the Archangel—which she loved because he looked like a strong and fearless warrior, and of course, Saint Christopher, the patron saint of travelers. Her grandmother had worn them every day, pinned to the slip beneath her housecoat or day dress. And now Assumpta did, too.

*Thank heavens.*

She was certain Dan had burned his hand on them and that was what had sent him fleeing. She rummaged through her jewelry box and found a long chain to secure the medals onto and put it around her neck. She wasn't taking them off anymore. Not even at night.

She pulled off her skirt and hose, changed into a white T-shirt and thick, navy blue sweats, then sat cross-legged on the floor. With her back leaning against the bed, she picked up her pendulum. From the top nightstand drawer, she retrieved a piece of paper with a semicircle drawn on it. The alphabet was written along the arc, each letter precisely drawn and equidistant. Assumpta placed it on the floor in front of her, the alphabet facing her so she could easily read it. If she asked the pendulum anything other than a yes-or-no question, she would read the answer as it swung back and forth over the message chart. *Yes* and *No* were signified by a clockwise or counterclockwise rotation.

The pendulum had served her well in the past, helping her answer difficult questions and find missing objects. Finding things was her talent. Usually, someone else paid her to do the finding. That was how she had met Greg. It wasn't often she was her own customer.

She wrapped the thin, braided cord of the pendulum twice around her second and third fingers and let the teardrop-shaped crystal drop to the length of its string, about ten inches. She held it steady and waited for it to stop swinging. When it hung perfectly still, she closed her eyes and let the question develop in her mind.

Then she asked, "Where's Jak?"

Silently, she used his full name, always careful not to say it out loud in case something evil listened. In the spirit world, knowing someone's name meant having power over him, power to command or enslave. She was careful to keep Jak's full name a secret.

The pendulum hung slack. She didn't like that. The pendulum not responding meant it didn't know the answer. If it didn't know the answer, it meant Jak wasn't on this plane of existence. Well, she knew he hadn't gone to Hell—so Jak was probably in Purgatory. Maybe he'd even moved on to Heaven by now. She could only hope.

"We'll start with something easier," she said aloud. "Was my visitor Dan a demon?"

With barely a moment's pause, the pendulum started a clockwise rotation.

She nodded. "I knew that. But it's always nice to have confirmation when dealing with evil spirits."

"Will he be back?"

The pendulum continued its clockwise motion.

*Great.* "How can I get rid of him?"

The pendulum jerked and hung slack again. No answers there, at least not yet. She'd try again another time.

She thought to ask why he was following her, but she already knew the answer to that: the mark. Apparently, it made her susceptible to any demon that crossed her path. It must give off a scent or signal or *something* that alerted demons to her presence.

Usually, humans were off limits to the creatures unless they invited evil into their lives somehow. That line in the sand, for her at least, didn't mean anything to roving demons.

The mark, apparently, made her fair game.

"How do I get rid of the mark?"

The pendulum hung slack for a moment, then began a back and forth motion over the message chart.

"S," Assumpta said, guessing by the trajectory what letter the pendulum moved above. But, the pendulum continued swinging back and forth. S was wrong.

"R?"

The glass teardrop hiccupped on the string, then changed direction, signaling that she had guessed correctly. It veered left.

E was the closest vowel in that direction. "E," she said.

The pendulum changed again, back to a similar pitch as the first direction.

"T." It continued to swing.

"S," she said. And then it changed to swing toward E again.

"R, E, S, E...*research*?"

The pendulum swung clockwise and Assumpta threw it aside. It slapped the wall in front of her and fell in a crumpled heap.

"What do you think *this* is?" she asked, referring to using the pendulum. Then she felt bad about throwing it. She retrieved the pendulum, checking to see if she'd chipped or broken the glass, and then, satisfied she hadn't, wound the cord around her hand neatly, peeled it off and sat it on the night stand. "I'm sorry," she said. "I appreciate your help."

Dowsing wasn't foolproof. You got your answers from the universe, or rather, spirits in the universe. And sometimes, the spirits just didn't have the answer. She knew that, but knowing it didn't make things easier to bear when finding answers was slow and frustrating.

"I wish Jak were here," she said.

# CHAPTER 3

ASSUMPTA MIGHT BE A DEMON MAGNET, BUT SHE still needed answers. She had to leave the apartment, despite the risk she might encounter other demons. *No one can stay cooped up in their house forever*, she thought. Even if she had every amenity known to man, she was sure to go crazy without some external contact with someone.

And besides, whatever she needed to get rid of this mark was outside the apartment. She had to go and obtain it. It certainly wouldn't find its way to her by itself.

Still, she took precautions. She wore her grandmother's medals on the long chain around her neck—and the chain was never coming off again, if she could help it—but she'd pulled two Miraculous Medals off the wad, her least favorite, and the ones she had the most duplicates of, and attached one of them with metal twist ties to the bottom of a ring on each hand so they dangled down into her palms. If a demon materialized anywhere near her, she wanted to be able to burn it through with a touch.

She took the bus downtown to the main branch of the Enoch Pratt Library, one of the oldest free libraries in the United States. The Roland Park branch would have been closer, but it was a modern affair opened in 2007. She needed access to the older collections from the building built in 1931, where everything was moved after the original 1830s building was shut down.

She loved the main branch with its marble floors and columns, map rooms, musty card catalogs, and the genealogy center with its old-fashioned microfilm readers still in use. The building on Cathedral Street was as long and wide as the city block, and held more history than she could fathom.

And while Pratt had made great strides to meet the electronic age, many of its treasures were still buried in the stacks. *If I want the most obscure information*, Assumpta thought, as the bus rattled and wheezed its way down St. Paul Street, *I need to visit, not just jump online.*

Surely there would be a book on demon marks there. Something obscure that Mr. Enoch Pratt and his donated million would have acquired. (When one donated money in the 1800s, a million-point-five bought an awful lot.)

Hopefully she'd find something with a local angle in the collection. Demons were like ghosts, right? Haunting one particular area? She wasn't certain about that, but she aimed to find out.

Assumpta stepped off the bus and headed through the front door of the library, her footsteps echoing on the marble floor. She could have bypassed the reference desk and headed straight for the computers in the back, something she'd done a hundred times before. But now she needed access to the library's *hidden collections*, those which hadn't yet been added to the electronic database. She'd need a librarian's help.

It used to be that libraries didn't talk about the books that hadn't made it to the electronic software yet. Instead, they'd brag about all the items available electronically. (*We have four million records on line!*) Then they realized their foot traffic was diminishing. And so was the advertising money and the cash they made on copies and vending.

They needed an incentive to get people to return to the brick-and-mortar buildings, and *voila! Hidden Collections* were born. The ugly stepchildren got their day in the sun, albeit only locally.

*It's amazing how the right spin on things makes everything seem so different*, Assumpta thought.

The woman behind the desk looked up as Assumpta approached. Assumpta smiled. "I'm looking for something on the occult," she said, "breaking curses, hexes, that sort of thing."

The librarian nodded, shuffling through a few papers on her desk. "You should start with the Poe collection. Up the stairs and to the left. Here, take this." She handed Assumpta a photocopy of a newspaper story about the collection published in the *Baltimore News American*. The paper had stopped publication years before she was born, but her mom and dad still mentioned it every once in a while. She glanced at it as she walked up the stairs.

And then she saw the room containing nearly four thousand books related to Edgar Allan Poe in some fashion or another. According to the news story, Poe's small collection had been added to over the decades by family members and then donated to the library. So it wasn't really just Poe's collection. But with this many books, she was bound to find what she needed.

"Can I help you?" A young woman with blond hair pulled back in a low ponytail, and wearing a badge that said *Librarian*, approached Assumpta.

Assumpta repeated what she'd told the triage librarian downstairs and added, "I'm specifically looking for anything about demon marks. Do you think there might be something in the collection?"

The woman ushered her over to a small section in the back corner of the dark-paneled room, then handed Assumpta a pair of white cotton gloves to wear while she touched the books. The librarian showed her how to handle the aged volumes in order to prevent damage, then left Assumpta alone to do her research.

Assumpta pulled off the gloves. *How can you turn pages with gloves on?* She'd just be super careful with the fragile edges.

Judging from the titles, only three or four volumes in the small area the librarian indicated looked like they might have information she needed. She'd start with those, then read the contents or thumb through indexes—if there were any—to see if any others fit the bill.

She chose three and sat at a scarred wooden table to do her research.

Despite the fairly recent renovations, this room was poorly lit. In fact, Assumpta felt a bit uncomfortable alone in a room with Poe's musty books. The solid marble floors and walls of this place made her feel entombed. The air fairly echoed with sounds from the past. No doubt Poe would be laughing at her if he could see her right now.

She wondered if the place was haunted.

"I understand you're looking for information on demons," said a man from the doorway.

She gasped, knocking a book from the table at the unexpected interruption. Her heart leapt to her throat, then plummeted, beating riotously. She hadn't heard any footsteps on the marble floor of the hallway.

"You scared me," she said, looking at his feet. He wore hard-soled shoes. Why hadn't she heard him?

"My apologies." He smiled with even, white teeth, bright against the chocolate of his skin, but his smile didn't reach his mocha eyes. Was he angry about having to help her? He wore a fashionable—and probably expensive—suit, unlike the more casual employees of Enoch Pratt. From this distance, she couldn't read his name tag. "I'm an expert on demons," he added, when she didn't speak.

Assumpta waited for her pounding heart to quit playing a cadence against her ribs before she responded. "I wasn't aware the library had an expert on demons."

"Demons, the occult, things that go bump in the night. Enoch Pratt employs many experts." He smiled again, barely there and insincere. "I can probably tell you everything you need to know—without cracking a book."

Assumpta studied him for a moment, then concluded it couldn't hurt to ask. "Demon marks," she said. "I need to know how they work. And, I need to know how to get rid of one."

He quirked an eyebrow. "There's no such thing as demon marks, miss."

"I'm not certain you're the expert I need," Assumpta said. "Thank you, though." She looked back at the book she'd been studying.

"You're a believer, then?" He took a step into the room. When Assumpta looked up, he gestured to the chair across from her. "May I?"

She nodded cautiously. But when the man got within ten or so feet of her, she felt a distinct itch between her shoulder blades. Her heart thumped anew. *What good is a demon detector if it's got such a short range?* She scooted her chair back, putting more distance between the two of them, wondering how fast she could get to an exit if she needed one. The mark on her back itched and fluttered like crazy as the demon sat down across from her.

"Well, believing..." He laced his fingers together and rested his hands on the table. He leaned toward her. "*Believing* means something different. It is belief that gives a demon mark its power. The more you fear—the more you hate—the stronger it is. You can't be harmed by a demon unless you've got a mark. Once you're marked, *beware.*"

Yeah, she got that.

But what he said didn't exactly ring true. She was thinking about the minor demons that had followed her and Greg around before they were able to banish them. They had certainly caused both her and Greg pain. "I'm not sure that's entirely right," she said, her voice tight and dry. She swallowed. "I didn't used to believe in demons until I was attacked by one. Literal pain and blood tend to make one a believer."

"You've been demon cursed." His eyebrows rose. He looked interested in that bit of information.

She nodded. Apparently she had—cursed *and* marked. How did she get so lucky? "What's the difference between being demon cursed and demon marked?

"A demon curse is the only other way a demon can harm a human. It's misfortune and hurt—and most definitely pain— visited upon you by demons, because you've gotten in their way, or crossed them, or just happened to be in the wrong place at the wrong time. But at the end of the day, you still own your soul." He looked her up and down. "You're certain you haven't made a deal with a demon?"

*Wait—soul? I no longer own my soul?* That thought had her heart jumping anew. Yes, she and Jak had made a deal: she helped him escape from Hell in trade for information. But Jak wasn't a demon. He wasn't evil. She knew that in her gut.

Assumpta shook her head, denying any pact-making.

"Then how did you get marked?" he mused, more to himself than her.

"Who says I'm marked?"

He leaned in close. "I could smell it on you all the way from the lobby."

And now she caught the pungent scent of sulfur. A bead of sweat broke out on her forehead. It took everything she had not to raise her hand and brush it away. She needed to show strength here, not weakness. Demons were a bit like dogs weren't they? Striking at the runners? The cowards? The weaklings?

"Who are you?" she asked.

"As I said, an expert on demons."

"You *are* a demon."

"Which makes me an expert," he said with a wry smile. "There are only two ways to get a demon mark. The first is to do something so heinous that you cannot be forgiven. Something you'd hate yourself for, if you'd realized you'd done it. Something that would make evil smile." He chuckled. "You'd be surprised how little that actually takes. The mark in this case is almost invisible. It looks quite natural, like a mole or a freckle."

"And the other?"

"You become marked if you make a deal with a demon—though you deny you've done this. Once you obtain your part of the bargain, the mark appears." He looked at her thoughtfully. "If you didn't make the deal yourself, my sweet, then you must have been made party to the deal after the fact."

*Oh.* She felt the blood drain out of her face. *Now it was starting to make sense.*

"Think hard," he said, looking her up and down. "I can't picture you doing anything evil, not even by accident. You smell too good." He leaned toward her and breathed in deeply. "You're wearing something blessed. If you'd done something so horrible, I suspect you wouldn't find whatever it is so comfortable to wear."

She lifted her hands to show him her palms with the Miraculous Medals dangling from her rings, and he sat back abruptly. He looked frightened for a moment, then regained his aplomb. "Funny that you can't remember. Maybe you were tricked, unknowingly, into the bargain."

She thought of Jak. He'd seemed so sincere when she helped him. Had he been telling her tales? No. She couldn't believe it. She'd helped him escape Hell, and he'd saved her life at least once. There was no way he had tricked her into anything. He simply hadn't realized that he'd drawn her into his own pact with a demon. That had to be the way of it.

"The how of it doesn't really matter right now," Assumpta said. The fact that she'd lost ownership of her soul did. "I really need to get rid of this mark. Can you remove it?" *It didn't hurt to ask, right?*

"Oh, no," he replied with a twist of his lips. "Only the originating demon can do that. You can renegotiate, of course, though that's seldom done. Your circumstances must change dramatically to tip the scales. More often, a demon-marked individual will make a more amenable deal with another demon. Someone who can protect her from the first demon—" he paused, drawing out the inevitable "—for a price."

He reached into his left breast pocket and pulled out a white business card. He laid it on the scarred wooden table, turned it around to face her, then pushed it in her direction.

"Who are you?" she asked again.

"My name's on the card."

She picked it up and read the name aloud. "Pournelle Ahb—" As she said the syllables, the name disappeared off the paper, burned away as she articulated the letters. She dropped the flaming card to the table where it burned briefly before the flames extinguished. All that remained was a small pile of ashes.

"Now that was just a waste," Pournelle said. He waved his hand, and the ashes twirled around like a dust devil, then danced off the table where they fell in a heap. He leaned toward her. "I'm already here and ready to deal."

"You can leave now," Assumpta said. "I don't need what you're offering."

"You don't even know what you're up against."

"Neither do you! And I'm fairly certain I don't want to take the deal you're so eager to make."

He stood. "You won't get a better deal than what I'm offering now. The deal gets worse the longer it takes you to accept it."

"Go away," she said.

He smiled, reached into his breast pocket for another card, and pushed it across the table to her. "Call me when you're ready to talk."

Then Assumpta remembered from when she first met Jak that she had to dismiss him three times. "Go away, go away, go away."

Pournelle disappeared in a puff of smoke, but his card stayed where he'd left it.

Assumpta closed the book she'd been looking at and pushed all the books to the center of the table.

*Woe betide mankind if deals can be made so casually in the afterlife,* she thought.

But maybe there was hope. She had a sudden idea: could the mark be erased in the confessional? All sins were forgiven if you repented them...even the ones for things you couldn't remember doing. Maybe she worried for nothing. Maybe the absolution of a priest could remove the mark.

She'd make an appointment to see Father Tony in the morning.

# CHAPTER 4

ASSUMPTA NOTICED GREG'S DUFFELL BAG DROPPED
in the foyer as she performed her homecoming ritual, looking
for signs the apartment contained unwanted guests. He was home
from his trip, and her cleansing rituals hadn't been breached.

Another roommate might have thought she was crazy, but it had
been Greg who came to her with a demon problem to begin with.
He didn't just *put up* with the blessed salt and protection spells; he
*participated*. Greg had learned firsthand the power of a demon curse
and appreciated her knowledge. He'd even converted to Catholicism
based on her beliefs, but not because she'd asked him to. He'd made
that decision on his own.

They'd fought demons together and won. Too bad she didn't feel
for him what she felt for Jak, because Greg was the total package:
smart, rich, and handsome. And he liked her, too. She felt bad she
couldn't reciprocate.

Which was why she needed to move out. She'd moved in to help
him solve his demon curse. And now that she'd succeeded, it was time
to move on. Literally.

She pushed the door shut behind her.

"Greg! I'm home," she said.

"In the kitchen!" came his reply. She turned right through the arched doorway and into the large kitchen. A pan heated on the stove while Greg, hair still damp from a recent shower, pulled ingredients out of the industrial-sized fridge—eggs, sausage, mushrooms, onions—and piled them on the granite counter top.

She smelled coffee brewing.

"Omelets?" she asked.

He stood back from the door and grinned. "Is there anything else?"

She laughed. "Don't you mean, it's the only thing you can cook?"

His eyes twinkled while he stood up tall and pretended indignation. "Is it a crime if the only thing I can cook is one of my favorite things in the world to eat?"

"I'm sure there's a correlation there somewhere."

"Probably," said Greg, "but I refuse to own up to it. I will admit to being an omelet genius, however. And if you'd care to join me, you'll agree."

"You are an omelet genius," she replied dutifully. "Can I help?"

"You can slice the onions while I brown the sausage."

"Done. How was your trip?"

Greg tore open the package of sausage, laid the ground meat in the warm pan, and used a spatula to break it up into smaller pieces. "We found another urn." He turned to her and raised an eyebrow. "It looks Roman and was probably once sealed, but it's long been cracked and opened. I have photos."

"Do you think it's related to the first?"

"Probably. But I also think we have nothing to worry about. Whatever was in this jar is long gone."

"Or maybe still in the area?"

Greg gave the sausage a stir and reached for the mushrooms. He tore the plastic covering from the blue Styrofoam tray and walked to the sink to wash them. "What makes you think whatever was in the urn—if there was anything in there—stayed in the area? It was finally free. Wouldn't it want to go back to where it came from? Or go back to take revenge on whatever imprisoned it in the jar?"

"I'm not sure," Assumpta said. She dumped the diced onions into the pan with the sausage. "I'm investigating a local angle on demons. What if they, like ghosts, tend to stay in one area?"

"Are you suggesting there are some local demons around here?" He pushed the mushrooms in Assumpta's direction and stirred the sausage.

She dumped the mushrooms on her cutting board and started to chop. "I'm saying that I just happened to bump into two of them." She told him what happened on the bus and at the library.

"Are you all right?" He rushed toward her, looking her over.

"I'm fine." She gently pushed him back toward the stove.

"But if what you say is true, you didn't just *bump* into them," Greg said. "They can locate you based on your mark. How does it lead them to you? Can they get inside the apartment?"

"I don't know how the mark works...and I don't think they can enter the apartment, not with all windows sealed with holy water and blessed salt."

"Where's your *friend* Jak?" Greg stirred the sausage and onion mixture with the spatula, then raised the utensil to point at her. "Shouldn't *he* be helping out with this? He's the one that got you into this trouble." Greg lowered the spatula back to the pan and stirred again, chopping the sausage into smaller bits.

Assumpta could hear Greg's annoyance in the tone of his voice, but she couldn't blame him. It was tough for a flesh-and-blood man to compete with a spirit.

"I don't know," she said, keeping her tone flat. No sense alerting Greg that not knowing was killing her.

"He got what he wanted and he's gone," Greg said. "You'll note that *I'm* still here."

"Maybe Jak couldn't help himself," Assumpta said. "Maybe he's hurt somewhere, needing our assistance, and he can't come back to help." She felt herself getting a tiny bit hysterical. "Did you ever think of that? Or, maybe God reined him in, and now that his soul has lost its demon taint, he was ushered into Heaven. Or maybe he's been captured, and he's back in Hell."

"And maybe he just didn't need you anymore and he took off."

The coffeepot gave one last steamy gurgle as it finished brewing, and Assumpta reached for a heavy mug. "I think you've got it backwards, Greg," she said. "*You* got what you wanted, and *I'm* still here." She poured herself a cup of coffee and took a sip, letting the hot liquid cool on her tongue a moment before swallowing. "But now that you're no longer cursed, and apparently I still am, it's time I moved out. Consider this my official notice."

"Assumpta," Greg turned pleading eyes in her direction, his anger gone.

"Save it." She hardened her features. She had to stop giving in.

Greg took one look at her, tossed the spatula onto the counter—knocking over the pepper mill—and turned off the gas under the pots. Then he stormed out of the kitchen, leaving the eggs to scorch on the still-hot burner.

# CHAPTER 5

JAK STROLLED PAST THE REMAINS OF THE TEMPLE OF Saturn, remembering its full glory. Ironic that even a temple dedicated to a God of Time wasn't itself immune to it. *The passage of centuries brings even the mightiest of empires down,* he thought.

And Hell, he'd felt every bit of the snail's pace of eons ticking by in his Hellish captivity.

The urn had not been a place of darkness and restriction, instead it was as bright as Rome on a summer day, with an open window to the world—only cold—so cold that he burned from it, his bones radiating the chill, his frame rattling with each shiver. Inside the urn, the landscape was vast and desolate, and absent of everything. And though there were others trapped with him, there were times he'd been lonely enough to die—but he'd been sustained by the demon's curse to remain alive and sit idly by and watch eternity pass.

He'd seen all of Rome implode upon itself, and the rise of other nations. He'd seen everything he'd ever loved die, and the birth of all kinds of wondrous inventions as time marched on.

Still, Saturn's dilapidated temple saddened him, casting a pall on his mission. Knowing about its destruction and seeing it in person, were two different things.

*Could he ever make up for the mistake he made? The one that had condemned him to Hell and an eternity trapped in the urn?*

That was why he was here now. He couldn't help the men who were gone, but he could do something, *maybe*, for their descendants—even if it took this entire life to do so.

But he hoped it wouldn't. Because as soon as he found forgiveness, he'd be on the first plane to the States to help Assumpta. He no longer had powers in this human form, but he had knowledge—more knowledge than a man had a right to know, thanks to the time spent in the urn. And maybe when he'd finished what he came to do, he could help her, and himself, just one more time.

It wasn't as if she was the only one demon marked.

He looked over his shoulder, suddenly afraid. He wiped the sweat from his brow. The Roman Forum was an eerie place in the wee hours of the morning. The full moon shone down with spotlight glare, bouncing off the marble. It made the old monuments gleam, but he found himself chilled, sweating with the knowledge that he was more vulnerable now than when he'd been a legionnaire. He had no armor to protect himself and no weapon.

He wore black denim pants and a gray concert T-shirt with "Judas Priest" emblazoned on the front. A photo of a hand squeezing a razor blade was centered under the band's name. He'd preferred the irony of the *Hell Bent for Leather* shirt, but the graphic didn't grab him as much, and now given the freedom of choosing what to wear, he'd gone with a style he both liked and one that implied he was tough and could handle himself. He'd have preferred a military uniform, but he was no longer a soldier—and as much as he felt like one in his heart, he had no claim to the honor now.

Denim and leather were comfortable once they'd been worn a few times. They just didn't offer as much protection as armor, but he wouldn't need any armor. He hoped.

He hurried down Via dei Fori Imperiali, paved now and filled with cars even at this early hour. Already, the odor of petrol obliterated the fresh scent of morning. Where were these people going? He lost the worried feeling. Nothing would attack him in full view of others, right?

Fifteen minutes later, he found himself in front of the Pantheon and gasped. Though buildings and sidewalks had sprung up around it, it looked hardly changed despite the passage of centuries. Then he chided himself, *Why am I surprised?* In 609, the Byzantine emperor Phocas gave the building to Pope Boniface, and for that reason alone it remained one of the most well-preserved monuments of ancient Rome. The Pope had turned it into a church.

Marcus Agrippa had commissioned it as a monument to all the Roman gods. Hadrian had rebuilt it after a fire, and Trajan again after him. But only the Catholic Church preserved it. Jak wondered, *could any of its past remain?*

He jogged up the steps of the portico, past its sixteen Corinthian columns and through the rectangular vestibule, until he reached the large circular building of the Pantheon proper. Inside, things had changed mightily since he'd been here last. He knew the Catholics held Mass here on high holy days, but he hadn't realized it had also been turned into a tomb. Two kings of Italy and one of their wives were buried there, as was the painter Raphael. Gone were the statues of the Roman gods. He felt a pang of regret to have seen this. Sometimes, the reality of memory was best left untouched.

He turned to the left and was stunned to see a monumental painting depicting the Assumption—the Catholic belief that Mary was carried physically to heaven by angels—and Assumpta's namesake. *Could this be a sign?*

Moonlight shown down from the oculus—a hole in the ceiling— in the center of the rotunda. Its brilliant whiteness cast light into the center of the large chamber, but not quite to the boundary of the circular wall. He pulled a tiny flashlight from his pocket, one of the many fine conveniences he loved about this century.

He cast the light on the painting. Mary, depicted in her usual blue, was being bodily lifted to Heaven by cherubs. The painting was gorgeous, as was most Renaissance art. It might have moved him, were he a Christian, but he was a child of his pagan upbringing. He believed more in the Roman pantheon of gods than a single ruler of men.

Perhaps that was what had led him here.

He approached the painting, paying careful attention to the marble to the left of the frame. It had been eons since he'd stood in this location, but he hadn't forgotten. He ran his fingers down the crack of marble, feeling for the catch between the stones, a place where the marble appeared to meet perfectly, but left room for his index finger to push.

*Click.* He found it.

He heard a distant sound of rumbling gears, felt the marble beneath his feet vibrate softly, as if a truck passed by on the street outside. The sound of stone on stone overpowered the gears, and a large marble block indented into the wall.

Jak had to bend to fit into the crevice made by the three-foot-tall block. But he wedged himself into the black hole, then pushed it shut from inside the hidden tunnel. A set of stairs led down below the portico, then turned and led beneath the rotunda.

In his time, there had been no paintings and no statues of the Virgin. Instead, there had been sculptures of Mars and Venus, and people marveled at the roof—which mimicked the heavens—instead of just seeing it as some architectural wonder.

He shook his head. How could one god have completed such splendor on earth? Only a pantheon of gods, working in concert, could have done so. *How weak the philosophy of modern man,* he thought.

The stairs led farther down, each marble tread worn by the passage of a millennia of sandaled feet, for surely none other had passed this way since his time. His *original* time. The scent of decay, overlaid with dust, grew stronger the further he descended.

Another turn, and he was at the bottom.

Jak turned to his left, shining the flashlight on the wall, hoping a torch still resided in the sconce. He was in luck. Pulling a lighter from his pocket, he put it to the torch, and was rewarded by light suddenly blazing through the square cellar. The torchlight glared off strategically placed mirrors hanging on the walls and several central columns, the design engineered to light the entire space.

A sea of brass shields awaited him, covering the bones of the best of the Roman army. Here lay leaders and foot soldiers alike, those judged worthy enough to be buried here. Leaders among men, by word or by deed. Many here had been betrayed by him when he'd been fooled into releasing the captured demons. His bones weren't here.

He knelt. Wordless. Thoughtless. Taking in the solemnity of it all. Cold seeped through him. He wasn't certain if it were the literal temperature that chilled him or the graveness of this place, the site of all his fallen comrades.

"I'm sorry," he said, his words gruff, his voice unused for so long. "It was wrong, and I beg your forgiveness. I know I cannot put it right. I accept your hatred, but know that no one can hate me more than myself. I know I am the cause of Rome's fall."

He bowed his head. From the distance of the far wall, he heard a scuffling among the bones. He stood and moved closer, waving the flashlight beam in that direction for better sight.

Then he stumbled backward, falling on his ass as he retreated from the skeleton rising from the dead: a femur here, a tibia there, a jawbone from somewhere else, pieced together from various corpses.

No sun shone here to bleach the bones. Damp stains pervaded their exterior to a mottled brown. Wet earth and wisps of cloth or hair clung to the skull. Beetles played jail in its rib cage. When finally a complete skeleton stood before Jak, flames erupted in its eye sockets. It bent to pull a red Roman cloak from another corpse, and draped it Greek-style over one shoulder. A scythe appeared in its hand, and its jawbone clacked as if it practiced for speech.

"Samael." Jak recognized the reaper instantly in his skeletal guise. A millennia ago Jak would have called him Mars, god of war, and bowed down to him on bended knee. Jak stopped his backward crawl. He found his footing and stood. Heart beating wildly in his chest for the first time in eons, he wondered, after all these years of a half-life trapped in Hell, if he would finally meet his end.

# CHAPTER 6

A SSUMPTA TOOK A DEEP BREATH AND KNOCKED on Father Tony's office door.

She smiled when he opened it. "Hi, Father. Do you have a few minutes? I need your help."

"For you, *always*," he said, stepping back to let her pass.

She took a seat in front of his desk. He'd obviously been hard at work on something when she arrived—*Sunday's sermon?* Stacks of books littered his desk, and several others lay propped open beside piles of documents, all strewn about as if he'd been doing intense research. His Waterman pen lay on top of a few blank sheets of paper. He didn't type.

"What can I help you with?" he asked, turning back into the office but leaving the door open. Now that Father Hughes was gone—possessed and killed by a demon—they had no worries about anyone listening in.

Assumpta forced a bright, sunny smile, though inside, she didn't feel cheerful at all. How should she broach this? There was no easy way to tell Father Tony about the demon mark. She could tiptoe all around it, but in the end, she'd still have to tell him she was *marked*. She should just get it over with, she decided, so she plunged in. "I've been demon-marked. And I need to know if you can remove it, perhaps by a rite or holy water or maybe in the confessional."

Silence.

He looked at her hands, and she smiled again, not quite as sunny.

"It's not like last time," she said, lifting her right hand and wiggling the fingers.

The last time she'd had such a problem, she'd been fighting demonic gargoyles—minions of a high demon of Hell. When Greg had shattered one, she'd touched the broken pieces with her bare hand and they'd been absorbed under her skin. Her hand had turned to stone—until Jak had fixed it for her.

"Then I'm not sure what you mean, dear."

She squared her shoulders. "I'd better show you," she said. "Maybe you'll understand then." She started unbuttoning her shirt.

"What are you doing?" Father Tony practically shouted. He stood from his chair and came around the desk. "You can't disrobe in here."

"I'm not *disrobing*," she said, undoing another button. "I only need to undo one more. I can slip this down off my shoulders and you can take a look. The mark is on my back."

He looked dubious but walked behind her chair. Assumpta pulled her hair to the side and shrugged her shirt down a few inches. "Do you see it?"

"I see a tattoo," Father Tony said, censure in his voice. "When did you get that?"

"It's not a tattoo. It came from a demon."

"Assumpta…" He sat down in the chair next to her, his expression disappointed.

Irritation evident in her voice, she said, "I know it looks like a tattoo, but you've got to believe me on this. How many demons do I have to fight before you'll take my words at face value?"

He sighed, running his hands down his thighs to his knees. "You're right. Forgive me, please. Old habits die hard. Tell me what's going on."

Assumpta told him about Dan and about meeting Pournelle in Enoch Pratt Library.

"I assume you haven't tried blessed salt or holy water?"

"Well, no," she said, "but not because of the same complications as last time. I have no problem handling either, or my Bible, or anything else that's been blessed." She offered him a wry smile. "I just can't reach the mark."

"Well, I can remedy that. Let's try a few things and see where we get."

He stood and walked to the other side of his desk, and bent to reach the bottom drawer on the right. He retrieved a chrismatory—a glass bottle containing holy oil—a small plastic bottle with a white cross on it containing holy water, and a glass jar of holy salt similar to the one that Assumpta carried: the one Holy Rosary sold by the case during their May Day carnival and celebration. Father Tony stood and toed the drawer shut, then walked back around the desk and sat the oil and salt containers on the chair next to Assumpta.

"Let me see your back," he said, unscrewing the lid on the holy water vial and putting his thumb across the opening. He tilted the bottle and wet his thumb and started reciting a prayer in Latin.

"What are you saying?" Assumpta asked him.

"A cleansing prayer. I normally say it on the altar before Mass, asking God to wash the sins from my hands...I figured it couldn't hurt. It's the first thing I could think of. Although, I suppose we could simply ask God to remove this without resorting to prepared prayer." He reached for her back and then hesitated. "I'm afraid I'm going to hurt you."

She wondered if he were really afraid of hurting her. Maybe he just had a major aversion to touching female flesh. But it wasn't as if they were strangers. He'd baptized her, for heaven's sake. Could it really be that much of a problem?

"You're not going to hurt me," Assumpta replied.

The priest gave her a skeptical look.

"Okay," she amended. "I hope you're not going to hurt me." *I couldn't get that lucky,* she thought.

Father Tony took a deep breath, then touched the holy water to her skin, rubbing his thumb across the top of the mark. "Dear Lord, please remove this demon mark from your child, Assumpta. Help her to walk in thy grace, and protect her from all the evils of the world."

The water felt cool on her skin; his touch, soft. She gave an involuntary shiver, her shoulders quivering.

"Do you feel anything?" Father Tony asked.

"Nothing out of the ordinary."

"And nothing has happened," he said. "I can still see the mark, but at least your skin didn't blister and smoke as your hand did when you were cursed before."

"Thank heaven for small favors."

"Let's try the oil."

Father Tony held his thumb over the open mouth of the chrismatory and upturned the bottle. Then he sat it carefully on the chair. She felt him brush aside a stray hair, then place his thumb between her shoulder blades and rub it along the lines of the mark—quickly as if he wanted to get this over with as fast as possible.

"Anything?" he asked.

She shook her heard.

"Again, nothing here either." Father Tony replaced the lid of the chrismatory.

Assumpta's shoulders slumped. Outside, a car horn penetrated the window, two honks, and then there was silence. "I'm afraid the salt's not going to work, either."

"We can forgo it, if you like."

She shook her head. "No. If we don't try, I'll always wonder if the salt might have done the trick. We've got to try it, if for nothing else than completeness," she said. "If it doesn't work, at least I won't be wondering if it might have."

"Only if you're certain."

"I am."

The tin lid on the salt jar stuck. Father Tony rapped it on the edge of his worn, wooden desk and then tried it again. It popped open with a metallic *thump*.

"All right," he said, and dumped a pinch of the salt into his cupped palm. "This is going to get messy."

"Just do it."

He flattened his palm against her back and rubbed. The salt crystals scratched against her skin. *Maybe he could scratch it off my back*, Assumpta thought.

"Nothing's happening," he said.

"Okay, you can stop." She waited for him to brush most of the crystals away, then shrugged her blouse up over her shoulders and buttoned it. "I don't know what to do, Father. If I don't get rid of the mark, the demons will continue to come after me."

"How did you get away from them yesterday?"

"One left of his own accord. The second touched my holy medal juju."

"Holy medal *juju*?"

Assumpta sighed. Poor choice of words, she thought, but how would she ever bring him around to her thinking if she didn't cross his boundaries once in a while?

She explained about the holy medals, then pulled the chain from around her neck to show him. She hadn't explained the medicine bag, but he frowned when he saw it.

"And the leather pouch?"

"American Indian medicine bag."

"I know what it is," he said, a tone of exasperation in his voice. "You disrespect God by—"

"This one was made by a woman of the Apache tribe in Idaho. It contains some healing herbs and some items special to me. If God made the Indians, too, as I suspect he did, he should have no problem with me respecting their religion."

"You want to add blasphemy to your list of sins?"

Assumpta sat back in the chair. This wasn't like Father Tony. He wasn't usually *open*, per se, to other religions when they butted up against his Catholic sensibilities, but he wasn't usually so vitriolic—or bigoted—either.

"Is something going on, Father?"

He moved the blessed items from the chair and sat down next to her. "I am afraid for you," he said. "Consorting with demons, fighting minions, poor Father Hughes's demonic possession and murder—"

"None of which I asked for. But I'm in the fight now, and I can't pull out until it's all done."

"I can't help but feel if you counted on the Lord to help you..." He turned his hands palm up and shrugged. "Let Him guide you back to the Catholic faith and all would be well."

"You mean give up the pendulum? And the medicine bag?" She felt her simmering anger rise. Something must have happened, because she really thought she'd been getting through to him about this. Was it the new Cardinal on staff? Maybe it was Sister Michael.

"Yes," he said. "I think it's the best way."

"I don't. Especially about my pendulum. I think my abilities are a gift from God, not something to be shunned. We've been over this ground before, Father. I'm not going to change my mind about it." She stood. "I've got to go."

"You should confess before you leave."

"So that if I get hit by a car I'll go straight to Heaven?"

"That," he nodded, "and so that your conscience is clear about the methods you use to find your way."

"My conscience *is* clear," she said. "I think it's you who needs to do some self-examination. But, I'll confess—because I'm hoping that doing so will help remove the mark on my back. But I won't confess the wrongness of the pendulum, the medicine bag, or anything else I might seek to fix the problem. I'd only be lying."

"But not confessing them is lying."

"Unless you come up with a better argument than *it's against the Catholic faith*, Father, then we're at an impasse. Will you hear my confession on the other items and at least absolve me of *them*?"

He nodded and stood, and took his folded purple stole from the corner of the desk. Lifting it to his lips, he kissed it while the long ends unfurled almost to the floor, then he placed it around his neck.

Assumpta knelt on the carpeted floor a few feet from him and recited, "Bless me, Father, for I have sinned. It's been about eight weeks since my last attempt to confess."

He raised an eyebrow. She said, "I tried to confess the night Father Hughes was killed by the demon. But it turned out to be the demon in the confessional instead of you."

"You never told me that."

"It wasn't relevant."

"How long was it before then?" he asked.

"Several months." And it would have been several months longer than that if she didn't think that confessing might have helped her cause then. She did it now only to see if confession might somehow affected the mark.

"I should have known that," he said, giving her a weak smile.

"I hope not. You don't keep score with the other priests or anything, do you?"

He pulled his shoulders back, standing taller. "I will not dignify that with an answer. Let's continue. What are your sins?"

Assumpta thought. "I have skipped Mass, I have taken the Lord's name in vain, I have disrespected my father..." *Who heartily deserves it.* "I have lied. I have questioned my faith."

She began the Act of Contrition, a prayer expressing sorrow for having sinned: "Oh my God, I'm heartily sorry for having offended thee..."

Her back began to itch.

"...and I detest..."

The itch became a burn. She squirmed, shrugging her shoulders to slide the material of her shirt against her demon mark, hoping to alleviate some discomfort.

"Is something wrong?" Father Tony said.

"It hurts. The mark hurts." She began unbuttoning her shirt again. "You'll need to look at it."

"Assumpta—"

"Please do this for me, Father."

He walked around behind her. She pulled her hair aside and he gasped. "The mark has burned through your shirt," he said. He slipped a finger into the collar and gently pulled it down to view her back. "It looks as though you've been branded."

*Oh, no,* she thought. She had a terrible suspicion about the mark. "Absolve me, Father."

He continued to stare at her back. "You'll have to finish your prayer."

A chill danced across the back of her neck. Involuntarily, she shivered, and a ripple of pain spread across her shoulder blades. She got the feeling that finishing the Act of Contrition would be a very bad idea.

"I think we can agree that I've shown I'm sorry," Assumpta said. "If the Lord is as omnipotent as you say, he understands. Now absolve me. *Please.*"

Still behind her, he held his hand above her head and recited, "God, the Father of mercies, through the death and resurrection of His Son, has brought forgiveness of sin to the world; through the ministry of the Church may God give you pardon—"

The demon mark burst into flames. Assumpta screamed and fell forward on her hands, arching her back, as if she could twist away from the pain. Father Tony patted at the burning material and flesh, using his stole to extinguish the fire.

"God, it burns." Tears ran down Assumpta's face.

"You're no longer on fire." He started to say a blessing.

"Don't, Father."

He looked at her, stunned.

She wiped the tears from her eyes. "I just think it would make it worse."

"But we've got to try."

"Do you want to see me go up in flames again?" she asked. "And if it kills me, do you think I'll be welcomed into Heaven with this mark on my back?"

"Well…no," he conceded. "But I don't know what else to do to help."

Assumpta got to her knees, then crawled back into the chair, straightening her shirt and re-buttoning it. She took a deep breath, willing the pain to go away. "Does Holy Rosary have a private library? Maybe you could search for a solution to a problem such as this."

"No, but I could write to the Vatican. Their library is vast."

"And they'd just send you what you need?"

He shook his head. "They'd probably send a delegate here to ask some questions first. They might want to see your mark."

"An inquisition? Are you kidding me?" That scared her more than the demon mark. How messed up was that? She stood, bending to reach her purse, and immediately regretted it as she jarred the burns on her back. "Who knows what they'd do once they see the mark. Would they pray over me? That just might get me killed sooner." A heaviness filled her chest—dread like she'd never felt it before. She hurried to the door. With trembling hands, she turned the doorknob and pulled.

"Wait." Father Tony fingered the edge of his stole where the fire had scorched it. He slid it from around his neck. "At least let me bandage the burns."

Assumpta paused. She didn't want to take the time. Perversely, the anxious feelings she was having made her want to get away. She felt a need to *do*, not sit. But he was right, she couldn't run off with an open wound.

"Okay." She returned to the chair in front of Father Tony's large desk.

"Stay here." He dropped the ruined stole on the chair beside her. "I'll get some supplies from the hall cupboard."

As he walked away, she fingered the leather pouch at her neck. Maybe Father Tony was right about it. Except, the problem wasn't the medicine bag, it was *her*. She wore it like a lucky charm—a worthless talisman—because she didn't really believe it would help her. It had seemed like a good idea at the time when she'd bought it, more of a pragmatic purchase than anything. It couldn't hurt, she had thought. But it wasn't right.

She pulled the leather pouch from her neck and dropped it into her purse. She'd find a respectful way to get rid of it later.

Father Tony returned with gauze, peroxide, white medical tape and what looked like a brown, knit cardigan. "You won't even have to unbutton," he said, coming around behind her. "The burn goes clear through your shirt." He dropped the supplies to the chair next to Assumpta, then she felt cool air on her exposed back as he parted the burned cloth.

He worked in silence, pressing a compress of peroxide gently to the burn for a few seconds, then he covered the wound with gauze and taped it.

"Let me help you put this on," he said, holding out the sweater so she could slip into it. It was too large, but the soft knit felt comforting against the gauze on her back. He helped her into her coat and lifted her purse to her shoulder. "Assumpta, what if an inquisition is the only way to get rid of the mark?"

"If it is, I'll deal with it. But let's leave it as a last resort. I need more information. If you can learn anything without involving the Vatican just yet, I'd much appreciate it."

He nodded.

"I'm off to the library."

"Be safe."

"Pray that I don't get hit by a bus on the way, Father, because this is much worse than I thought. Not only am I to be visited by demons whenever they like, but I can't be absolved of my sins." She looked Father Tony in the eye. "And if die before I remove this mark, I'm headed straight for Hell."

# CHAPTER 7

THE BURN PAINED HER ON THE BUS RIDE THROUGH every pothole and jostling turn on the way to Enoch Pratt. But twenty minutes later, when she arrived, the initial torture had subsided to a dull throb.

Assumpta found her way back to the Poe collection and the same scarred table she'd used before. Setting her satchel on top, she pulled out a notebook and a pen, then found the small section of books that might have the best information.

Ignoring the box of white cotton gloves, she pulled a thick, leather-bound volume from the collection, rubbing her thumb along the raised lettering on the spine. Hoping she wouldn't be bothered by demons this time, she sat down at the table and flipped to the back for an index.

The light flickered overhead, and she glanced up.

"Hello," said a woman seated directly across the table from her, scaring Assumpta half out of her wits. He heart thrummed in her chest. She hadn't heard the woman enter the room, pull out the chair, or sit. And she knew she hadn't been that engrossed in the book. Slowly, she inched one hand toward her purse. Maybe she could get to her blessed salt before anything happened.

But, her demon mark wasn't itching, so it couldn't be a demon, right? God, she hoped that its catching fire didn't diminish her demon-sense. She suddenly realized what an asset it was.

But how could the woman have sat down without her realizing it? And what could she possibly want?

"Hello," Assumpta said, shivering. The temperature felt as if it had dropped ten degrees. "Can I help you?" She stared at the woman. Something about her didn't look right. Her face was far too pale to be healthy, and though she was youngish, maybe ten years older than Assumpta, her clothes were ages out of date. Maybe she shopped at the local thrift store. Her long, golden-blond hair was gathered in a loose braid and tied with a ribbon half-way down her back.

"It's more a matter of what I can do to help you," the woman said in a faint Irish accent.

*Where have I heard that before?* Assumpta thought.

"I don't have time for games," she said, hand around her blessed salt, tired by the thought of helping anyone else right now. *Tired? Exhausted* did not begin to describe how she felt. "Why don't you just tell me what you want, and what you're willing to give me in return? I'll let you know if I can help you out."

The light above them flickered again, and Assumpta spared it a brief glance before turning her attention back to the woman.

"Very well," the woman said, leaning forward in a conspiratorial manner. The books that Assumpta had pushed to that side of the table melted right into the woman's jacket, just below her Enoch Pratt Library identification badge. It was then that Assumpta could tell that the woman was not quite solid. She could see the faint outline of the bookshelf behind her with the texture of the books making dimples on her collar.

Assumpta gasped. "You're a ghost!" *That explained the temperature and the flickering lights.*

"It's not a secret," the woman said. "Practically everyone here knows me. I've been at the library forty-three years."

"I must have missed that memo."

"You don't have to be snide about it," said the ghost. "I really can help you."

"I'm sorry," said Assumpta, releasing the salt and running a hand through her hair. "I'm a bit pressed for time and it's making me anxious." *Among other things.* "How do you think you might help? And why are you wearing a badge?"

The ghost sat up straight and smiled. "Apology accepted. I guess introductions are required. I'm Brona Daly. I was killed on the job here at the library, so I'm stuck here for now. I can help you because I've read nearly all the books in this room—most of the books in the library, in fact. There's not much else to do when you're trapped in a library." She winked. "Thank goodness they keep getting new ones."

"I'm—"

"Assumpta Mary-Margaret O'Connor," said Brona, her accent much more pronounced. "I know. Word travels fast."

"Word travels fast?"

"Among the undead." She nodded, then lifted a hand to tick off the names on her fingers. "Ghosts, angels, demons, vampires—"

"I get the idea," said Assumpta. She closed the book she'd been studying and sat up straighter. "Just how many of these *undead* creatures have you had contact with?" Assumpta looked around the room. It appeared empty. She could see nothing through the doorway into the hall. Were any of them here in the room with her and Brona?

"Well..." Brona looked uncertain about how much to reveal. "I saw an angel right after I'd been killed. Fierce-looking, he was, scared me to death. I told him I wouldn't go with him." She ducked her head. "I'm not certain that was the right decision, at the time. I've seen another ghost or two. They usually wander in on their way through to somewhere else."

"Vampires?"

"Never." Brona tucked a stray hair behind her ear. "Thank goodness. Though, I'm not exactly sure I'd be able to identify one even if I did see one. A few days ago, I would have said the same thing about demons. And now we're practically overrun with them, though we're quite alone right now."

Assumpta could only focus on one thing Brona had said. "Overrun?"

"Well, perhaps not *overrun*. And I've only seen them while you're here, which stands to reason."

Assumpta gave her a hard look. "Why do you think it's logical that you only see demons when I'm here?"

Brona pressed her lips together and turned away for a moment, as if needing to think about how to phrase things. Facing Assumpta again, she said, "I do a wee bit of scouting among the library's patrons. Invisibly."

"You spy on people!"

Brona shrugged, an unapologetic lift of a single shoulder. "I like to think I'm doing my part to protect the staff. When I saw you chatting so casually with the demon, I was going to warn you away from it. But then I heard what it said—"

"No more spying on me," Assumpta said, thinking through the ghost's words. But she breathed a sigh of relief. The city wasn't being *overrun* by demons. And maybe, there was light at the end of her demon-marked tunnel.

Brona nodded. "No more spying."

"Which leads me back to my original question," Assumpta said. "What is it you can do for me? And what do you want in return?"

The ghost smiled. "I've a good memory for remembering what I've read in the books. If it's here, I'm certain I can help you find what you need to get rid of your mark. In return, I'd like you to help me get into Heaven."

# CHAPTER 8

OH, BOY, ASSUMPTA THOUGHT, *THAT'S JUST WHAT I need—another deal that could land me in hot water.* Jak had asked a similar request of her: he'd wanted her to help him get out of Hell. And look where she'd ended up: demon-marked and chatting with ghosts. Things could only get better, right?

"How am I supposed to do that?" Assumpta asked.

"You have to find what it is that's keeping me here," Brona said. "Once we figure out what that is, I can be free to move on."

"Are you certain?" Assumpta asked, sitting back in her chair. "You were already offered that path—with angelic escort to make sure you got there all right—and you turned it down. What makes you think you get another chance?"

The ghost blushed. Assumpta hadn't known that was possible. A little color in Brona's cheeks made her look more human—less transparent.

"It all happened so fast," Brona said. She twisted her hands in her lap, turned anguished eyes toward Assumpta. "I'd placed a large stack of books on the automated lift to take them up to the second floor. I hadn't realized that my scarf had gotten caught in the mechanics. When the lift started moving, my scarf tightened around my neck and I couldn't breathe. There was no one around to see me, and I couldn't yell for help. The head librarian didn't find me until after lunch." When

Assumpta didn't say anything for a few seconds, Brona added, "It's not like I planned to die here, you know."

"What makes you think there's something we need to find in order for you to move on? Why don't you just…go?"

"Do you think I haven't tried that?" Brona asked, her voice rising. "I've prayed for someone to come back and lead me to Heaven. I've tried closing my eyes and wishing myself there. I've begged God for another chance. I'm stuck. It's got to be something else." She reached into her hip pocket, pulled out a sheet of paper, and smoothed it on the table in front of her. Tiny script filled the page, with multiple things crossed off.

"I told you, I've read nearly every book in the library. I *have* read every book on ghosts, the occult, and religion. I've made some notes on the existence of ghosts, why they're still here on this plane, and how you can usher them into the next. I've tried everything—every idea—from every book in this library." She pointed to a circled item on the list. "The only thing I haven't done is find something that might be keeping me anchored here. I don't know where to begin." She looked at Assumpta. "And since you're a finder, I think you might be able to help me. In return, I'll write down everything I remember about demons. And while you're helping me find out what it is I need to find, I'll re-read all the demon and occult books in the library for you, starting with those in this room."

It was an attractive offer. Assumpta looked at Brona's list. "May I see that?"

The ghost pushed it across the table to her.

The paper reminded Assumpta of the elementary school handwriting paper with its solid blue lines separated by dotted ones. Instead of using both to write on, Brona had crammed two items in her narrow, precise script between each line and written around the margins of the thin paper as well. Assumpta was surprised to find she held two sheets of paper, written on both sides in tiny writing, the creases worn so much from folding and unfolding over the years that they were in danger of separating into tiny squares. Brona had been hard at work. There had to be hundreds of possibilities written here, and the majority of them had been tried.

Every item had been neatly crossed out except the one: *Bindings: find the thing that is binding you to Earth, a tangible object or the completion of some deed.*

"You've been busy."

"I've had more than forty years to be busy."

Assumpta gritted her teeth and carefully folded the sheets before handing them back to Brona. "I don't have forty years."

"It won't take me that long to go through all the books for you," she said. "Remember, I don't eat or sleep. I read a lot more books in twenty-four hours than even the most voracious of readers. And a lot of books won't need to be completely read," she added. "I'm sure I can help you."

"But I'm not sure I can help you," Assumpta said. "That's the problem."

"Then I can only ask that you try."

"If it's an object or deed that's keeping you here," Assumpta said, "then why did the angel come for you to begin with? Wouldn't you have been ignored by Heaven until you'd finished or found whatever binds you here?"

"I've been giving that some thought. I think maybe I would have been allowed to go immediately after death, but since then, something's happened, and I'm the only one who can fix it. So, I think it's a deed that I need to perform."

Assumpta reached into her pants pocket and pulled out her pendulum, letting it dangle over the table. "Let's see what we can find out."

"Oh, you can't use that now."

"Sure I can."

Brona shook her head. "Not in my presence. It won't work right. Just like your phone isn't working. Or the lights." Just then they blinked, as if to prove her point. "Electronics just don't work right around ghosts."

"My pendulum isn't electronic."

"But it works on electric impulses. Just like plant cells in nature have electric impulses, just like our own nerve cells do: it's abundant in nature. Trust me. Your pendulum works on electric impulses. It's not going to work."

It just didn't seem possible. But then, she'd never given too much thought to how her pendulum functioned. She thought it was sort of a cross between prayer and begging for answers from the universe. But didn't Foucault prove that a pendulum's movement was due to the earth's rotation? Assumpta shook her head. "It's gravity that causes the pendulum to swing and forces in the universe that tell it which way to go."

"And my electric forces will prohibit it from working. Go ahead, try it."

Assumpta held the pendulum a few inches above the table and held her hand still until it hung slack. "Does Brona need to find a physical object before she can ascend to Heaven?"

The pendulum jumped about two centimeters, then hung slack again.

"Well, that's not right." Assumpta said, giving Brona a withering look.

"If I step further away," the ghost said, "the pendulum will work better." She stood and walked to the door, her steps so slow and smooth she almost appeared to glide. "Try it now."

Assumpta ran two fingers down the cord to straighten it, then asked the question again. This time, the pendulum gave a small lurch, started what might have been a counterclockwise motion, then stopped again.

Assumpta laid the pendulum on the table. "All right—I believe you. Go away and come back later. I'll let you know what I find."

"Best you leave the library before you try a reading," Brona said.

"Because you're too afraid that your presence will interfere with my research?"

"Because you never know what other ghosts are lurking about."

Assumpta gave her an astonished look. "There's no mention of ghosts at the Enoch Pratt Library. That kind of publicity would get people here in droves."

"Maybe not, with the kind of ghosts we have lurking around here," Brona said cryptically, and turned off down the hall.

"Wait!" Assumpta stood and sprinted around the table to the doorway, but when she stepped into the hall, Brona had vanished.

Assumpta walked back to the table and packed up her things. There was no sense staying when the ghost obviously wanted her gone. As if to punctuate her thoughts, the light above the table flickered again and Assumpta caught another chill.

Had an invisible Brona made her way back into the room? She had no way of knowing. On a hunch, she pulled her spiral notebook from her bag and tore three sheets from the back of it. Then she dug out a sharpened pencil, and left them on the table.

"For your notes," she said to the room at large as she left.

# CHAPTER 9

JAK FACED SAMAEL WITH RESIGNATION, THE GROUND soft beneath his feet.

"So are you here to take me away?" Jak asked. That depressed him. And it didn't make sense. Why would he be allowed to earn his freedom if the Angel of Death would come so soon after?

Since he'd died a traitor, he would be sent to Tartarus, where the Furies would torture him until they decided he'd been punished enough. Only then he could join his brethren in the Elysium Fields.

Or, would he be sent back to the Christian Hell, since he was demon marked? There would be no open arms for him in Heaven. Unless the Angel of Death was here on God's behalf, and God meant to accept him despite it?

If he had a choice, he'd take Tartarus, because at least there was the hope of redemption.

The skeleton opened his mouth and a wind sprang out, battering Jak. Samael's voice was the combined dissonance of every voice of every soul he'd reft over the millennia. Jak put his hands on his ears to drown out the cacophony. Still, the voices echoed in his head. "Do you forget your history? Where you came from? I am not here to take your soul. I am here as a Guardian of Rome, and of you, by extension. Today, I am but a messenger of Mars, instead of him himself."

Of course, he'd not forgotten his history, but it seemed a little moot at this late date. "Haven't the Roman gods been usurped by the one Christian God? Are you not *His* minion now, an archangel of death?"

"As long as one such as you, one who worshiped the Roman pantheon, walks upon the earth, then so do the Roman gods exist. If you die now, you will ferry across the river Styx and set foot in Pluto's underworld. But you're not destined for that." Samael closed his mouth and let the winds die down before uttering, "Yet."

"I'm confused," said Jak. "How is it that the gods that I was raised with still exist? The Christian God demands that He is the one true God. He has obliterated the pantheon. In fact, this building has been taken over by a Christian sect, which removed all traces of the gods I knew. He must be all powerful. His angels rescued me when I was thrown from Hell. They have given me this chance to right my wrong. Even you are more *His* messenger now than a messenger of Mars. Or even Pluto."

Samael laughed, and the bones lying on the ground in front of him were caught up in the spinning vortex escaping his mouth. He turned his head, and directed the bone devil to dance a path around Jak and collapse into a heap. "And yet doesn't this new God sit on a triumvirate of thrones?" The voices howled in Jak's ears. "Does he not claim to be the Father, the Son, and the Holy Ghost?"

"Indeed."

Samael raised a skeletal hand, turned it palm up and shrugged his shoulders, his bones rattling together. "A god of three, a god of twelve. He is nothing if not adaptable. *They* are nothing if not adaptable. First they were Roman, then Greek, and now they are Jewish and Christian. *They* are all one. *He* is all the same."

"Then are you a messenger of *Him* or Mars?"

The flames in Samael's eye sockets dimmed as they bore down on Jak, as if assessing the question, or the man. He lowered his hand to his side. "Whom are you more comfortable serving?"

*Mars, of course,* Jak thought, immediately. Even a millennium in the Dark One's Hell did not diminish that he was a son of Rome. Things learned as a child cannot be unlearned so easily. And yet… Mars's angels had not rescued him. And Assumpta knew only one god. If he was to help her, maybe he needed to serve her god.

*"Him."*

"So be it," spoke Samael.

The wind ceased. The Roman cloak fell from the skeleton's shoulders. Flesh formed over the bone, heavy and muscled. Hair, curly and dark, grew from his scalp to his shoulder blades. Silver armor covered his flesh, nearly blinding in the reflected light. Ivory wings unfurled behind him, the ends tipped golden, nearly touching the ground. And a halo appeared—a thin, golden band, hovering inches above his head. His entire body radiated a blinding, golden aura.

When all the transformations ceased, a spear appeared in his hand, fully two heads taller than the messenger himself.

"Saint Michael, the Archangel," Jak breathed, and sank to his knees in the damp earth, his head bowed to the ground and the remains of his brethren scattered across the floor.

"Kneel not," spoke the archangel in a single tenor. He crossed the distance between them and offered Jak a hand to help him rise. "I am not one to be worshiped."

Jak nodded, taking Michael's hand, and stood. "Why are you here?"

"To request your help—because He needs an emissary on earth to do His will. Someone who can protect His children. Someone like you, with a warrior's training."

"Someone who might be dangled at the end of a leash with the promise of a place in Heaven?" Jak could not keep the bitterness from his voice.

"Your place is already assured. Of course, you have free will and might squander it."

"God would allow me into Heaven, marked as I am?"

The Archangel Michael closed his eyes and tilted his chin upward, as though he received a private message. Then he nodded, and slowly lifted a hand toward Jak.

Jak tensed, then felt a luxurious warmth pool in the center of his back. It spread upward over his shoulders and downward, following the path of his trapezius muscles. After a moment, it ceased. He felt utterly relaxed. Was that because he'd been touched by God, or because the threat of Hell no longer scared him? Perhaps a bit of both, he decided.

"Is that your only objection?" Michael asked. "The mark is gone."

Jak flexed his back, resisting the urge to feel for the mark. "Could you do the same for Assumpta Mary-Margaret O'Connor?"

Saint Michael smiled. "You are truly good of spirit, Jak. Sadly, I cannot grant your request. This is something she needs to accomplish herself. If she succeeds, she does more work for Him in a single span of time than legions of so-called Christians have done in lifetimes."

"What is it you want of me?"

"Protect Assumpta. Keep her from harm's way. Help her on her journey."

"I betrayed my brothers-in-arms a lifetime ago. What makes you think I can be trusted to do as you ask?"

"If not you, the she-demon would have seduced another. You're not blameless, but you have learned a hard lesson and come through it stronger. You are seasoned and tested. Your skills will help us."

"I'm a warrior, but brute strength won't protect her from demons."

"I will loan you this," Michael said, leaning his great spear toward Jak. "This will defeat any demon it touches."

Jak viewed the spear with awe, taking in the ornate scrollwork on the shaft and the razor-thin edge of the lengthy blade. It blazed with the fire of the righteous. He lifted a hand to touch it, but hesitated, dropping it back to his side. "I cannot."

"You must," said Michael lifting Jak's hand and placing it on the shaft himself. "It is but a weapon."

"A holy weapon."

"But a weapon nonetheless. Take it."

Jak grasped the spear in both hands, the etched designs on the haft enabling him to grip it firmly. He held it horizontally, weighed it, and tested its balance. "It's a fine weapon."

"And to be used with caution." Michael touched a spot just below the flanked cutting edges, and in an instant, it shrank and transformed into a switchblade knife. "Easier to carry," he said, grinning.

Jak smiled. "And to transform it again?"

"Press the button to release the blade, and it will turn back into a mighty spear."

Michael closed his eyes and looked toward the ceiling again. He stepped back. "I have to go now."

Jak nodded, putting the switchblade into his back right pocket.

"Before I go, there's one thing you should know. You still have the ability to contact the souls that haven't moved on," Michael said.

"I do?"

Michael nodded. "And you can allow Assumpta access to them as well."

Jak licked his lips. He'd done this once before. The only way Assumpta could experience the voices was if they were joined in sex. He'd enjoyed the intimacy of the act, though he couldn't feel the pleasure of it, since the body he'd used to join with her was not his own. He'd made certain she'd enjoyed it, though.

Together, they'd found answers, but Assumpta had forgotten them immediately when the sex act was over, and he had disappeared, released from his Hellish prison. How joyless that had been for both of them.

"It works the same way as last time?" Jak asked. *Perhaps, this time in his own body, he would receive as much pleasure as he gave.*

Michael's grin grew wide, his eyes twinkling, his expression one of wicked glee. "Yes. For yourself, simply open your mind to the area around you. To enable Assumpta to hear, then you need join the two of you together. Though a simple clasp of the hands will work—as it would have done the last time."

Shocked, Jak stepped back. "What?"

"Demons are tricksters, Jak. They delight in leading innocents down a path to a fiery eternity."

"But to be released from my prison, I needed to *sleep* with a woman."

"Indeed, but you needed only to have held her hand for her to hear the voices. Is it no wonder the two of you were marked afterward?"

Jak felt like pulling his hair out. He had been damned either way, and he'd snared Assumpta in their net as well. He had much to be forgiven for. He hoped she would accept his apology. "But I don't hear the voices now."

"You'll have to concentrate this time, Jak," Michael said. "Having a physical form makes it more difficult for them to reach you."

Jak closed his eyes and focused his mind. There was silence for a brief moment, and then all the voices came roaring at him, a cacophony of pleas and cries for help, all trying to out-shout each other in order to be heard. He shook his head, opened his eyes, and the voices were still there, much more faint, like a low droning. He'd been ignoring them. "And Assumpta?"

"Her need to concentrate will be greater."

Jak nodded. He tapped his back pocket. "How do I get the spear back to you?"

"It will return of its own accord when your job is done," Michael said, fading from view. In seconds, Jak was alone again with the bones.

He had a mission, but he still hadn't found forgiveness.

# CHAPTER 10

GREG WAS REVIEWING A NEW DIG PROPOSAL ON his laptop on the kitchen table when Assumpta got home. "Any luck?" he asked.

She shook her head, then told him about Brona.

"How do you know she was a ghost?"

"Well, she wasn't a demon. Not a single itch of the demon mark the entire time I was there, not to mention the fact that I could see through her. I just don't know if I can trust her."

Greg pushed the cover of the laptop down to give her his full attention. "What makes you think you can't trust a ghost? Have you ever met one before?" He shrugged. "She seems willing to help you."

Assumpta gave him a puzzled look.

"What?" he asked.

Was he yanking her chain? It wasn't quite the stance she expected him to take. But she decided to roll with it.

"Well...I've never met a ghost before—in the flesh—so to speak. I've talked to several spirits via the pendulum. I've just never seen them. But what else would you call them other than ghosts?" Assumpta dropped her satchel on a chair and went to the fridge for a drink. She poured iced tea into a tall, narrow glass, added sugar and a squeeze of lemon, then joined Greg at the table. She didn't know how to explain what she was feeling. "It just felt weird, making a deal with a ghost."

Greg gathered his papers together to give her more room. "You know what I think? I think you're so used to asking ghosts or spirits for help, that you've never actually considered having to help one back. Maybe you'd rather take than give."

That was kind of harsh, she thought. But could he be right? "Maybe I just don't know what it will cost me. I helped Jak and look where I am."

"I'm pretty sure it's not going to cost you anything but a little bit of your time."

"How can you be so certain?"

"There's a ton of folklore—in many cultures—warning people about making deals with the devil, or demons. I can't think of a single similar story about ghosts. Can you?" He gave her a pointed look. "If it were a problem, we'd know."

Assumpta drank her tea, fiddling with a napkin on the table. Greg's assumptions were logical. They seemed sound. Suddenly, she felt lighter. "I do believe you're right."

"I know I'm right," Greg said, smiling. He changed the subject. "Caroline called while you were out."

"Oh?" Caroline was her on-again, off-again friend from high school. "What did she want?"

"She said she has some exciting news for you."

Assumpta laughed. "And she's calling to rub it in. Sounds like Caroline."

"Give her a call; invite her over."

"So she can see just how good *I've* got it right now?"

Greg wiggled his eyebrows. "Well, you don't have to tell her we're dating. You can just let her assume."

"I'm not going to use you that way."

"It wouldn't be using—"

"—if I agreed to go out with you. I know." *How many different ways could they have this conversation?* She dropped her eyes. "I'm just not ready to do that yet."

"When are you going to understand that Jak's not coming back? And even if he did, he's not going to be a living, breathing man like me?" Greg stood and slammed his chair under the table with enough force that Assumpta's iced tea sloshed over the edge of her glass.

"Greg—"

"Forget it. I'll talk to you later." He walked out the door as stone-faced as one of the earth mother statues he collected.

# CHAPTER 11

AFTER SAINT MICHAEL LEFT, JAK SANK TO ONE KNEE again, bowed his head, and opened his mind to the souls of his brethren who might be here with their bones, the souls of those who had not passed on.

He lifted his head and looked around the room. "I know you're here," he said in old Latin.

From the far corner, a few bones tumbled from their resting place as a shadowy figure rose from the grave and came toward Jak. The shade floated more than walked, though it gave the appearance of walking. It wore the cloak and sandals of a Roman soldier. His well-muscled chest bore a wide bloodstain and scratches covered his bare legs from ankle to thigh. No sword hung by his side.

Jak didn't recognize him, but then he didn't expect to. Thousands of men had served in the Roman army. A man couldn't know them all.

Seven more ghosts shook themselves from their graves, all in various states of dress, tunics ripped, sandals missing, bracers and greaves bearing the imprint of weapons. All would have looked hale and fit, despite their injuries, if they hadn't have been mere shadows of their former selves. They joined the first ghost in a semicircle in front of Jak, who stood to greet them.

"I need your help," Jak said. "You've witnessed my discussion with Saint Michael. You know I must battle demons and protect a woman. I formally ask you to assist me in this task."

The soldier with the bloodstained tunic stepped forward. "How can you expect us to help?" he asked in a raspy voice. "We are mere shades of our former selves."

"You can help by finding answers for me, by talking to others who have not passed over, and relaying what you find back to me. I fight a battle over knowledge as much as by brute strength. We are Roman warriors, brothers on the battlefield. We have trained together and fought for the same Republic. Perhaps you can find a way to use that strength and cunning. I know I can trust you to help me, should you take up the task."

"But why *should* we help you?" another one asked. He wore a rag wrapped around his head, covering one eye.

"To aid a brother in need," Jak said, "and to alleviate an eternity of boredom on this plane." He raised his eyebrows. "To help a pretty woman. There are many reasons for you to decide to join my cause." He shrugged. "And when you're done, I'm certain Pluto would welcome you to the underworld with open arms."

"He would welcome us now," said a third. "There's nothing stopping us from crossing over."

"He might welcome *you*," said the ghost with the covered eye. "But many of us are bound here until we do penance for our misdeeds in life—"

"I'll help you," said a female voice in modern Italian from across the room. A shadow peeled itself away from a column with a sinuous movement and drifted over to the group. A young woman with long, dark hair—the bangs pulled back and fastened away from her face—and sun-bronzed skin offered a hand for him to shake. Her form grew solid, and Jak took her hand and shook it; then she faded back into semi-transparency.

Jak and the other soldiers looked at her in amazement.

"You can become corporeal," he said.

"For a few minutes, sometimes longer. It takes a great deal of energy to do so. I could teach these sad warriors a thing or two," she said, gracing them with an impish grin.

"But how? And how did you get here? In this burial place?"

"I've had more than a hundred years to practice," she said, shrugging. "I was killed here in the Pantheon, part of an archeology group in 1859. I found the secret passage to this burial chamber and came down to explore. When the wall closed behind me, I couldn't make it open again. I starved to death amid these bones."

"I'm so sorry," Jak said.

She shrugged. "I've had plenty of time to get used to the idea. So what do you say? Can I help?"

"Why would you want to?"

"Reason number two," she held up two fingers. "'To alleviate an eternity of boredom on this plane.'" She adjusted the collar of her button-down shirt and crossed her arms over her chest. "There's nothing left for me to explore here, and I'm ready to move on."

"You speak Italian perfectly," Jak said, "but your accent is slightly off. Where are you from?"

"Georgia, originally," she said, lapsing into English with a Southern drawl. "I'm from the States. Do you speak English?"

"Yes—and several other languages," Jak said. "You will indeed be an asset. I'll be happy for your help."

Her face lit up. "Excellent. I'm Vesta. And I need you to do something for me, too."

She beckoned him over to the column. "My body is over here. Can you take my notebook with you? Maybe we can find some descendent to give it to."

Jak squatted down by Vesta's body, seated with its back to the column. She would have looked relaxed, if she weren't so obviously dead. And beautiful—the cool dry air having preserved her remarkably. He lifted the book, still clutched in her skeletal hand, and ruffled the pages. The diary was nearly complete, with pale, spidery writing on all but a few pages in the back. Curious, he asked, "May I read this?"

"Of course," Vesta said, smiling. "You can tell me if there's anything there that hasn't been published already. Maybe I know something someone else doesn't." She gave him a quizzical look. "Is publishing still important in your day and age? We could write a paper."

"I have no idea," Jak said, pocketing the book, "but I know of someone who might."

He turned to the ghostly soldiers. "Are any of you willing to help?"

The one-eyed soldier stepped forward. "I am."

The ghost with the bloodstained tunic raised his hand and moved toward the first. "I'll help as well." His raspy voice filled the underground space. "Even if Pluto doesn't accept us, it's a respite from an eternity in this graveyard."

Jak waited. Three additional soldiers stepped forward to join the line formed by the other two.

When no one else moved, Jak nodded. "That's all, then. Let's get moving."

In a blink, they disappeared.

# CHAPTER 12

GREG AND ASSUMPTA WERE MAKING LUNCH WHEN
a knock sounded at the door.

"You expecting anyone?" Greg asked. He put down the bow knife
he'd been using to cut slices of French bread.

"Not me." Assumpta continued to pull lunch meats and cheese from
the refrigerator. She looked thoughtful as she laid the cold cuts on the
granite counter. "And it's damn tough for a salesman to get through…"

"And I'm fairly certain a demon wouldn't knock," Greg said.

Assumpta gave him a wry look. "I think my mark would let me
know if there was a demon in the vicinity."

"You think?" His expression said that he didn't.

She shrugged. "As much as I hate the damn thing, I can't believe
that a little fire would prevent my demon barometer from working. It
is, after all, a product of Hell."

The knock came again.

"Little fire?" he asked, wiping his hands on a dishcloth. "I've seen
what that *little fire* did. You look practically branded."

"It *is* healing rather quickly, though…"

Greg walked to the door and then looked through the peephole.
"I don't recognize him." He undid the deadbolt, but left the chain in
place, then opened the door a crack.

"Yes?" he asked.

"I'm looking for Assumpta. Is she around?"

Greg looked back over his shoulder. "Someone is here to see you."

Assumpta came to the door, and her heart gave a little flip-flop when she saw who it was. She would have recognized him anywhere, the spirit of her dreams. *Jak.*

When he had come to her the first time, bound by the chains of Hell, he'd tempted her by appearing in many guises. Now he wore his true face: dark curly hair, low brow, straight Roman nose, full lips. Of all the faces he'd worn during her seduction, this was the one she loved the best.

"Jak!" A smile split her face. "Why are you knocking? Why didn't you just materialize? I've been calling for you." She unhooked the chain and pulled the door wide, stepping back so Jak could enter. A cool breeze whipped through the door as he came through, and she shivered. "Why didn't you come sooner?"

His face grew serious, and he reached out and briefly touched her arm. She looked down to where they touched and her eyes grew wide.

"You're flesh and blood! Like Pinocchio!" She leaped against him, giving him a hug. "But how?"

Smiling, he pushed her away gently.

"You freed me from my prison, and I was allowed to leave. But where was I to go? I could wander like the other souls who are either unable, or unwilling, to cross over. Or, I could pay Charon, the ferryman, and be judged for my sins in Hades. After spending an eternity trapped in Hell's urn, I wasn't willing to submit to the Furies' torture."

"Torture?" Assumpta asked, scrambling to remember what little Roman mythology she'd learned in school.

"I beg you, let me tell you later." Jak glanced at Greg, and Assumpta immediately understood. He didn't want to share his past with Greg. She nodded. He was entitled to his privacy.

Jak took her hands in his. "I'll tell you this: God has removed my demon mark, and so I've been allowed into Purgatory—"

Greg leaned his back against the wall and crossed his arms over his chest. "Purgatory is not a place."

Assumpta glared at him. *New convert*, she had to remind herself. Greg was flush with knowledge and righteousness. She needed to give him a break, but honestly, she wanted to kick him in the ass. Their guest was more forgiving.

Jak nodded. "You're right, it's not literally a place. It's a time period, if you will, while I wait for purification of my soul."

"But you didn't die in a state of grace," Greg said. "How can you even be allowed the option?"

Jak told them briefly of his conversation with Saint Michael—about a pantheon of gods versus a trinity—and how he'd been given the choice to serve one god or many.

Greg didn't look convinced. "So what are you doing here now?"

"In short? Helping Assumpta—because toiling in Purgatory to work the stains off my soul could take me centuries. Oh, someone could have prayed for me to exit Purgatory sooner. But there is no one on earth who would do that for me now. Everyone I have ever known has been dead for centuries." He gripped Assumpta's hands more firmly, looking into her eyes. "You might have been able to help me again, but I had no way to contact you to let you know what had happened. So I asked for an indulgence instead: the ability to make amends. I was granted that, and tasked to help you, Assumpta. And now I am here to do so—grace notwithstanding."

"And you've gotten yourself a fancy new body. How convenient."

"Greg!" Assumpta shouted at him. "What's wrong with you?" But she knew what was wrong. Greg was jealous. He couldn't compete with the spirit of Jak, and now here Jak was in the flesh. That had to stick in his craw. Her moving out needed to become a higher priority.

"It's okay," Jak said. "I know it's hard to believe. But this body is temporary: it might look like flesh and bone and feel like flesh and bone, but it's still an illusion. Once I'm finished doing what I need to do, I'll return to spirit."

"So why don't you take care of it and be gone already?"

"Greg!"

"I am sent here by God's messenger, Samael—the Archangel Michael—to protect Assumpta." He squeezed her hands again. "And I must be honest with you," he said, looking into her eyes. "By helping you, I also hope to receive the forgiveness I crave for letting down my fellow soldiers of Rome so many lifetimes ago. By helping you, I help myself."

Assumpta felt a hopeful flutter in her belly. "So you can remove my mark?"

Jak sobered, and his face said it all. She felt tears prickle as he sadly shook his head.

# CHAPTER 13

G
O AWAY, SPIRIT BOY," GREG SAID. "ASSUMPTA'S
given you enough of her time and effort, and look where it got
her: demon-marked and a target for any wandering soul who might
cross her path. If your *protection* is the price she'll pay for helping you,
she doesn't need it. Not when it keeps getting her into trouble."

Jak turned a worried look in her direction. "You've been
visited? Already?"

Assumpta nodded. "Twice."

"I didn't think they would come for you so soon."

"You didn't think," Greg said, stepping toward him. He looked like
a bantam rooster itching for a fight. "You didn't think when you asked
for her help the first time. Didn't you realize what would happen?"

"Greg!"

"You're one to talk," Jak said, anger flaring in his eyes. "You came
begging for Assumpta to help you clear a curse. And look where that
got her: fighting one of the major demons in Hell face-to-face. It almost
got her killed. It almost got *you* killed."

Greg backed down.

Jak said, "We're both at fault for putting her in danger. But at least
I'm equipped to protect her. I'm here to help. What about you? Are you
just a taker in this equation? It's no wonder she likes me better."

"Jak!" Assumpta held up her hands as if to push them both away and took two steps backward. "You're squabbling like kids over candy! And I won't have it." She looked at Greg. "The fact is, I need Jak's help as much as he needs mine. You're no longer cursed and don't need me at all. I've got to help him."

Greg pulled himself together, schooling his face into a placid expression, he said, "I *do* need you."

*Oh, he had it bad,* Assumpta thought. She felt for him, she really did, but at the present time, she didn't return his feelings. She didn't know if she ever could, not with Jak in the picture, and maybe not even when he was out. She liked Greg, a lot, but *like* didn't necessarily turn to *love*.

*What a mess!* She could try to let him down easy, but she didn't want to give him any hope...and yet there might be. *What to do?*

Assumpta said, "And that's why I've got to move out. My presence here is only making things worse between us. And if I've got to help Jak, you're only going to get more resentful."

"Where will you go?"

"I don't know. But I'll find something soon."

"Don't," Greg said, reaching for her. "We can make this work."

"I'm not sure how we can," Assumpta said. She held up a hand to fend him off. "You don't like Jak on principle, and you don't like that I'm helping him. He's going to be hanging out for as long as he needs my help, and for as long as I need his. How can we possibly make this work?"

"There's more," Jak said to Greg. "If you're sincere in your offer, you should know that I come with others—"

"This isn't a hotel," Greg said.

"They're ghosts," said Jak. "They won't take up much space."

*Well, that explains the cool air that entered with Jak,* Assumpta thought.

Greg paled. "They're here now? In the room?"

Jak nodded.

Assumpta squinted her eyes and looked around. Jak had a double aura—first time she'd seen that—the blue color of the first convincing her he was sincere. The second glowed a brilliant golden yellow, surrounding the blue completely. That shade of yellow was usually reserved for divinity. He must have it since he was working for God.

*Jak's gone from demon-marked to marked by God.* She pondered that for a minute.

Greg's aura was quickly fading from an angry red to a calm blue. *Good*, she thought. *He's beginning to accept things, if only for the moment.*

A group of auras blended together behind Jak—she couldn't tell the number since they stood so close together; three or four, maybe. She could not discern what they might look like, but saw only green and blue lines mixing around in a crowd-like shape.

A single ghost had wandered over to the glass cases on top of a waist-high bookshelf that divided the foyer from the living room. It seemed to study the archeological artifacts Greg had displayed there. The aura of that ghost was a strange mixture of brown and blue... not quite the usual fare. If she had to guess, she'd call it *ambitious*. A relatively good soul driven to succeed and willing to break a few rules along the way.

"I see the tight-knit group behind you, Jak," Assumpta said, "but there's another who's not a part of them," she guessed. "It's inspecting Greg's finds."

"That would be—"

"Vesta," the ghost said, answering for Jak. She materialized slowly in front of the last case, which held a plaster cast of Greg's hand from when he was little boy. "Darling."

"My mother's idea," Greg said. Assumpta thought he might have looked a bit embarrassed to admit such a thing. And she was certain that he'd told her it was his idea. She made a mental note to ask him later.

"I adore it," Vesta assured him in her Southern drawl, "though I much prefer the antiquities. I didn't know there would be a fellow archeologist along for the adventure." She moved closer to Greg and smiled brightly. "I think we're going to be kindred...spirits." She winked at him. "Jak," she said, not taking her eyes off Greg, "why don't you give Greg my notebook. I think he and I are going to have a lot to talk about."

Assumpta watched the interchange with close attention. Was Vesta coming on to Greg? What could she possibly have to share with him? Or was she simply curious to learn about the latest archeological discoveries? Why would an archeologist—a dead one—be interested in such things?

# CHAPTER 14

J AK PULLED THE LEATHER-BOUND NOTEBOOK FROM
his back pocket and handed it over to Greg. Greg leafed through
the first few pages.

"Your notes are quite detailed," Greg said to Vesta. He turned a few
more pages, looking over the sketches. "Roman study." He looked up at
her. "Pantheon? I didn't know there was much to find there."

"Ask Jak about the hidden cellar in its depths," Vesta said. "He told
me no one today knows of it. There's a crypt of Roman soldiers beneath
it, and my body, of course. It will look a strange site when you find it
buried among the armored bones. Can't be helped though."

"When *I* find it?"

"Of course," Vesta said. "When you ask the Italians if you can
explore." She ran a ghostly hand up his arm—a lover's caress. He
shivered and stepped away.

"I'm afraid they'll need plenty of convincing to allow me to do so,"
he said. "It won't be as easy as you might think; besides which, the
Catholic Church now owns it. It's them I'd have to petition."

"I'm sure if you authenticate my diary, it will go a long way to
convincing someone," she said. "We can start right away."

*Definitely ambitious,* thought Assumpta.

Greg looked intrigued, but he said, "It's not my typical area of study."

"Oh? Can't you broaden your study a bit?"

"Of course." He leafed through the book again. "I can't go anywhere knowing Assumpta's still in danger, but I can write some letters this week, and—"

Assumpta cut in. "I think we need to get back to the project at hand, which is getting rid of my demon mark."

Greg nodded and closed the journal.

"God removed mine," Jak said. "I will ask him again."

"Again?" Assumpta asked.

At the same moment, Greg said, "You've got a direct line to God?"

"Of course, not," Jak responded to Greg, "that's what prayer is for." To Assumpta, he said, "Yes, I've asked Saint Michael, but maybe if I pray directly, with you—"

"He's not listening right now, Jak," Assumpta said.

"*He* always listens."

"Well, then," Assumpta said, "He's not feeling so charitable toward me right now. He's not answering *my* prayers." And then she wondered, had she actually prayed to God to ask him to remove the mark? Father Tony had prayed on her behalf. Had probably *continued* to pray on her behalf. But had she done it herself? "I'll beseech him again tonight."

"Beseech?" Greg said.

"I prefer that to begging," she replied.

"It's the same thing," Jak said.

Assumpta shrugged. "*Beseeching* sounds more formal, but if that doesn't work…" She looked at Greg, raising her eyebrows inquiringly.

"I can put out some university feelers, check with the archeology community, if you think that would help," he said. "You and Brona have the library research covered. Jak's got his conduit to God." He shrugged. "I suppose I could pray."

"Thank you." Assumpta squinted at the group of ghosts behind Jak. "How many of you are there? Can you show yourselves?"

Five watery apparitions appeared, weak and insubstantial. If one didn't look closely, they would be very hard to see.

"And how are you going to help?"

A ghost with a large bloodstain on his chest stepped forward. "In any way we can, Citizen," he said. "We will be Jak's eyes where he cannot see and his ears where he cannot hear. We will help him protect you if we are able." He unsheathed his sword and gave her a salute.

Greg whistled through his teeth. "If that were real, it would be worth a mint. How much damage can a ghostly sword do?"

The ghostly soldier slammed it down on a throw pillow tossed casually on the sofa. The sword cleaved the pillow in half, the spongy insides spilling out like brains.

# CHAPTER 15

ASSUMPTA OPENED THE DOOR TO REGRETS TATTOO Removal Parlor and walked to the receptionist's desk. Hundreds of before-and-after photos graced the walls of the lobby area.

She ignored them. She didn't need to look at how well a job the technicians did. In her case, this procedure would either work, or it wouldn't.

"I'm here for my 10 a.m. appointment," she said. "Assumpta O'Connor."

The receptionist, a thirty-something nurse in hospital scrubs with a stethoscope hanging around her neck, tapped a few keys on her computer keyboard and nodded.

"You filled out the medical questionnaire on line?"

Assumpta nodded back. "There were a few questions I didn't know how to answer."

The receptionist gave her a bland smile, as if she got similar responses all the time. "Dr. Barnes will go over those with you. I'll page him now. He should only be a minute."

She picked up the phone, pressed the intercom button, and spoke quietly into the mouthpiece.

Assumpta wondered where the intercom speaker was located. She certainly didn't hear any page in the lobby area.

"Follow me." The nurse rose and motioned Assumpta through a door behind the desk. She led Assumpta down a short hallway and into the second room on the right. The room was small, the examination table pushed against the back wall, leaving just enough room at the foot of it to stand in front of the sink. From a cabinet beneath the examination table, the nurse pulled a paper covering and handed it to Assumpta. "Where's your tattoo?"

"Between my shoulder blades."

"Take off your blouse. You can leave your bra on. I'll be back in a second to take a photo."

"Is that really necessary?"

The receptionist blinked. "You get a discount if you allow us to use your before-and-after photos on line or in the lobby."

"No thanks," Assumpta said. "I'd prefer to remain anonymous."

"Oh, it has to be anonymous anyway. HIPAA laws, you know."

"Still not interested," said Assumpta. She gave the nurse a smile to soften the finality of her tone.

The nurse nodded. "Dr. Barnes will be here in just a moment."

Next to the examination table was a wheeled cart with the laser sitting on it. It was smaller than she thought it would be, taking up slightly more room than her toaster oven. It had a keyed ignition start, but the key was already in the slot, with a second dangling down from a ring connecting the pair.

*Looks like they don't pay too much attention to safety around here,* she thought. *I could start the machine myself and try my own hand at removal.*

It was chilly in the small exam room, uncomfortably chilly. Assumpta suppressed a shiver. She shrugged out of her blouse. Chill bumps erupted across her shoulders and down her back. Normally, she'd ignore the paper wrap. She didn't worry about modesty with a doctor, especially if she was still wearing her bra, but the cold was really uncomfortable. She wondered if it had anything to do with the laser they used to remove the tattoo. *Did it get really,* really *hot?*

She tucked her holy medals into her bra, shook out the paper covering and slipped it on, leaving the opening in the back. Wearing it hardly affected the cold. The demon mark seemed especially susceptible to the temperature—it almost burned. *How badly was the cold affecting it?* She wished there were a mirror in the room so she could take a peek.

A quick knock sounded on the door, which then opened. "I'm Dr. Barnes," said the man, dressed in hospital scrubs. Not a blond hair looked out of place. The eyes behind his silver wire-frame glasses were a cold, emotionless blue. He carried a manila file folder, presumably containing her questionnaire, and held out his hand for Assumpta to shake. She took it and squeezed.

"Your application said your tattoo is on your back? Why don't you lie down so I can take a look?"

Assumpta laid chest-down on the table, turning her head so her eyes focused on the pens in the doctor's breast pocket, and pulled her hair out of the way. She tensed and released the muscles of her back, over and over, trying to ease the ache she felt there. She was starting to get a bad feeling about this.

"It's hardly noticeable," said the doctor.

"But that's not the point."

"You're right," said Dr. Barnes. He noted something in the chart he'd carried in. "I'm just making small talk. As tattoos go, this one should come off fairly easily."

*"Should" being the operative word*, she thought. *If only the mark was a tattoo.* "How many sessions do you think it will take?"

"Well, that's hard to say," said Dr. Barnes. He sat on a wheeled stool and rolled over to the laser. He turned the key, then pulled the wand from its resting place and punched a few buttons. The machine hummed audibly in the small room. The doctor donned a pair of latex gloves, snapping them to fit, and rolled back to Assumpta's side.

He ran his fingers lightly across her back, and she got chills. She clenched her jaw. She'd read about laser tattoo removal on the Internet.

It was supposed to be painful, more painful than getting a tattoo. But since she hadn't ever had a tattoo, she had nothing to compare. On the other hand, her mark had not been made by ink. So, would she feel the same pain? Would it be worse?

The doctor leaned closer. "You realize this isn't going to work," he said, circling one finger around and around the demon mark.

The muscles in her back tensed and the demon mark fluttered weakly. "What do you mean?" Assumpta got a sinking feeling in the pit of her stomach. Did she smell sulfur, or was she imagining things? Her heart began to thump.

"You can't remove a demon mark as easily as a tattoo." He stopped touching the mark and slid the stool forward. They were practically face to face. "Nice try."

He smiled at her and dropped his façade. In an instant, his clothes disappeared. Black-and-purple mottled skin burst through the doctor's tanned human skin. A thick vein bulged in his forehead. Eyes, entirely black, smoldered with lust. Horns pushed through the skin on the top of his head. The sound of ripping flesh sent chills down Assumpta's spine.

The room grew ripe with the odor of sulfur. Assumpta gagged from the nearness of him. She rolled up on one arm, pushing herself away from the smell, and from him.

"Not so fast," he said, grabbing her left arm and pinning her to the table. Assumpta felt the holy medals fall out of her bra and *clink* against the table's thin padding. "I want a little piece of what you've been giving Jak all these weeks. When we're done, you're not going to want him anymore. You and I are going to fuck for so long, and so hard, you won't remember what Jak felt like. My cock will consume you—you'll begin to crave it."

He slid his free hand down to his crotch and grasped his large, engorged penis. He gave it a yank, then smoothed his hand down the length of it.

Assumpta eyed the thing in terror. It would rip her in half!

He taunted, "Soon, you'll be begging for my cock, and I will give it to you over and over and over." He released himself, then leaned toward her for a kiss, his thick tongue lolling out of his mouth before their lips even touched.

Assumpta recoiled, pushing up on one arm and putting her back against the wall, wishing she'd not removed the Miraculous Medals from her rings. But she hadn't wanted to explain them to the doctor.

The demon grabbed her shoulders with pocked and twisted hands, black claws at the end of each finger digging into the tender flesh, and pressed his face closer to hers.

"Sweet," he said, licking around her lips. "You could make this very easy for me, and therefore very easy on yourself…" He licked her again. "Or I could take what I want, and hurt you very, *very* much in the process."

Assumpta gagged. The demon looked like it would enjoy causing her pain.

"Well?" it prompted her. "What's it going to be?"

*As if she had a choice!*

She pulled her knees to her chest, then kicked at his groin. Her feet glanced off his hip, but the blow loosened his grip. She grabbed the holy medals dangling from the chain around her neck and thrust them at the demon. They sizzled against his skin, and she smelled the odor of rotting, burning flesh.

He bellowed in pain, swatting aside the medals. "You bitch! I'll—"

A knock sounded on the door. A man said, "Miss O'Connor? Are you ready? It's Dr. Barnes."

In an instant, the demon fled. Only a whiff of sulfur lingered to remind her it had been there at all. The temperature in the room rose at least ten degrees, probably more. *So, the demon had been keeping the room cold to stop my mark from alerting me,* she thought. *I won't fall for that trick again.*

Assumpta tore off the remaining bits of the paper gown and pulled on her shirt. She pulled her hair out of the collar, straightened it the best she could, then wiped the demon saliva from her face with the back of her shaking hand.

"Miss O'Connor?" Dr. Barnes entered the room, clipboard in hand—a carbon-copy of the demon's human facade. The demon had stolen its look from the doctor.

"I've changed my mind, Dr. Barnes." Assumpta jumped off the table. "I'm sorry to have wasted your time."

She couldn't do this now, she thought. Another time. Maybe at another shop.

On shaking legs, she brushed past the real doctor and ran out the door.

# CHAPTER 16

**I**T TOOK ASSUMPTA HALF THE AFTERNOON TO CALM down after meeting the demon at the tattoo removal parlor. And she'd thought the demon Dan had been bad. Was this the way of things to come—larger and more powerful demons would attack her? Demons with more on their minds than just the capture of her soul?

She shivered, collected herself, then spread holy oil and blessed salt around the entire perimeter of her bedroom, creating another barrier against the damned creatures. Then she said a prayer and asked for protection. Finally, she'd made a cup of tea and curled up on her bed. And that's what made her feel the best, the hot liquid pushing away the coldness in her chest. When she felt warm again, she knew she would get beyond this latest assault.

Finally, her nerves calmed, and she could think more clearly.

Assumpta pulled out her pendulum. What could she do for Brona?

She retrieved the semicircle of paper with the letters on it, straightened the cord on the glass teardrop, and held the pendulum over the paper, then took a deep, calming breath.

She started with an easy question to make certain that nothing interfered with the pendulum's movement, as it did in Enoch Pratt in the presence of Brona.

"Is my name Assumpta?"

The pendulum swayed back and forth, then started turning clockwise in tiny circles, signifying *yes*. The longer Assumpta waited, the wider and wider the circles became. She waited a moment longer, then asked a *no* question: "Did I receive my chemistry degree from the University of Pennsylvania?"

The fact was, she had no degree yet, and when it was conferred, it would come from the University of Maryland.

The pendulum skipped, then traveled in awkward arcs until it reversed itself and made counterclockwise circles.

Convinced that nothing interfered with the pendulum's divining abilities, Assumpta let the pendulum drop to the paper to stop its motion, then she lifted it again, and asked, "Is the ghost, Brona, telling me the truth about herself?"

After a moment, the pendulum started its clockwise movement.

Assumpta nodded and moved on to her next question.

"Must Brona complete some mission before she can move on to the afterlife?"

The pendulum swung clockwise.

"Yes," she said, smiling. *Perfect*. This was easier than she thought it was going to be. She moved the pendulum over the center of the lettered paper. "What does Brona need to do?"

The pendulum jumped to stop its circular motion, then began a back-and-forth motion over the semicircle of letters.

"G?"

The pendulum continued on its path.

"H?"

The pendulum changed direction. Swinging toward D-E-F. "E," she said, knowing she needed a vowel. The pendulum changed direction once more. It swung back and forth over L-M-N.

"Hem?" She asked and paused.

"Hen?" It continued on its path.

"Hel...Hell?" *God, she hoped not. What would that mean?* The pendulum changed again.

"Help," she guessed, from the next trajectory. Instantly, she felt better. *Help* was a thousand times better than *Hell*. "Who does Brona need to help?"

The pendulum jumped, swinging wide, then moved to another path by X, Y and Z.

"Y?" She couldn't think of any names that started with X or Z. Come to think of it, she couldn't think of any names starting with Y right now, either.

The pendulum changed direction.

"O," she said, naming the vowel closest to its current path. It changed again.

"Yov?" she said. "Yow?" It continued. "You? Help You? Help... *me*?" Well crap, she knew that already. That would teach her not to be specific.

The pendulum leaped and started moving in a clockwise circle.

"How is Brona going to help me?"

She hated this part. It always took so long. *Yes/No* questions were so much easier, but they didn't always provide the detail she needed.

The pendulum swerved.

"R..." Assumpta guessed. It changed its movement again.

"E." The pendulum changed.

Several frustrating minutes later, Assumpta yelled, "Research!" and the pendulum leaped, then hung slack. She resisted the urge to toss it across the room. Instead she wadded it into her hand, string and all, and shook her fist. "That's what I've got *you* for," she told the pendulum, "to find the answers for me."

# CHAPTER 17

SEATED AT THE SCARRED WOODEN TABLE IN THE Poe room at Enoch Pratt Library, Assumpta combed through the most recent demonology book the library had acquired. Finally, the lights flickered overhead. The temperature in the room dropped at least five degrees. Assumpta stuck a piece of scrap paper in the book to save her place, then reached for her sweater. She was about to have a visitor.

Brona slowly materialized in front of her.

"Did you like that?" she asked, a bit of her Irish brogue coming through. "I waited until the lights warned you I was coming."

"Better than just *popping* in," Assumpta agreed. "I can't stand that."

"Noted," Brona said, nodding. She looked at the book Assumpta was reading. "Don't bother with that one; I've already read it."

"But I pulled it off the new arrivals shelf on my way in."

"I read it last night. Not much to it, anyway."

Assumpta yanked a bibliography of demon books out of her purse. Twenty-five pages of anything that might contain the key words of *demon, demon mark, summoning demons, hexes, curses*—and more— that Enoch Pratt shelved. She figured she would work her way through the list, crossing off the items Brona had read, but following up on them later if she needed to and had time. "How many of these have you read recently?"

Brona looked over the document and crossed off twenty-nine books while Assumpta waited. Several others she starred, then pushed the list back to Assumpta. "The starred ones don't circulate anymore. Leave those to me."

Pulling some folded sheets of notebook paper out of her jacket pocket, Brona smoothed them down on the table. "So...I do have a few ideas from the books I read last night: douse with holy water."

"Tried it."

Brona drew a line through the item. "Blessed salt?"

"Tried it."

Another line.

"Holy oil."

"Doesn't work."

Brona looked up from her papers. "It seems you've happened on to quite a bit of the lore already."

"Just a few things. But I'm certain I haven't found it all."

"How about fire?"

Assumpta didn't like the sound of that. Nonetheless, she asked, "How does that work?"

"You burn the mark off with an open flame."

"Like a blowtorch?" *Yeah, like that's going to happen.*

"Well, this author suggests holding the affected area over a candle's flame, though that might be awkward in your case. I suppose a blowtorch could work quite well for you, considering the flame shoots horizontal."

"I was kidding," Assumpta said dryly. "And I'm not sure I want to go that route. I've already experienced the pain of the mark on fire." She explained what had happened in Father Tony's office. "Leave it on the list, but it's definitely a last resort."

Brona nodded. "Just consider that the holy fire probably came from within, not without. It could make a difference." She circled fire and moved down the list. "There are a few witchcraft spells you could try."

"I'm not certain they'd work," Assumpta said. "It's sort of like a non-Catholic asking Saint Christopher to protect him on a journey. Would such a prayer work for him?"

"Are you saying that prayers are like spells?" Brona asked. "You've got to believe in them to work? Or are you saying that Saint Christopher would turn his back on someone just because they're not Catholic?"

Assumpta had never thought about it that way. She countered, "Do you mean to imply that spells are like prayers? And that a witch's god or goddess wouldn't ignore me, even if I don't really believe in them?"

"Would Saint Christopher ignore a plea?"

Assumpta laughed. "I don't believe he would. I've certainly talked to plenty of non-Catholics who've buried Saint Joseph when their house wouldn't sell in a bad real estate market, then swore by his ministry when they had contracts right after. If good old Saint Joe won't ignore a non-Catholic, I guess Saint Christopher wouldn't either." She sobered. "But I don't know how to cast a Wiccan spell."

"I didn't say *Wiccan*." Brona emphasized the last word. "As a religion, it's only been around about sixty years or so, but like most other religions, it derives a lot of its belief and ritual from others. I think we need to go *more* pagan—something much, much older." She pushed a sheet of paper toward Assumpta.

"Witches?" Assumpta asked.

"These are all the names of self-proclaimed non-Wiccan practitioners I could find in the area who advertise that they'll help people," Brona said. "There were a few others, but once I cross-referenced their businesses against the Better Business Bureau database, I couldn't put them on the final list. These look like the ones you could trust."

"You really think I should visit a witch?"

"Either that or get some confidence in casting spells. If your non-Catholic friends can bury Saint Joe, I don't see any reason why you can't cast a spell. But it's your choice. I'm just laying out your options."

"Are there any more *easy* items on the list I can try myself?"

"I don't have anything else for you today. Most of the books came up empty, or duplicated information, and then I spent some time researching local witches and copying down some pagan spells." Brona pushed another piece of paper toward Assumpta. "Here they are, in case you decide to do them yourself." She gave Assumpta an expectant look. "Did you find anything for me?"

Assumpta smiled. "Yes. According to the pendulum, you need to keep doing what you're doing: research for me."

Brona offered her a disbelieving smile. "Really?"

Assumpta nodded. "I wouldn't lie to you about something like this. But I don't know how to prove it to you, since the pendulum doesn't work in your presence."

Brona nodded slowly, then grinned. "I guess I'll just have to find out how to fix you."

# CHAPTER 18

ASSUMPTA STIRRED HER TEA ABSENTLY, THE HUM of the stainless steel refrigerator keeping her company while she looked over the spells Brona had found for her. Two were hex-breaking spells. One required ingredients—*components?*—that she didn't have. She'd have to go shopping.

Would it be easier to ask a witch to cast the spells? Or should she just try herself? Maybe Brona was right: that as far as religion and belief were concerned, spells were prayers and prayers were spells. It couldn't be that easy, could it?

Supposing she cast the spells herself and nothing happened? Would that mean they hadn't worked? Or, would it mean that she'd worked the spell incorrectly? She had no way of knowing—but a witch might.

She really needed to see a witch.

Assumpta pulled out the list Brona had compiled and perused the names. The third on the list had three stars on it, Brona's shorthand for the best. Luckily, this woman also owned a store. If Assumpta decided she wanted to try things herself, she could purchase what she wanted there, and if she decided she wanted help, she could ask the expert. Good, solid advice never hurt anyone.

She got up and wandered to the pantry where Greg kept the phone books.

*I really need to get myself a laptop, or an Internet-connected phone,* she thought. *If only I had the cash. It always comes down to the cash.*

She flipped open the book and turned to the blue pages with the city information in them. Bus schedules and timetables were printed on the last few pages. She cross-referenced the address of the shop, found the times it was open for business, and hoofed it to the bus stop at the end of the block.

Thirty minutes later, she found herself in front of Jo's Turning Wheel.

Assumpta pulled open the door, stepped over the raised threshold, and entered into a store jam-packed with dried herbs and lush, growing plants, books and tarot cards, candles and altar supplies, clothing and jewelry. A wave of strawberry-scented smoke wafted over her as she passed an incense burner. An armada of glass baubles, feathered fairies, and brilliantly colored dragons hung from the ceiling. Assumpta felt sheltered—protected, even—rather than hemmed in from all the merchandise in the small shop.

To her left, a woman waved from behind a glass counter, phone glued to the side of her head. Multiple silver studs pierced the cartilage over the top of her ear, and her spiky black hair stuck out in all directions. The woman smiled and waved, and Assumpta couldn't help doing the same. Was that the woman she'd come to see—Jo Byrne? She'd look around the shop until the woman was free.

Assumpta wandered over to the herbs. The mixture of aromas almost overwhelmed her. She took a step back, away from the cloying pungency of sandalwood, sage, berry, and apple. Many more she couldn't identify blended together in a wall of fragrance. Punching through the odor of all the herbs, she smelled the cool, clear scent of mint.

She pulled out the list Brona had made her to see what she needed. Some of the herbs came pre-packaged, but others could be bought in bulk. Most were fairly inexpensive. She could work with that.

She moved to the altar supplies, thinking again how similar they looked to her own Catholic altar items. Here were altar clothes and chalices, statues and bells, and a large selection of candles in various colors. Two things stood out which she didn't use on her own altar: cauldrons (although she used a bowl sometimes) and athames, knives used ritualistically in spells.

She picked one up by its smooth, black handle and gripped it firmly, waving it in the air a few times to feel the balance. The nine-inch knife weighed more than it looked, but felt comfortable in her hand. She had an urge to pull the plastic sheath from the blade to test its sharpness, but she didn't dare. A surreptitious glance at the price tag dangling from the hilt told her it cost more than she was willing to spend.

She heard footsteps behind her and turned to see the woman from the counter approaching. The woman's earrings ringed both ears, and she wore a beaded choker low around her neck. It should have clashed with the silver, but it looked great.

"Hi," she said brightly. "Let me know if you need anything. There's a lot more here than meets the eye. If you're looking for something in particular, I can probably help."

"Actually, I'm looking for someone who might be able to help me break a hex or a curse." Assumpta returned the athame to the display on the counter and unfolded her list again. "I was directed to come here and ask for Jo."

"I'm Jo," the woman said, losing her smile and crossing her arms over her chest. "Who referred you?"

Assumpta knew that look. She pasted it on every time Caroline sent someone in her direction for help in finding something or to calculate their numerology. She never knew if the customer was sincere or coming to ridicule.

"I'm genuinely seeking help," Assumpta said. "But you won't know who sent me."

"Try me," Jo said.

"Brona Daly."

"The ghost at Enoch Pratt?" Jo smiled again. "How did she hear about me?"

*Does everyone know about Brona?*

"I don't want to burst your bubble," Assumpta said, "but in a more mundane fashion than you think—she looked you up in the phone book."

Jo burst out laughing.

"If it makes you feel any better," Assumpta continued, "she starred your name three times on my list, based on feedback and references from other folks and the Better Business Bureau."

Still smiling, Jo said, "Well, I'm not going to knock it. Too bad I can't put that on my business cards: *Recommended by local ghosts.*" She offered her hand to Assumpta, who took it and shook. "Why don't you tell me your name and what Ms. Brona Daly seems to think I can do for you. Come on up front. We can sit behind the counter while I mind the shop."

Assumpta introduced herself and explained about the demon mark.

Jo raised an eyebrow, but didn't say another word until they were seated on stools behind the counter. Jo flicked the switch on an electric kettle and said, "The mark has a physical manifestation?"

Assumpta nodded. "I'll be happy to show it to you, but I'll need to unbutton a few buttons." She lifted her hands to her shirt.

"You can show me later. How did you wind up demon-marked?"

"It's a long story," Assumpta said. *And not altogether a believable one*, she added silently. "It started with an archeologist who brought me an urn he'd broken transporting from a dig site. When the urn broke, it released a horde of demons."

Jo measured loose tea into strainers and dropped them into mugs. "And why did the archeologist come to you?"

"We have a mutual friend. She told him I could help him find things. He needed to find the demons and seal them back into the urn, or something like it."

Jo glanced at her. "You're a dowser?" She looked as though that information might be useful to her later.

Assumpta nodded. She pulled her pendulum from her purse. "I use this."

"And you tracked the demons and one of them marked you."

"No," Assumpta said. "One of the trapped souls was not evil. Even though he was released from the urn, his soul remained the property of a powerful demon. He asked for my help to get free. I agreed—but in gaining his freedom, we found ourselves marked. Until I get rid of the mark, I'm doomed to be plagued by demons...and there's the possibility I'll spend my afterlife in Hell. I need to get rid of it as soon as I'm able."

"Here," Jo said, placing a cup of strong tea in front of Assumpta and pushing honey toward her to sweeten it. "I have to be honest," she said, "I'm not sure there's anything I can do to help you. We can try a couple of hex-breaking or evil-repelling spells. But a physical representation on your body is strong magic. I can't name a witch who might have the power to remove one."

"I was worried about that," Assumpta said.

"And then there's the problem of belief. If you don't believe the spells will work, then they won't."

Assumpta smiled. "I've had this conversation with Brona already. The fact is, I do believe they will work."

"Then why don't you cast the spells yourself?" Jo asked. She took a sip of her tea, then set the cup down. The bell over the door jangled, and a pair of high school girls walked in. Jo smiled brightly and waved to them. "Let me know if there's anything you need."

The girls giggled and waved back.

Assumpta dismissed them. Even she could tell they were interested in the novelty of the store more than anything else.

Jo turned her attention back to Assumpta. "There is lots of information on the Internet."

"There are a number of reasons why I don't just troll the Internet and look for a spell to do the trick," Assumpta said. "One of which is, you never know if what you're reading on the 'net is true—not to mention that there is so much to wade through. But the main reason is because I've not had any formal training. I was raised a Catholic—no room for exploration there." She shrugged. "The truth is, if you work the spell, and it fails, then it's likely that the spell itself isn't powerful enough. If I work the spell, and it fails, it could be because I chose the wrong spell, or I messed up the incantation, or I didn't focus enough when I cast it." She took a sip of her tea, savoring the steaming clove and allspice. "Or because I just don't know what I'm doing.

"My intention was to ask you to cast the spells for me, but now I think it would be better if perhaps you helped me to cast the spells. Maybe we could cast them together. Would you be open to that?"

Jo nodded. "I would. In fact, I was going to suggest it."

The two high schoolers made their rounds around the shop and came to the counter, their baskets filled with temporary tattoos, strawberry incense, and some glittery tank tops from the few items of clothing on the racks in the far back of the shop. Jo rang up their purchases, wished them a good evening, and checked the watch on her wrist.

"Last customers of the day," she said, smiling, and went around the counter. She turned the *Open* sign to *Closed*, pulled down the shade on the front door, and locked up: turning three locks clockwise to set the bolts and then secured the chain.

She returned to the counter, reseated herself on the stool, then bent and retrieved a three-ring binder from under the counter. "I take a lot of notes," Jo said. "Something from just about every book I've ever read is in here—and lots of things said to me by my customers. You never know who you might learn from. There are some spells in here that we might want to try." She quickly turned several pages in the book, the silver bangles on her wrist clapping together musically.

"You don't know if they'll work?"

"They'll work," Jo said, closing the book slowly and turning to give Assumpta her full attention. "The question is: will they work for you?" She took a deep breath. "We should have probably began with this conversation."

"I don't understand—"

"Right," Jo said. "Let's start with this: you already know that you just can't cast a spell and have it work. You need to believe, to have intention, to draw on the energies around you. But how do you focus your energy and all that surrounds you? There are many paths in this craft—"

"Like there are many religions," Assumpta said. "The truth that I buy into won't work for everyone."

"Exactly." Jo nodded. "A lot of Wiccan spells are beautifully ritualistic, and I might have pointed you in that direction because I find Catholicism ritualistic, except that Wicca is a religion with its own deities—which is where the focus is. Spell casting is only part of it. But like any religion, there are rules. We can't just take a Wiccan spell and follow it like a recipe."

Assumpta was nodding now. "I need to find my own path." A sudden thought came to her. "I don't have that kind of time. It could take years!"

Jo said, seriously, "Absolutely. It's a journey, but we can narrow things down. You're Catholic—do you enjoy the ritual? Does it help you focus on your faith?"

Assumpta found herself smiling at Jo's words. She heard the question that Jo hadn't actually asked: *Does the repetition of ritual feel restrictive?*

"Actually," said Assumpta, "that's one of my major objections to Catholicism. All that ritual feels like a wall between me and my God. Why can't things be simpler?"

Jo opened the book again and began turning pages slowly. "What about family celebrations and such? What traditions do you follow?"

*Oh, sly Jo,* Assumpta thought, admiring the other woman's investigative skill. *You don't really care about traditions. You're probing to see if anyone else in my family walked a particular path.*

"My grandmother burned candles," Assumpta said. "Every day."

"Candle magick," Jo murmured, thumbing through the page dividers and turning to a particular section. "It makes sense, and easily walks beside Christianity..." Her words trailed off. "You'll need to purchase a few things for the spells: candles, herbs, and tools. I could lend you some of my items, but I firmly believe that you should select your own. You'll own the power that way, not be borrowing it. Gather whatever in the shop appeals to you. The spell will be more powerful, because if you open yourself to the choosing, you'll pick something that complements your own power."

Assumpta nodded. "Just like when I chose my pendulum. There was a much prettier one in the case that I really wanted, but something kept telling me to choose this one."

"Exactly," Jo said. She advanced the cash register tape a few inches and tore it off, then made a list. Handing it to Assumpta, she said, "Start with these. Take your time. While you find what you need, I'll look through the book for spells to start with. Whatever isn't perfect, we can adjust to our needs. The spell will be stronger that way, too."

Assumpta nodded. She set her teacup on the counter and stood, reading the list: cauldron (bowl), black candle, bamboo, chili pepper, oil.

How big did the cauldron have to be? Five gallons? *Imagine lugging that home on the bus,* she thought with a smile.

She nearly kicked the first one she came across. About eighteen inches tall, it stood on three squat legs and looked like it had escaped from a fairy tale. She bent and lifted it by the handle. She managed, but couldn't conceive of having to carry this around. It was simply too much. But on a low shelf just above it, she found a collection of cauldrons in various shapes, colors, and materials. One caught her eye right away, a red-metal affair about ten inches tall, with cork feet. She lifted it to feel its weight, and then spotted a smaller white cauldron hiding behind it.

She set down the red one and picked up the white. She smiled as soon as she had it in her hands. It was enameled and reminded her of the pots her grandmother used to cook with. It felt like a pleasant memory. And it was small, barely six inches tall on its three squat legs. She could put it in her sweater pocket to carry home.

Assumpta dropped the little cauldron into a woven basket that Jo kept handy for shoppers, and made her way to the candles. She called to the front of the store, "What kind of candle, taper or votive? And does it really have to be black?"

Jo looked up from turning pages. "The candle should be taller than the cauldron is deep. We need a black candle because we're going to have to break an evil spell, *not* because we're practicing black magic. Okay?"

"All right," Assumpta said. That relieved some of her worry. Deep down, she knew witchcraft wasn't bad, but it didn't hurt to ask about what she didn't know.

She'd never seen such a large collection of candles. Jo sold long thin tapers, short squat votives, tall pillars, and all shapes and sizes in between. And both came in scented and unscented varieties.

"Scented or unscented?"

Jo looked up from her book again. "It doesn't matter for this spell," she said, "but I'd go with unscented. We're going to burn it until it extinguishes itself. Some aromas can get overwhelming over time."

Assumpta chose a slender black taper about as thick as her pinky finger and only five inches tall, then wandered to the herbs.

Again, how much? Jo looked engrossed, so she grabbed pre-packaged bamboo and chili, and on impulse, rosemary. Then she joined Jo at the front of the store.

"Do you have everything?" Jo asked.

"I think so." Assumpta reached into her purse and pulled out her blessed oil. "Can I use this for the oil?"

Jo stared at the jar of oil for only a second, then grinned. "Do you always carry that around with you?"

Assumpta wondered how much she should tell Jo. She wanted to avoid the whole looking-like-a-nutcase-thing, but Jo would probably know exactly where she was coming from. She returned Jo's grin. "Yep, and these, too." She pulled out the wide-mouthed jar of blessed salt and the opaque plastic container of holy water.

Jo whistled. "There's a story there."

"Long story. Can I fill you in later?"

Jo nodded. "I'm going to hazard a guess here and say that there must be something special about that particular oil for you to have it with you all the time. That gives it power. It will be an asset to your spell casting."

"Good," Assumpta said. "Do I need an athame or other ritual tools?"

Jo shook her head. "You can use them if you want to, but it's not necessary. I look at it this way: our ancestors didn't have the cash to spend on separate tools for crafting. They used the same knife they cut their meat with to chop the herbs for a spell, the same cup, the same bowl." Jo pulled a few pages from her notebook. "Honestly, you don't even need the cauldron for candle magick, but I'm terrified of starting a fire, especially in my shop. It's simply precaution. And when you do this on your own, you may find that you don't want a cauldron or even a simple bowl. You'll learn how the magic works best for you and do it that way."

Suddenly, Assumpta's demon mark itched like crazy. "Uh-oh," she said, scanning the shop.

"It won't work, you know," said Pournelle. His suit was a navy blue pinstripe tonight, more stylish than the dapper look he had sported at Enoch Pratt. The librarian badge was missing, and he looked completely out of place in the small shop. He walked toward them from the front door. "I really wish you'd consider my offer, Assumpta." He reached into his breast pocket and pulled out a tri-folded piece of buff-colored paper and shook out the folds.

"How did you get in here?" Jo asked, her voice loud and harsh. She reached for the phone.

"9-1-1 won't help," he said.

Assumpta stepped in front of Jo to protect her. "We've discussed this already. I won't be put in a worse position than I already am."

Pournelle put the paper away, then snapped his fingers and a business card appeared between them. Assumpta ignore the proffered card.

"When the spells don't work, I want to be the first one you call." He grinned broadly, his teeth gleaming white against the backdrop of his black face. Stepping closer, he leaned toward Assumpta, his forehead nearly touching hers, the scent of sulfur overwhelming. "You're out of options."

"I'm calling 9-1-1," Jo said, pushing buttons on the phone.

"There's always hope." Assumpta reached into her purse for her blessed salt.

"Except where there's none," Pournelle countered, and disappeared. His business card fluttered down to the counter.

# CHAPTER 19

JO SLAMMED DOWN THE PHONE. "WHAT THE HELL was that?" she asked, her voice tremulous.

Assumpta released the bottle of blessed salt, which she hadn't even cleared from her purse in the short moment it took for the demon to pop in, threaten her, and pop out again. She turned to Jo. "That was one of the demons that feels compelled to visit me due to my mark."

"He looked rather charming for devil spawn." Jo seemed to regain her composure, though her face remained pale. "I never imagined a demon in a three-piece suit."

"Trust me, it's a façade. Nothing is what it seems when it originates in Hell. I've seen what they look like up close and personal. It's not pretty."

Jo nodded once, a determined gleam in her eye. Then she brushed past Assumpta and into the store, first grabbing a basket by the door. "I'd like to cast a protection circle before we work any spells," she said, taking some candles from the nearby rack. "Go to the back of the store and get some chalk. Meet me in the office once you've got it."

Assumpta nodded, pocketed Pournelle's business card, and walked past the athames and cauldrons to the shelves in the back of the store. There was a miscellany of items here: books, henna products, honey-based hand cream, clearance items, and the chalk: a small cardboard display of flat chalk sticks instead of the schoolroom round ones. She grabbed a few sticks and returned to the front of the store and the office, a room just to the right of the counter.

The office also served as a store room. Half the room contained shelves full of boxed items. Many of the labels indicated they were inventory. The other half contained a wooden desk, a swivel chair and a freestanding altar comprised of a small marble table on a metal tripod base.

Jo had already pushed the desk chair against the wall, and with a handmade broom, she was sweeping a large circle in the open area. She tossed the broom on the desk.

"Do you have the chalk?"

Assumpta handed it to her.

Jo bent and drew a chalk circle on the floor about five feet in diameter—as large as she could make it in the space she'd cleared between the desk and storage shelves.

"I don't normally cast a protection circle," she explained, "but it seems prudent from what I just witnessed. My Wiccan friends would be ecstatic."

"Wait," Assumpta said. "You really don't have to do this. I could see the demon scared you. And if you don't want to get involved, I understand."

Slowly, Jo finished drawing the circle. She kept silent for a moment, as if choosing her words carefully, or perhaps giving the idea more thought. Finally, she said, "It's not my way to run from danger or ignore someone who needs help. You need help. I'll do what I can."

"It's not your fight," Assumpta said.

"I couldn't live with myself if I didn't try." Jo rummaged through the basket and pulled out four white pillar candles. "I can't guarantee that what I do will help you, but I promise I won't harm you."

"I wouldn't be so sure about that," Assumpta said. She explained about Father Tony's attempted absolution.

Jo looked stunned. "I've never heard of anything like that. Are you certain *you* want to try this?"

"I have to," Assumpta said. "The demons will keep following me until I get rid of this mark." She looked at Jo's chalk circle.

Jo nodded. "Then let's get this done. Do you have your oil?"

Assumpta handed her the bottle she kept in her purse.

Jo sniffed. "Do I smell rosemary?"

"I couldn't pass it up." Assumpta showed her the sprigs she'd grabbed along with the other herbs. "I love the way it smells."

"Perfect," Jo said. "Rosemary is excellent for protection. You've got good instincts." She accepted the offered sprigs, crushing the needles between her fingers and releasing the sharp scent of rosemary into the air. "Rosemary oil," she said, lifting her hand to show Assumpta her shiny fingertips.

Next, Jo uncapped Assumpta's bottle and wet her thumb and fingers with the holy oil, mixing it with the rosemary. "First, we're going to *dress* these candles," she said, indicating the tall, white pillars. "That means rubbing the oil on them and rolling them in herbs. I'll do two and you can do the others." She showed Assumpta the correct way to rub the oil on the candles. "There are several herbs that can be used for protection, and you'll learn them, but tonight we're using bamboo, chili, and rosemary—in conjunction with rosemary oil, it's doubly powerful. It's important while you're dressing the candle to think about what you want from the spell. Since we desire protection, meditate on that while you work."

Assumpta closed her eyes as she rubbed the oil on the candle, focusing on protection and the ability to remain safe.

When they were done, Jo set the pillars in a cross pattern on the lines of the circle on the floor.

"Will it hurt your spell if I add a circle or two of my own?" Assumpta pulled the bottles of holy water and blessed salt out of her purse and held them up for Jo to see.

"Christian ritual and pagan magick working in concert? I guess it can't hurt, especially if you think it will keep the demons out. Just don't—"

"Break the circle. I know," Assumpta said, already turning the uncapped bottle of water over and wetting her fingers. She drew a circle outside of Jo's, re-wetting her fingers as needed. When she was done, she spread a thin line of salt on top the holy water. "I think I'll have just enough salt to go around. Would I make you uncomfortable if I called upon Saint Michael to protect us, too?"

Jo shook her head. "You've been physically marked by a demon and have been visited by them. If you have the power of Saint Michael at your disposal, use it."

*If you only knew*, Assumpta thought. But did she? Saint Michael was working with Jak, so was he working with her by extension? Yet, as a Catholic, she could call on him at any time. And if she did call on him, how would she know if he came? Still, she had to try.

Assumpta said the words of the traditional prayer: "Saint Michael the Archangel, defend us in battle. Be our defense against the wickedness and snares of the devil." While she prayed, Assumpta continued to spread the salt around the circle. "May God rebuke him, we humbly pray. And do thou, O Prince of the Heavenly Hosts, by the power of God, thrust Satan into Hell, along with all the evil spirits, who prowl about the world seeking the ruin of souls. Amen."

"Amen," Jo echoed. She moved her altar into the circle, lifting it over the chalk, salt, and water, then brought in the basket of supplies. "Step inside with your items. We'll light the candles to close the circle."

Assumpta stepped into the circle and waited for Jo's lead.

Jo pulled a cigarette lighter from her pocket and bent to the first candle, pausing over it a moment. She handed the lighter to Assumpta. "Light each wick and concentrate on protection as you do so. Think about a wall or shield surrounding us and keeping us from harm."

Assumpta bent and lit the second candle, invoking Saint Michael again. Out of the corner of her eye, she saw a shadow enter the room from the door and slither along the wall to the back. She lost sight of it behind the shelves. Her heart thumped almost painfully in her chest. She wondered, *protective spirit or threatening demon?*

The mark on her back was silent. Maybe she was protected within the delineated space of the circle and the mark *couldn't* activate?

She lit the third candle. As the flame took hold, Assumpta saw shadows rise up like seeping gases from the floor outside the circle, then slither to the back of the storeroom to join the others behind the shelves.

"Assumpta?" Jo called out in a shaky voice.

"I saw them. Is this normal for circle casting?"

"I've never seen a physical manifestation of anything while working magick," Jo said. "I'd have called you a liar if you came to me with a story like this."

Assumpta nodded. "It's a pretty normal day for me, lately. I'm going to assume that it's my presence that brought them here. Do you have a banishment spell for spirits?" More shadows rose up through the concrete floor, this time standing their ground about eighteen inches from the protection circle.

"I do," Jo said, rummaging through her basket. "We'll cast that first."

"One more candle," Assumpta said, kneeling to light. Again, shades—like shadows come to life—whispered up from the concrete floor. These stayed in place and gently flickered in time with the candles on some invisible air current.

Jo smiled shakily. "Okay, we can start the banishment spells now."

# CHAPTER 20

ASSUMPTA ASKED, "WILL YOUR BANISHMENT SPELL do anything about the spirits we seem to have attracted?"

"I have no idea," Jo said. "I've never seen anything like them. I've never seen anything manifest. Ever. But if the spell I've chosen doesn't work," she said, "there are others we can try."

Assumpta nodded. "What can I do to help?"

"Not a thing. I'll cast this spell alone to get us started. Then we'll work together on your hex-breaking spell." Jo took a black candle, a small bottle of oil, and some chopped herbs from her basket and set them on the altar. "I'm using a black candle to break the hex, and olive oil and onion—both good for banishment—to dress the candle."

She closed her eyes, oiling the candle with the olive oil. Then, she opened her eyes and rolled the candle in the dried onion, using the plastic packaging to press the onion tightly to the candle. She lit the wick and said, "Unwelcome spirits be gone, I command you. Your presence is unwelcome." She looked around the room. The shades remained where they were. She repeated, in a firmer, louder voice, "Unwelcome spirits be gone, I command you. Your presence is unwelcome."

"How long does it take?" Assumpta asked in hushed tones.

Jo shook her head. "I don't know. It depends on the strength of my spell—and the strength of those I'm casting it against." The shades flickered, then rose up higher. Jo looked worried.

"Do you mind if I try?" Assumpta asked.

"Be my guest."

Assumpta lifted a small bowl of salt from Jo's altar and said, "In the name of the Father, and the Son, and the Holy Ghost, I command you to *depart*." She took a pinch of the salt and threw it on the shadows.

With a hiss—the sound of wind moving through saw grass—the shadows shrunk to only inches off the floor. She repeated herself, this time louder. "In the name of the Father, and the Son, and Holy Ghost—"

Jo joined in, and together they said, "We command you to depart." Assumpta threw the salt again, and this time the spirits vanished, slithering away and then sinking into the concrete.

"That was impressive," Jo said. "I've never seen Christian magick work like that."

"Prayer, actually," Assumpta said, "though I can see how it might qualify as magick." She held up the small bowl. "The consecrated salt was pagan, so I'd say it was a combination of things that did the trick. I'd have used my own blessed salt, but I used it up on the circle." She took a deep breath. "Shall we try your other spells on my mark?"

"Let's," Jo said. "Would you mind showing it to me now?"

Assumpta turned her back to Jo, unbuttoned a few buttons on her shirt and shrugged it down to give the other woman a peek.

"If you hadn't have told me what it is," Jo said, "I'd have mistaken it for a tattoo."

She tugged upward on Assumpta's collar, and Assumpta shrugged the shirt the rest of the way up and turned back around to face the altar, rebuttoning. "You don't need me to keep the shirt off during the rite?"

"Would it make you feel more comfortable?" Jo asked.

"Not particularly."

"Then leave it on." She rummaged through Assumpta's basket and took out a sprig of rosemary. Assumpta could smell the cool, sweet flavor before she even saw the sprig as Jo handed it to her. "Carry this with you at all times," Jo said.

"For how long?"

"At least three days. We'll know by then if the spell doesn't work. That's the thing about pagan magick: like prayer, it doesn't always happen immediately. So, we'll cast a hex-breaking spell tonight. And a personal protection spell, if you'd like. If we don't see results, we can cast them again in a few days or try a different spell."

"So long?"

"Sorry. It's not like we're spraying grease remover on a stain. These things take time." She rummaged in her basket while she talked and pulled out a small yellow notepad, a red felt-tipped marker, a pair of plastic-handled scissors, a red scarf, a jar of what looked like paprika or red pepper, and a spool of red cotton thread. She stacked these on the already crowded altar.

Jo handed the paper and red pen to Assumpta. "We're going to try a little sympathetic magick."

"Sympathetic?"

"Magick based on correspondence. We'll make a symbol that corresponds to your demon, who is then affected magically by actions performed on his symbol. Hopefully, once we break its hex, the mark will disappear."

"Like a voodoo doll."

Jo nodded. "Very much so. Write the name of the demon who hexed you in the center of the paper, then draw an outline of his form around his name."

"But I don't know his name!" Assumpta said. "If I knew his name, *he'd* be under *my* power."

"It's okay," said Jo, her voice low and soothing. "Just write 'enemy mine' in the center of the paper."

Assumpta uncapped the pen and wrote *ENEMY MINE* in bold, capital letters in the center of the page. But what shape should she draw around it? The demons usually came to her in human form and stayed that way as long as she didn't piss them off. But it wasn't their true appearance.

"Does the spell require me to draw their true form or the form in which they appear to me?"

"Is there a huge difference?" Jo asked.

"Vast," Assumpta said. And if you counted the minions that the first demon had brought with them, then it would seem that demons could take on any shape they wanted. She had no idea what to draw.

"Draw them how you think of them," Jo said.

Assumpta drew a vaguely human shape with a head, two legs, and two arms, but then she added a thick, heavy tail, like the one on the first demon she'd battled in Holy Rosary Church. She added a set of horns pushing out of the flesh of the forehead and giant wings spreading the width of its shoulders and reaching nearly to the floor. She capped the pen and laid it down.

"Cut it out," Jo said, handing her the scissors. When Assumpta finished, Jo pulled a short length of thread from the spool and showed Assumpta how to tie it around the drawing's waist. "We're binding the demon with this string," Jo said. "Next, sprinkle it with paprika and tie it in a red scarf." When Assumpta had done as she directed, Jo said, "We have just created the demon's own private hell."

"Now what?"

"Now you grip the bundle in your hand and say in your own words, 'Enemy mine, your power over me is gone. Your hex is broken, your mark is gone, the spell is undone. Enemy mine, you have no power over me from this moment forward.' The important thing is to visualize the spell broken," Jo said. "Imagine your energy flowing out of you to repel the demon and break the spell."

Assumpta spoke the words with her eyes closed, focusing deeply on the words. She opened her eyes a minute later. "Nothing happened," she said. She'd been hoping for the appearance of a demon, or at least some minions—anything to show her that she was getting to them in some way. Even a tingle or itch of the mark would have been nice.

"We don't know that," Jo said. "You've cast the spell and sent it out into the universe. Now, we wait for it to bear fruit."

"What do we do in the meantime?"

"You cast the spell tomorrow and the next day. On the fourth day, unwrap the paper doll and tear it into nine pieces, then burn it. Scatter the ashes far from your home and throw the scarf in the garbage. Whatever you do, don't re-use it for anything. And don't even consider wearing it."

"Should I burn it?"

"It wouldn't hurt if you did," Jo said, "but I'd burn it separate from the effigy. And if this spell doesn't work, we'll look for something else. Are you ready to cast a protection spell?"

*God, I'm tired.* She just wanted to peel off her clothes and crawl into bed. "Yeah, but then I've got to get home."

Jo must have sensed her fatigue. "This won't take much time at all."

Assumpta nodded. "Where do we begin?"

"Outside the circle," Jo said. "It seems strange to me to cast a protection spell within a protective circle. So—" She blew out the candles and took a step toward the chalk.

"Wait," Assumpta said. "What about the shades? Do you think they might be hiding, waiting for us to step outside the protection of the circle?"

"I think they're gone," Jo said, stepping over the chalk. She shrugged. "They enjoyed taunting us. If they were still here, I think they'd be gathered as close as they could be around the circle."

Cautiously, Assumpta stepped outside the ring. She took a deep breath. "All right. What next?"

"We need a candle, and some rosemary. Traditionally, a yellow candle is chosen for power, but I get the feeling yellow might feel off to you. So choose a color that, for you, symbolizes power. Then meet me up front. I've got the rosemary."

Assumpta walked back into the shop and over to the shelves of candles, considering them. There were so many! She closed her eyes, breathing in the warring scents of the candles to the left. They felt anathema to her. Scented wouldn't do.

She opened her eyes and took a step to the right. The candles were arranged in chromatic order, yellow and gold at the top and spiraling down through all the colors of the rainbow toward black. White candles occupied an entire shelf to the right, coming in many shapes, sizes, and molded forms.

She thought, *What color is power?* She lifted a hand and lightly touched each of the candles to see if any *felt* right. Nothing, but her eyes kept drifting right to the white candles. White was the color of light, of brightness. It blasted away the shadows. White *felt* right.

She chose a slender taper, then walked to the front of the store.

Jo had pulled a small table and two stools out of a corner and thrown a green scarf over the table. There was a small vial of clear liquid and a box of wooden matches in the center of the scarf. When Jo saw Assumpta carrying the taper, she grabbed a clear, crystal candle holder from off the nearby counter and, pulling the purple candle from it, set it on the table.

"I had a feeling you would choose white," Jo said.

"Why?" Assumpta asked. "I didn't have any idea—with so many choices—what I would end up with."

"White just seems right," Jo said, shrugging. "It looks correct in your hand."

Assumpta smiled. "And it just *felt* right for me to choose it."

Jo smiled back. "Please sit. This spell is quite simple, but it relies heavily on your will. It will work regardless, but the stronger you believe, the stronger the protection will be." She handed Assumpta the vial of clear liquid and laid some crushed, dried rosemary on the table in front of her. "You're going to prepare the candle similarly to the ones we used for the protection circle. As you're dressing the candle, close your eyes and picture a protective shield around you, which grows outward as you push your fingers toward the wick. The shield should be whole, without defects, surrounding all of you."

Assumpta opened the vial and inhaled the strong, pungent aroma of rosemary oil. She'd always loved the scent of rosemary, and now it made her feel safe as well. She poured some of the oil on her fingers, rubbing them against her thumb to coat it as well, then grasped the candle. She closed her eyes to concentrate. Her fingers, slick with oil, slid to the top of the candle. She turned the candle and made the motion again, picturing a shield forming around her body; a strong, thick shield, created by her will. She did it a third time, strengthening the vision. And again, making certain to anoint the entire candle.

"Once you have a clear picture of the shield," Jo said, "open your eyes and light the candle."

Assumpta placed the candle in the crystal holder, struck a match, and lit the wick.

"Focus on the flame," Jo said, her words soft and soothing, almost mesmerizing. "See the flame as strengthening and hardening your shield. The white color becomes brighter and brighter, imbuing the shield with its strength, too." She waited a few seconds, then said, "When you're certain of the shield, when you feel its solidity protecting you, when you're certain there's no crack or fissure, blow out the candle."

Assumpta closed her eyes once more, imagined hardening the shield to titanium strength, then opened them and blew out the candle.

"Excellent," Jo said.

"I feel safer already," said Assumpta said. Strangely, she felt better protected than if she had prayed for aid. Praying was like signaling into the wind, hoping someone would hear...who knew who listened and heard? Maybe she got protection, or maybe she'd signaled someone or some*thing* out to do her harm; someone or something that now knew how unprotected she was.

This protection was her own, borne of herself. She could rely on it. And she was more than okay with that.

# CHAPTER 21

FOUR DAYS LATER, WHILE JAK AND ASSUMPTA walked to Enoch Pratt, Assumpta pulled out an envelope containing the ashes of the burnt effigy and dumped them into a city trash can. She also tossed the rosemary sprig, now brown and dry.

She had thrown the ashes from the scarf in which she'd wrapped the effigy into the trash in Greg's apartment. Jo had told her to burn them separately, so she wasn't taking any chance on co-mingling the ashes in the same trash bin. And the likelihood of the ashes being mixed together at the dump seemed fairly slim—she was satisfied that she'd done everything right.

She took a deep breath, held it a second, then let it all out, hoping this would be the end of it. "You're going to love this," she told Jak, opening the library door and ushering him in.

Assumpta loved arriving at Enoch Pratt just as it opened. Early in the morning, she could almost feel alone among the books. The library seemed to breathe differently; the air felt more still, more serene. The solemnity felt almost like a church.

Jak seemed to sense her mood, remaining quiet as they headed through the lobby to the marble-stepped staircase.

They got to the Poe room without seeing another patron.

"I've never seen so many books in one place," Jak said, standing in the middle of the room and turning a circle. He walked to one high shelf and brushed a reverent hand down the spines of several books. "Amazing."

Smiling, Assumpta said, "Wait until you see the rest of the library."

They'd come straight up the stairs to the Poe room. He hadn't seen the literal miles of books shelved in the remainder of the building. The Poe room held but a fraction of the library's entire collection.

While Jak examined several books in awe, Assumpta pulled out the bibliography of demon-related works and reviewed the ones she wanted to examine based on the brief bibliographical data available in the catalog. There was one she really wanted to look at, but it was checked out for at least the next two weeks. Maybe Brona had already read it.

The lights flickered, and Jak glanced up at them. But before Brona appeared, Assumpta felt her demon mark tingle. There wasn't a demon in sight, and that worried her. The mark appeared to be getting stronger. And that was good for its demon-detecting abilities, but what else did it mean?

"Something's coming," she whispered to Jak.

He tensed, and reached for something in his back pocket. "A demon?"

"Yes—" She shivered as the mark on her back fluttered and itched.

The light bulb over the table shattered, and bits of glass flickered down over the table like snow. Assumpta brushed a shard from her face with one hand while reaching for her salt and holy water with the other.

A curl of smoke materialized on the other side of the table, rose higher, and coalesced into the form of a tall, leanly muscled man. The pressure in the room expanded, Assumpta's ears popped, and he appeared: young and smiling, his dark hair combed back in a pompadour away from an appealing face. He kept his hands in the pockets of his navy blue Dockers, and with his matching long-sleeved shirt buttoned all the way to his neck, he looked as though he might have stepped off the lot at Bethlehem Steel.

"Sorry about that," he said, glancing up at the light. "Happens every time I enter this plane. Can't figure out why."

The temperature dropped ten degrees, and the demon looked over his shoulder. He smiled, then turned back to them. "Didn't know we'd be having company, but I do like a cool breeze for a change of pace."

Brona looked him up and down. "I haven't seen this one before."

The demon turned back to her. "Because I haven't been here before." He *tsk*ed. "Poor wee *ghosty*...trapped like an animal in a snare." He didn't look very sympathetic.

The demon turned back to Assumpta and offered her a cheery smile. "I've got a proposition for you."

She nudged Jak with her elbow. "Where have I heard that before?" When he didn't answer, she looked at him. He stared intently at the demon. "What's wrong?"

"I know this one," Jak said. "Kuna."

"Kenny," the demon corrected, losing his cheery smile. "Jak?" Recognition dawned. "Jak!" He stepped back two paces into Brona's space. Her outline curved around him, and with the gentle pop of a soap bubble, they merged. Brona shrieked and disappeared in a puff.

Her departure seemed not to phase the demon. "What are you doing here, Jak?"

Jak crossed his arms on his chest and gave Kenny a hard look. "I could ask the same of you."

"Just delivering a message from my master—"

"So spit it out and get out of here," Assumpta said.

A crafty look came over Kenny's face. "But your presence here," he nodded at Jak, "might change things, so I'll be keeping it to myself. Oh, and Assumpta—" He gave her a sad look. "That banishment spell isn't going to work."

And with that, he was gone, another bulb popping in the overhead fixture with his departure.

"How do you know him, Jak?" Assumpta asked, shoving her demon bibliography back into her purse. She was afraid she already knew.

"We were trapped for an eternity together within the urn Greg found. None of us were freed until the accident he had on the highway. And although I was free from the incarceration of the jar, I remained a prisoner of Hell. That's where I found myself once the seal on the urn had been broken."

"And you appealed to me to free you from Hell." Assumpta stepped away from him to evaluate their relationship. "I always wondered how it was you chose me to beg a favor from. If not for Greg, you wouldn't have found me."

He nodded.

"And how do you feel about me now?"

"You can ask that?" he said with a note of incredulity in his voice.

"Absolutely," she said. "We met by chance, and you handily had me agree to fuck like rabbits to release you from your Hellish prison—"

"You weren't so easy—"

"Then you disappeared without a word for months—except for a *dream* visit—and now you're back, offering to protect me, on some mission from God." She put her hands on her hips. "You probably have no idea how ludicrous that sounds." She stopped, feeling herself getting somewhat hysterical. If she didn't, she might just burst into tears. And she didn't want to do that in front of him, not when she didn't know where she stood. Where *they* stood. Even though the only thing that mattered right now was that she get this damned mark off her back. She didn't have time for complications.

Assumpta had a feeling she was in love and felt tears well in her eyes. She blinked rapidly, stemming the moisture before it grew too great and leaked down her face. *Complications.*

Jak stepped toward her and pulled her into his warm embrace. Beneath her cheek, she could feel the warm, hard muscle of his chest covered in soft cotton. His warrior arms held her tightly against him. It felt so good, she didn't want him to let go.

"I care for you deeply," he said softly, kissing the top of her head.

She wondered if that were man-speak for love or if caring was as far as his emotions ran. Maybe he tried to protect her in that, too, by not admitting to love. It would make his departure that much more difficult this time around.

She could live with caring, she decided. Better to have loved and lost and all that.

And she might as well make good use of the time while he was here, too, she thought, nudging him to release her. Brona was gone, the lights were out in this section of the library, and she was in no mood to do additional research. She needed a break from all this demon bullshit.

Assumpta stepped out of the circle of his embrace. "C'mon," she said. "I'm in the mood for a snack."

"What are you in the mood for?"

"A little *afternoon delight*," she said, giving him a smile.

He looked puzzled, then brightened. "Is that anything like heavenly hash?"

She burst out laughing. "Fudge?"

"I love chocolate and marshmallow together," he said. "It's sticky and sweet and melts on my tongue. I try to savor it, but I just want to gobble."

She laughed again. "This isn't quite the same, but you might want to gobble it anyway."

# CHAPTER 22

ASSUMPTA DREW JAK INTO HER BEDROOM AND locked the door.

"You're certain none of the others are around?" she asked.

He nodded. "I would see them, even though you can't. They must all be out with Greg."

"Let's hope they stay out for a good long time," she said, pushing him against the door and standing on tiptoes to reach him. She raised her lips to his and kissed. A fire spread through her body the moment their lips touched. God, she'd missed this. She'd missed *him.*

"This," she said, breaking the kiss, "is afternoon delight."

Jak needed no urging. He joined the kiss with equal enthusiasm, raising his hands to her shoulders to pull her closer. His passionate response sent a wave of instant arousal sweeping through her. Hot and wet, she pulled him closer for more.

Breath mingling, Assumpta brushed half-open kisses against his mouth, tasting his sweetness. At the same time, she pulled the soft, black T-shirt from the waistband of his jeans, running her hands beneath it, sliding her palms across the taut muscles of his waist and back, feeling his flesh for the first time.

When they had come together as human and spirit months ago, she had felt his weight, the power of his kiss, even the sense of touching...*something*. And it had felt so good—but touching him now, she realized there had been something lacking then, something her own inexperience didn't realize she was missing.

Now that she had the real Jak, the *in-the-flesh Jak*, it felt sweeter than ever. She ran her hands up the front of his chest and felt the muscles ripple beneath his shirt. His body was hard and warm, solid, like a military man's body should be. In spirit form, he'd tempted her in many guises—each face, each body, more seductive than the last. He'd felt real then, but he felt more real now. Perhaps that was what had been missing.

He pushed away from the door, nudging her toward the bed. She took a step backward, their lips still devouring each other. He nudged her again, but she preferred to dally in the sweetness of the kiss, standing firm.

Still kissing, she inched her hands down to the bulge in the front of his jeans and rubbed, just a little tease, then she curled her fingers over the top of his pants and clutched the firm flesh she knew they both wanted freed.

Jak gasped. "Slow down," he muttered against her lips. "Let's take our time."

She pushed her tongue into his mouth, then snaked her hands to the button of his fly and, grasping the material tightly, she yanked him closer to her.

She broke the kiss. "I don't want to go slow. Not this first time."

"Wait."

He pushed her away slightly, separating their bodies only by an inch or two. It was enough to allow her skin to cool and Assumpta groaned. She didn't want to stop, now that she had him in her arms again. She gave him a puzzled expression. "Why?"


He wanted her, he really did, more than anything. But he wasn't willing to have sex with her—no matter how good it might feel—

unless she knew the kind of man he was. "Remember when we *came together* before?"

Her eyes grew wide. "The voices." She looked him up and down. "They're still with you, even though you're no longer a spirit trapped in Hell? We could ask—"

He nodded. "The spirits are always here, but—" He took both her hands in his own and held them together between them. "Let me show you. Close your eyes, concentrate."

"But Jak, we're right in the middle—"

"*Please.*"

Assumpta gave him a half smile, then nodded and did as he asked. Jak opened his mind, breathing deeply, and invited the spirits in. Almost immediately, they flooded his mind. "Can you hear them?" he asked Assumpta.

He opened his eyes and watched her face, knowing the exact moment she heard them—saw the quizzical little wrinkle on her brow give way to a brilliant smile. "I hear them! But—" the wrinkle was back, "they're so quiet, it's not like last time. Is it because..." Assumpta dropped her voice, speaking almost in a whisper, "we're not having sex?"

He chuckled and said, "That's part of it, but not all." He told her what Saint Michael had revealed to him—that a simple touch of their hands was all they ever needed to share the voices.

Assumpta burst out laughing.

"It's not funny," Jak said, indignant. "It's probably what got us marked."

"I don't know about that," Assumpta said. "I don't think there was a thing either one of us could have done to prevent us from being marked. Don't worry, I'm not holding it against you." She squeezed his hands. "So...shall we get on with this?"

"Not yet."

"Not yet?"

Her crestfallen look nearly broke his heart. "We will, I promise you. At least, we will if you want to. But first, I want you to know how

I came to be in the urn, the kind of man I was: a traitor, a betrayer of my countrymen—"

"Stop," she said, disentangling her hands from his and pressing her fingers to his lips. "You're none of those things."

"I am."

"Okay. Spit it out," she said, her looking telling him she still didn't believe him, but that she was willing to listen.

"It's better if you hear it from them," Jak said sadly, "from the spirits. That way you can be certain I've left nothing out." She nodded, and he gripped her hands again. "Concentrate."

Assumpta gripped his hands and closed her eyes. The voices came flooding back almost instantly, faint, and then a little louder.

"Ask them," Jak said.

Assumpta licked her lips. "How did Jak come to be in the urn?"

At first, Assumpta couldn't hear anything. Then, she heard the softest of hums—a vibrating hum that grew louder, wavering, and then the dissonance evened out. She could hear distinct voices among the homogenous noise. The voices became louder still, a clamor of hoots and shouts. She listened for one voice, trying to separate one from the din, just as Jak had taught her previously. A moment later, she found that voice and focused on it. But then others joined in, determined it seemed, to relate to her all that happened...

Jak carried his laundry to the stream, grateful for a few moments alone to take care of his things. Blood and sweat caked the worst of it, and he was tired of battling the flies as they marched. Clean linen would go a long way to avoid the bloodthirsty insects. Let his less fastidious brethren bear their bite.

He dropped the soiled clothing to the ground, then lifted the leather belt and sheath of his dagger over his shoulder, dropping both sheath, belt and weapon to the ground. Muscles bulging, he pulled off his heavy cuirass—extremely difficult without the aid of another soldier—and laid the hinged metal armor gently on the loamy soil. He removed his belt and *baltea,* feeling vulnerable without the groin protection. But he wanted to swim, and he'd have to get vulnerable to manage that. His tunic was next, joining the other laundry, and finally his loin cloth.

He stretched, arms overhead, flexing muscles tired from marching and carrying everything he owned on his back. The setting sun, still warm, felt like a gentle massage on his skin. He relished the quiet by the stream—away from the noise of an army bedding down to camp. He savored the privacy, but hurried. It wouldn't do to be late for his watch.

He stepped into the river, the water chilling his ankles. Bracing himself, he dove in.

The icy water washed over him, wiping away the sweat, soothing his aching muscles and washing away the blood from the last battle and the accumulated dirt of three days march. He scrubbed himself with the fine white sand at the bottom of the river, staying under the water as long as he could, scouring away the toughest grime. Finally, lungs burning, he pushed off the bottom, and broke the surface of the water, breathing deeply.

He swam a few strokes, then noticed someone on the riverbank beside his things. *Mehercule*, he didn't have time for this now. Jak glided to the bank and stood, water sluicing down his chest. The cold braced him, and he felt re-made by the river. He could take on anything—or anyone. He swept back his hair and wiped the water from his eyes.

It was a woman—a beautiful woman—sitting on the ground next to his laundry. Her dark hair was braided away from her face, and she wore a beautiful blue tunic embroidered in silver. She clutched an urn in her hands.

"I'll do your laundry, *optio*, if you'll help me open this vase."

She flattered him. He wasn't second in command, just a simple soldier, doing as he was told.

Who was she? Most of the *lixae*—the camp followers—wore rougher garments. The lone women who followed the army were interested in easy coin for laying on their backs. Perhaps there would be time for—*no*. He didn't have the time—and already would have to race through washing his clothes simply because he had desired a bath. But guard duty wouldn't wait, and he'd already dallied too long.

Besides, the women of the lixae were used, hard. Not this one. She hadn't come to offer him her body for a few coins. *Pity—so what was she doing traveling with them?*

Apparently, she was a woman in some distress. But she couldn't be serious—she couldn't open the urn, really?

"How can I help?" he asked, picking up his discarded tunic and putting it on.

"The lid is sealed shut." She offered him the urn, pointing to the lip. "I've tried opening it with a knife, but it won't budge."

"Have you tried dropping it?" he asked.

"And spill the contents?"

She had him there.

Perhaps if he pried the lid off, she'd be willing to do his laundry and bring it to him later. But could he trust her? Probably not.

He took the urn and gave it a little shake. "It feels empty," he said.

"It's not—the contents are more valuable than you know."

She stood and gave him an enticing smile and he wished he'd had more time to get to know her better.

"Do you have the knife?" He might use his dagger, but he'd be liable to shatter the urn forcing a blade of its size under the lip.

She handed him a small knife, barely large enough to eat dinner with. Still, it should have been enough to crack the seal.

"I'll get started on your laundry." She gathered his things and walked to the river.

Jak tugged at the lid. She was right. It was stuck. He tugged harder. "I've a sliver of soap—" he said, turning. She knelt in the water at the river's edge. Her ass, plump and round, was the most beautiful thing he'd seen in weeks.

Quickly, he turned away. She was doing just fine on her own, and he couldn't afford to be distracted.

He placed the knife at the lip of the lid and jammed it into the urn, breaking the seal. There was a sucking noise, as if the urn breathed, and it rattled in his hands, shaking violently. Jak dropped it into the soft sand.

The woman's laughter, throaty and deep, caught his attention and he looked in her direction. She turned to face him, catching his eye, and her appearance stunned him.

The flesh of her face melted away, and beneath her lovely countenance appeared a green-scaled monster. Two horns protruded from her forehead. Her teeth elongated, her mouth rounded and her eyes all but disappeared. Hideous. Her body devolved into a many-coiled snake with the torso of a woman—and then she was beautiful again—smiling, the last rays of sun highlighting her braid, her red lips curved up.

The urn continued to rattle at his feet. Sand swirled around his ankles. The urn righted itself, and the lid popped off, tumbling to the ground. A fierce wind kicked up, thrashing his tunic around his hips, the sand abrading him as it whipped by.

Sand whirled around the urn, rising higher and higher. Blue smoke emanated from the mouth of the urn, rising, as if pulled upward by the spinning sand. It reached as high as Jak and spun away, coalescing into a man-shaped monster with purple-and-black skin and large leathery wings.

No sooner did it take shape than the blue smoke appeared at the lip of the urn and the process began again. The next monster was more bull than man, heavy chested and short, with solid legs and arms the size of small trees. It had no wings, but a cat-like tail, whisking back and forth, barbed at the end. When it finished solidifying, the she-demon abandoned Jak's clothing in the water and joined the creature, hissing with it in quiet whispers.

Jak leaped for his dagger, but just as quickly, the woman stopped him, her hands on his shoulders. Her hands were soft, but she had the strength of unyielding stone. He couldn't move.

"It's no use," she said. "You can't win." She nodded to the winged demon who bound Jak's wrists together in front of him with Jak's own belt.

Four more monsters escaped from the urn. The last was a scaled demon like herself, though obviously male, with broad shoulders and thick muscles bulging from chest to abdomen. As it coalesced, she walked toward it, changing from beautiful lady to snake-like demon, making the last few strides on serpents' coils. She wrapped her body around his, hissed, and open-mouth kissed him.

Jak looked away, disgusted.

She shifted back to human form.

"Demon," Jak said. "I've helped you, yet you truss me like a common criminal. Release me, and we can go our separate ways."

"You think you're to live after this? You've seen my true form, weakling. There's no release for you, only death."

"Then what's the sense in binding me? You should have killed me outright."

"And where's the pleasure in that?" She stepped toward him and bent, licking at a wound on his forearm where the sand had re-opened it. She licked the blood that accumulated there.

Her tongue was long and black, even in human form, and felt like sandpaper on his skin. His arm burned where she licked him.

"Ahhhh!" he cried out, reflexively bowing away from her, but his guard held him firm.

Blisters erupted on his skin.

She straightened and smiled at him. "I do thank you. The curse of the urn forbade me to open it myself. Had I done so, I would have killed my lover within, and all his friends."

"Then I beg a boon," Jak said. "Let me live."

"Oh, you'll live."

*She made no sense,* thought Jak, *telling him he would die, then telling him he would live.*

She walked up the short incline and through a small strand of trees to the flat plain where the army bedded down. One by one, the other creatures changed into humans, and followed her, the last pulling Jak along.

"Halt," said the soldier on guard duty, *Jak's* duty. "What's your business here?"

"Nicon, sound the alarm!" Jak yelled. "They are—" The creature imprisoning Jak punched him in the stomach, knocking the wind from him. His mouth gaped open, but he was unable to breathe—as though his lungs were paralyzed. He felt light-headed, and stumbled to his knees.

The she-demon changed again, and grabbed Nicon by the throat, her sharp talons leaving bloody trails on his skin. The guard's eyes widened, and he tried to speak.

"Yes, sound the alarm," she said to the guard. She thrust him away from her, and he flew to the ground and rolled over. "I love a good fight. Tell them *Jak* let us pass into your camp."

She looked back at Jak and winked.

His lungs unclenched, and he sucked in air like a dying man. He was incredulous. "You knew I'd be late for duty," he got out between strained breaths. "You planned this."

"Of course," she said.

He nodded, unable to make coherent conversation. Of course she'd known, and she'd turned him into a derelict in front of his friend, his army. At least she hadn't killed Nicon.

Cries of alarm spread through the camp.

Those who hadn't yet doffed their armor came to meet them first, running to the edge of the clearing. They carried shields and spears, or short swords, and met the creatures with battle cries. It was over in minutes, so many men lay dead or dying on the ground. Jak's sandals were soaked in blood, and he'd felt the hot spurt of it splash him several times. The bodies piled up, and the demons casually walked over them into the center of the camp, dragging Jak with them, making him witness the death of the entire army.

She sent the other demons forward and remained with the one who held Jak prisoner.

"The *lixae*—" Jak asked, "Will you kill them, too?"

The creature tilted her head and looked at Jak, as if considering. "Not all. Someone must live to tell this tale."

Well, that told him she'd lied about letting him live. So, what did he have to lose?

He fisted his bound hands together and struck his winged captor under the chin. While the demon reeled, he rushed toward the she-demon and wrenched his dagger from her hands.

She changed, and became...Nicon, just as a new wave of soldiers arrived.

But it was too late to stop his forward momentum. Jak struck the demon in the heart, and *Nicon* tumbled to the ground. "You've killed me," he said.

Jak knew it for the lie it was, but couldn't help the sharp surge of pain at the thought of killing his best friend. It seemed so real.

The battle had ceased. The soldiers gathered around.

"No," Jak said, backing away and dropping his dagger.

The she-demon, still in the guise of Nicon, said, "Traitor. You've killed me."

The soldiers turned from Nicon to Jak.

"Traitor," he heard the from the group of soldiers.

"No." Jak took another step backward, shaking his head. He raised his hands to show them he was bound, but the leather binding at his wrists melted away—another demon trick. "This isn't what it seems."

"Traitor!" he heard again, and this time, a soldier burst out of the crowd, running in Jak's direction. The soldier lifted his spear. Jak recognized him.

"No, Fidelus, it's not what it seems."

But Fidelus would not be deterred. He raised his spear and stabbed Jak in the chest, thrusting the spear through his ribs, then releasing it.

The pain was sharp, shocking, and Jak felt the force of it run through his body, a cold tingle from his ankles to his neck. He shivered once, and then his legs could no longer bear his weight. He collapsed to his knees, the end of the spear striking the ground hard, sending a second shockwave of pain through his middle.

Fidelus drew his dagger, and ran to Jak, grabbing his hair. He forced Jak's head back, and slit his throat. "This is what we do to traitors."

Blood poured down Jak's neck, falling hot and thick to his chest. And even as the blood warmed his skin, his body chilled. His eyesight dimmed, and he fell backward onto the ground. Fidelus stabbed him in the heart. Jak felt no pain, only pressure, as Fidelus ripped the dagger from his chest and stabbed him again and again, chanting, "Traitor, traitor, traitor," with each blow of the knife.

Jak heard the she-demon whisper in his ear, "That's what we needed Jak, the soul of a traitor."

But he wasn't a traitor...was he?

He considered the events at the river. His intention had been good, but if he had not opened the urn and released the demons, they wouldn't have destroyed the army. The she-demon was right. He had betrayed them—naively, innocently—but with treacherous results nonetheless. And the fact that many of his brethren died believing him a traitor must have made the demon's triumph sweeter.

"I see you agree." The she-demon yanked the spear from his chest, and thrust her hand into the gaping wound. He screamed, and he heard her chuckle again. She gripped his failing heart, and squeezed.

Everything went black.

A short time later, he awoke in the vast nothingness of the urn. It wasn't long after that he realized what the she-demon meant when she'd said, "Oh, you'll live." It hadn't been a promise, it had been a curse.

* * *

Assumpta gasped and opened her eyes, realizing her grip on Jak's hands had gotten tighter and tighter while she'd listened to the voices. Her fingers tingled. She released him, shaking her hands, trying to get the blood to circulate.

"And that's why I stopped us." Jak stepped away from her. "Now that you know the kind of man I am—"

"You were tricked," Assumpta said, reaching for him, but he pushed her away.

"That doesn't make me any less a traitor."

"The intent to betray was not there. You were seduced by a demon—"

"Making me weak—"

"You are *not* weak." She stepped toward him and pushed hard against his chest. He didn't move, proving her point. "You're strong! Think about how tough you have to be to live an eternity in Hell and come out fighting. The fact that you're here to help me is proof that your heart is good."

She stepped back to look him in the face. He didn't seem convinced. How could she make him see the truth?

"Jak, you need to forgive yourself for the things you've done. You can't shoulder the weight of it forever. Let it go."

He pulled her close again, holding her tight, resting his head against hers. She let him squeeze, allowing long minutes of silence to pass, giving him time to think. Softly, she said, "I've forgiven you."

Apparently, that was what he needed to hear.

He relaxed his hold, lifted his head, and gave her a brilliant smile. Without warning, he twisted, and pushed Assumpta hard against the door. She shrieked, laughing, pressing kisses to his face. He caught both of her hands in one of his, raised them above her head, then pushed her shirt and bra up to cup one aching breast in the palm of his other hand, teasing the nipple to attention with his fingers.

He ground his hips against hers, then bent to suck the jutting nipple, keeping a steady rhythm.

"Yes," she groaned. Her muscles clenched, her breasts full and heavy. The heat of his sex pressed against hers sent a thrill from her breasts to her hot, hungry core.

Jak released her hands, then cupped both her breasts in his palms. Squeezing her flesh gently, he took turns tonguing her nipples, then sucking them into his mouth. He turned his head to the side, catching her eye, then bit her nipple gently, sending a jolt through her. She almost came right then. When he'd come to her in spirit form, she'd loved the sandpaper feel of his gargoyle tongue rasping across her flesh, but this felt so much better.

Her hands moved to the snap of her own pants. Catching Jak's eye, she popped it with an audible *snap!* She slid the zipper down as Jak blew moist air across her nipples, then suckled each one before sliding his hands to her hips and helping her push her chinos and bright orange bikinis to the floor. Knees weak, she nearly slid to the floor with them.

Reaching for Jak's pants, Assumpta unbuttoned the remainder of the button fly and tugged them down over his hips. His cock sprang free, and he reached for her waist, lifting her high and bracing her back against the door.

Assumpta wrapped her legs around him, held on to his shoulders, and Jak slid between her thighs, her slick core aching for him. She arched her back and Jak slid deeper, filling and stretching her.

"Yesssss," she whispered against his lips.

He braced one arm against the door and thrust, pushing his tongue into her mouth at the same time. She loved the sweet friction of his sex invading her, loved his warm, musky scent. He pistoned in and out of her with a steady hard-and-fast rhythm. The pleasure started deep and moved like waves to her extremities, curling her toes. Her fingers clenched at his shoulders. Her body sang for him, and it wasn't long before she lost her fragile grip on control. She fractured into orgasm, keening low and long as the sensations continued.

Jak broke the kiss and caught her eye, offering her an impish smile, one that said, *But wait, there's more!* Kissing her again, he carried her two steps to the bed and fell with her onto the tangle of sheets she'd left that morning.

Hands seeking, arms holding, tongues dueling, they wrestled in sheets baked warm from the afternoon sunlight slanting through the window. Untangling her legs from Jak's, she pushed his shoulders into the depths of her feather pillow and glided one leg over his hips, straddling him—her sex nestled tightly over his.

She moaned as he arched his hips and slid his still-rock hard cock inside her, sending another wave of ecstasy rushing through her. Jak lost no time in sitting up, his mouth parted to take the tip of one breast, drawing on it with a gentle tug, then licking it gently, sucking and licking in a clever little pattern as he removed her shirt and bra and tossed them to the floor.

Assumpta pushed his shirt up and helped him pull it over his head. Finally, she thought, there was nothing between them but their skin. His golden flesh rippled beneath her touch, warm and silken. She bent to place hot, wet kisses on his collarbone. She remembered making love to Jak in his spirit form, remembered the heat and girth and weight of him, but had no recollection of the soft smoothness of his skin. This was ecstasy.

Jak grasped her shoulders, rolling them over. He pushed her into the tangle of sheets, resting his hips in the cradle of her thighs, and pushed her legs wide.

She groaned, then whispered, "You feel so good."

"You've no idea." He eased out, then thrust his hips forward, pushing farther into her.

He withdrew, slowly, then pushed in again, just as slow, setting a languid pace. He kissed her, sliding his tongue between her lips, thrusting in the same lazy tempo of his cock. She raised her hips to meet his thrust, feeling him reach and press deep against her soul. She wrapped her legs around him and squeezed.

Without warning, she exploded into orgasm, the muscles of her thighs and belly contracting. Jak pressed himself into her, holding her tight while the ripples continued.

"Don't stop now," she said, urging him to continue. "Faster."

"Feels so good," he said, resting his forehead against hers. "I can feel you all around me."

"We'll make it just as good for you," she promised.

He quickened his tempo—in, out, in, out—as fast as the beat of her heart. As fast as the beat of Jak's heart, which she felt drumming against her breast.

She came again, stronger than the last time. This time, she pulled him to her, tightening her legs around his waist and stopping his movement.

She breathed heavily into his ear. "Give me a moment."

He smiled and withdrew, nibbling on her hip, her thigh, her ankle as he sank back on his knees. "I have an idea," he said, and she smiled, remembering the last passionate time they'd come together. She rolled over and got to her knees.

Jak got behind her and slid home, his cock hotter and harder than before. Oh, God, she loved this, she thought. She missed the face-to-face intimacy in the other position, but the drag and pull of his hard, heavy cock as he thrust it in and out of her from behind felt so good, she never wanted it to end. Already sensitive and swollen from her previous orgasm, her muscles involuntarily clenched, cinching him tighter, bringing her even more pleasure.

Jak groaned. "Incredible," he ground out between clenched teeth, putting his hands on her hips and pulling him toward her even as he pushed into her. The double motion against her already sensitized core drove her crazy. Then, he bent forward and grabbed her breasts, pulling slightly at the nipples. She contracted around him, not quite an orgasm, but close.

He groaned again, released her breasts, and began a rhythm designed to bring him to his own climax quickly. He hammered into her, pulling her tight against him with each thrust. She felt her own orgasm building again. A few more strokes, and she exploded. He increased his pace, and a moment later, he exploded, too, clenching her hips to his with taught fingers on her thighs and muscled arms tensed hard, his hold almost crushing her. He half pulled out, then thrust in again, muscles rigid, his fingers squeezing her hips, sending her muscles clenching in another orgasm.

He bent and wrapped an arm around her waist, and she could feel the freight-train speed of his heart, hammering against his ribs, echoing the speed of her own heart. He pulled her against him, and collapsed to his side, spooning.

Nestled in the strength of his arms, she wished it could be like this forever.

# CHAPTER 23

ASSUMPTA WALKED HOME FROM THE LIBRARY. SHE'D spent all day in the stacks with nothing to show for it—probably because a certain somebody had returned—and rocked her world yesterday. Who could concentrate after that? She'd spent more time mooning over Jak than researching anything.

And she couldn't stop smiling. She knew she had some sappy expression on face—she could feel it. But she had to get it together. She had to be vigilant while she walked home. She didn't need anything—any demon—sneaking up on her.

And she sure as hell wasn't taking the bus. She had confidence she could outwit a demon again if necessary. But the thought of being confined in an enclosed area, with other people looking on at her strange antics, just didn't appeal to her at the moment.

She hurried.

The night was cool, and she was colder than she thought she'd be, her breath coming out in white clouds as she moved along, the muffled jangle of her wad of holy medals keeping time with her fast rhythm.

She passed the glow of the Victorian-era Observatory, known as *the pagoda* by Baltimore residents. The structure had once been so badly dilapidated that the city had planned to tear it down. She'd loved it then, and she loved it even more now, perfectly restored. Thousands of twinkling lights glowed around it making it feel like a Chinese wonderland, even in the wintry weather. Early frost glittered in the white light of the tiny bulbs. She'd walked this way a million times before, and the sight of it never failed to lift her flagging spirits.

Her back began to itch like crazy.

"The Big Guy has a proposition for you," the demon said, materializing beside her and keeping pace. He wore his Bethlehem blues and steel-toed boots. *Kenny*.

Assumpta screeched, then looked around to see if anyone had noticed anything. She took deep, slow breaths, trying to decelerate her thumping heart.

"There's no one around," he said. "I checked before I made myself known. Wouldn't want you to embarrass yourself in front of anyone."

That left her little comfort. No one else around meant there was also no one around to help her if she needed it.

*Now there's irony for you*, she thought. She would have been mortified had anyone seen her crazy act on the bus, but right now, she'd be overjoyed to see someone. *Anyone*. Not that the average person could help. They'd probably just run off screaming in the other direction. Or call 9-1-1. Just what she needed: a date with the men in white after the police witnessed the strange way she was acting.

"What's the proposition?" she asked. Then, her heart started thumping again, she asked, "Wait—did you say, 'The Big Guy'? As in, Old Scratch? The Father of Lies? The Prince of Darkness?"

*Why did she have a problem saying the Devil's name out loud? It's not like he could hear her. Could he?* She shivered. *Maybe he could. God could hear her prayers, right? So why couldn't the Devil hear her saying his name aloud?*

The demon burst out laughing, and for just a second, she saw his human flesh give way to red-and-purple mottled demon skin. His face became a grotesque parody of human with its twisted bones and razor-sharp teeth, and then he looked human again. He stopped walking, bending at the waist and holding his sides, he was laughing so hard.

Her heart stopped its adrenaline throb. How could you be frightened when the scary thing in front of you was paralyzed by laughter? She wished she had some kind of demon Taser. She'd stun him this very second, just to see who laughed then.

"Are you done?" she asked him. She'd gone from angry to simply annoyed.

He looked up at her. "You thought I was talking about *Lucifer* himself?" He laughed again, still holding his sides, but the force of his hilarity was waning.

"I hardly think it's a laughing matter," Assumpta said.

"Look, hon," he said, unbending as he got control of himself. "It's an easy mistake to make. You just don't know the hierarchy of Hell."

"But I'm sure you'll fill me in on it."

"That would take eons," he said. "The Prince of Darkness—" he paused and gave her a wink "—would never settle for a title as mediocre as The Big Guy. He likes...*grandiose*." The demon rubbed his hands together as if to warm them, then shoved them into his pockets and started walking again. "Look, The Big Guy's in charge of this region. Baltimore, mostly, but other parts of the Mid-Atlantic. Sometimes Jersey." He shrugged. "Alignments change."

"What about Delaware?" She had friends in Delaware.

"Armpit of the East Coast," he said, shaking his head. "Mostly old people there anyway. We don't care much for it. The fates of most of those old codgers are already sealed."

Assumpta wasn't certain she liked the idea of anyone's fate being sealed—even that of old folks—but she didn't have time to think about that now.

She let out a sigh. "So what does *The Big Guy* want?" she asked, feeling suddenly defeated.

Kenny shrugged again. "I'm not privy to that information. You'll need to ask him for yourself."

"I see." And she did, but she didn't like it. What kind of demon would send another to her just to set up a meeting? A powerful one?

Or one that simply wants to look powerful? "You don't have a deal for me, too?"

"I'm not like the others," he said. His tone was light. "I'm just an emissary from The Big Guy, himself."

"But you hadn't intended to be," she said, remembering the scene in Enoch Pratt. He'd been ready to throw his hat into the ring, too, until he'd recognized Jak.

Kenny looked at her sideways. She wondered if he were trying to decide just how much to admit.

"No, I hadn't," he finally said. "I was going to make you an offer of my own, but once I saw Jak…"

"You couldn't help yourself," Assumpta said. "You saw a way to curry favor with…" She swallowed, then said with rancor, "The Big Guy."

He nodded, looking crestfallen. "You have no idea what it's like in Hell."

"And I have no desire to find out."

"It's not like *I* ever intended to go there." His voice changed pitch at the end of the statement, almost pleading.

"But you'll make the best of it," she said, "Turning traitor on Jak just to help yourself."

"Are you trying to piss me off?" he asked, raising his voice, "because if you are, you're doing a really good job of it."

"It's not like I intended it," she said, echoing his words from a few moments earlier. "You're just such an easy target. Like Jak, I imagine."

He flushed. "I'm just trying to make eternity a little easier on myself. You can't blame a guy for trying."

"Of course I can," Assumpta said. "You don't have to stay in Hell at all. You're no longer imprisoned in the urn. You can choose another path." She waited for that to sink in. "I think you must like what you're doing down there. You've found some satisfaction. Anything else is unthinkable…and now you're going to make your situation a little better by turning someone else in, so to speak."

She stopped walking. "What's it going to get you, if you can get Jak back in Hell?"

He just stared at her a few seconds, and then continued walking, forcing her to catch up with him. *Strange business this*, she thought.

Finally, he said, "I'm not the one helping myself by turning Jak in," he said. "There's nothing in this for me. I made a deal with The Big Guy *for you*. You lead Jak back to Hell, and The Big Guy will remove the mark from you himself. All you've got to do is convince Jak."

"I can make my own deals, thank you very much," she said.

"Not very well, or you wouldn't be in this mess to begin with."

*He might be right*, Assumpta thought, but she couldn't even mention the deal to Jak, because she had a feeling he'd go for it. He'd turn himself in for her. She'd be damned if she let that happen. Literally. She'd worked too hard to free him from the cesspit of Hell just to send him back again to save herself. She wouldn't do it. There had to be another way to remove the mark.

The demon put a hand to his left breast pocket, unbuttoned the flap, then reached in and pulled out a notepad. Then he pulled a green pencil from behind his ear. She hadn't noticed that earlier. He flipped open the book and wrote something while they walked, then tore the perforated page from the pad. "Here," he said, offering her the paper. "This is where you can meet The Big Guy. He'll be there whenever you come looking."

She took the paper and saw that one side was plain white and the other side was printed like graph paper, fine blue lines crisscrossing the small sheet at even intervals. He'd written on the graph paper side in small, neat letters.

"Towson Town Center?" she asked, looking up at him. "That's outside the city. Mondawmin Mall isn't good enough? And why the employees' exit on the second level?"

"Inside or outside the city didn't matter," Kenny said. "The location just needed to be two levels. We used to use Golden Ring Mall until they tore it down."

"Harbor Place?"

"Too crowded—always a chance that someone would wander in unannounced and uninvited." He put the notebook back in his breast pocket and buttoned it. "I drew you a little map, too," he said, pointing at the paper. "The door is painted gray. Just take the stairs all the way to the bottom."

"Why don't I just start on the first level?"

He shook his head. "It doesn't work that way. Take the public escalator up to the second floor, then take the stairs all the way down from the employee stairwell."

She crumpled the paper in her hand, tempted to throw it down. "I don't want to meet with The Big Guy," she said, her voice trembling. She hated showing any sign of weakness, especially in front of a demon.

He shrugged. "It's the only way you'll get rid of that mark." He walked away, veering off the sidewalk onto the grass of Patterson Park. "Oh, and he wants you to bring some holy water, holy salt, and holy oil."

"And he'll take away the mark?"

"Probably not. But you should be able to bargain with them for something else," he said. He raised his hand to wave good-bye, then he disappeared with a fizzle and a *bang* like a firecracker.

The grass where he'd stood smoldered, sending curling eddies of smoke skyward.

# CHAPTER 24

ENOCH PRATT WAS NEARLY DESERTED THE NEXT
morning when Assumpta arrived. She waved at one of the librarians on the way in, but dashed up the stairs before the chatty woman could start a conversation. The woman could talk the handles off an old pot, and frankly, Assumpta didn't have the time to waste.

She threw her purse down on the old scarred table in the Poe room, and before she could pull the chair aside, the room's temperature dipped ten degrees and Brona materialized.

"That was fast," said Assumpta.

Brona smiled. "You look to be in a wee bit of a hurry this morning. What's lit a fire under your *toin*?"

Assumpta felt herself smiling at the Gaelic reference to her bottom, but got right to the point. "I've had an invitation from *The Big Guy* to visit him in Hell."

Brona looked aghast. She crossed herself. "Satan himself? Are you certain?"

Despite the wariness she felt, Assumpta couldn't help giggling, then explained what the demon in Bethlehem blues had told her.

"This sounds like just the thing you need," Brona said, sounding intrigued. She glided forward through the back of the chair facing Assumpta, then perched upon its edge, leaning her elbows on the table.

"You get to negotiate with the person who owns your mark."

"The bad part is, according to the messenger, the only way The Big Guy will remove the mark is if I give up Jak. I can't do that. I can't even mention the conversation to Jak because I'm certain he'll turn himself in for me. I won't let that happen. It sounds like a stalemate already, Brona. Should I even go?"

"Why not? Something else might come up in conversation."

"You make it sound so easy! Like I'm contemplating whether or not to have dessert with dinner—not stroll into Hell at the invitation of a high-ranking demon."

"Think of it as an adventure."

Assumpta barked, a bit of hysterical laughter forcing its way out of her throat. "Some adventure. What if he tries to keep me there? I don't want to be trapped like Jak was."

Brona rose and walked around the table to a bookshelf behind Assumpta. "But how many people can say they've stepped a foot into Hell and came back to talk about it? That adventure will keep you in beer at the local pub until you shuffle off your mortal coil." She tapped the back of a few books, checking the call numbers as she scanned the shelf. "Besides, there are rules about visiting Hell," she said. "As long as you follow them, and don't give cause for the local riffraff to consider you fair game, you should be able to return with no trouble."

"What kind of rules?"

"Well, off the top of my head, there's that old adage about not eating or drinking anything while you're there. It caught Proserpina by surprise, and she has to spend six months of the year there with Hades."

"You mean Persephone?" Assumpta said, turning around to see what books Brona perused.

"That's her Greek counterpart, but like Jak, I'm partial to the Roman pantheon."

"But they're myths!"

Brona caught Assumpta's eye over her shoulder and shook her head. "In a thousand years, they'll be calling Christ a myth. Hell, they've already started in some quarters. Then He'll be relegated to the has-beens along with the ancient Egyptian, Greek, and Roman gods. Ask Jak what he thinks of that the next time you see him. Ah! Here it is," she said, pulling a book from the lowest shelf.

She checked the index in the back, then hurriedly paged through the book to find what she sought.

"Got it," she said, and silently started to read. Then, "Hm. Lots of prayers listed here. It might be good for you to write some of these down and carry them with you...the one to Saint Michael the Archangel is a good one."

"I know it by heart."

"Good. Praying it while you're there couldn't hurt. But I'd suggest writing it down and carrying it with you. Maybe on some blessed paper?" She looked up at Assumpta. "Can a priest bless paper?"

"I imagine Father Tony could bless anything I asked him to, though he might find the request a bit unusual. I could just carry my prayer book."

"I wonder if that would seem like a threat—sort of like walking in with a gun? I'm thinking that if you carried a blessed prayer in your pocket and someone grabbed you, you could pull it out as a weapon of sorts," Brona said. "I could be off the mark about that, though." She skimmed a finger down the page. "Here are some other things you should consider obtaining: a scapular, a small crucifix to wear around your neck if you don't already, maybe have a larger one for your pocket. It also mentions holy salt, water, and oil. You've got those bases well covered."

Brona shelved the book and picked up another, skimming silently as Assumpta waited. She ran a spectral finger down the words on the page as she read. Suddenly, she looked up. "I should have remembered this. Do you have a Saint Benedict medal in that cache you keep around your neck?"

"No."

"You need to get one. You should be wearing one at all times."

"Who is Saint Benedict?"

Brona shut the book with a snap. "Don't they teach anything in Catholic schools these days?"

Assumpta rolled her eyes. "There are a bajillion saints. I can't know them all. And the school couldn't teach them all. There's not enough time in the school year."

"The Benedictine order was established following his precepts!" Brona shouted, clearly exasperated. Then, more quietly, she said, "You should at least know the important saints.

"Like you remember them all? Give me a break."

Brona looked like she wanted to growl. Instead she closed her eyes for a moment as if praying for patience, and then said, "Saint Benedict of Italy had been living as a hermit in a cave for three years when a religious community came to him after the death of their abbot and asked him to take over. At the time, he'd had quite a reputation as a holy man."

Assumpta withdrew the handful of holy medals she kept on the long chain around her neck and fingered them gently as Brona spoke.

"Benedict agreed. But a group of jealous monks provided him with poisoned wine and bread during a meal. It's said that Benedict made the sign of the cross over each and knew immediately they were poisoned. He toppled the cup and called for a raven to come and take away the bread."

"Like Snow White and her poisoned apple?" Assumpta chuckled.

Brona grew angry again. "Blasphemy!"

"Lighten up," Assumpta said, herself growing angry. "You're the one who mentioned myths earlier. Aren't myths just a step away from fairy tales?" She sighed. "Tell me about the medal."

"You'll have to do your own research for the entirety of it," Brona said, "but the most significant parts for you are the initials of the words, *Vade Retro Satana, Nunquam Suade Mihi Vana-Sunt Mala Quae Libas, Ipse Venena Bibas*, written around the edge of the reverse of the coin. It stands for, "Begone, Satan, do not suggest to me thy vanities—evil are the things thou profferest, drink thou thy own poison."

"But how does that help me?" Assumpta asked.

"The medal destroys diabolical and haunting influences, and it imparts protection to persons tempted, deluded, or tormented by evil spirits."

"Destroys haunting influences," Assumpta said. "Does that mean it will affect you?"

"I'm not haunting you; I'm haunting the library."

"Well, then." Assumpta sighed. "I guess I'll be getting a Saint Benedict medal."

# CHAPTER 25

*T*HE ROAD TO HELL IS PAVED WITH GOOD *intentions,* Assumpta thought, *but the hallway to Hell is tiled with cheap linoleum and painted institutional gray.* The hallway dead-ended at a nondescript, wooden door with a sign that read *Employees Only.*

Assumpta took a deep breath and pulled the chain of holy medals out of the neckline of her shirt. She touched the newly-added Saint Benedict medal. *Am I ready for this?*

She'd made the trip to Saint Benedict Church on Wilkins Avenue last night just to get it. Father Paschel helped her choose an appropriate, and inexpensive, version—it was smaller than the other medals on her chain—but just as powerful. The trip had cost her time, and she hadn't been able to visit Holy Rosary for Father Tony to bless a prayer for her as Brona had suggested. Instead, she'd copied one from her prayer book and sprinkled it with holy water. It was tucked into her jacket pocket.

She looked around, scanning for people. Few shoppers had made it to the second floor. She'd arrived at Towson Town Center just as the doors had opened for the day. And despite the lack of crowds, Assumpta wanted to make certain no one watched her. The last thing she needed was a run-in with a mall cop.

Seeing no one, Assumpta opened the door and found a set of steep, wooden stairs. They were poorly lit and descended into darkness. *Well, what did you expect?* she thought.

She stepped down onto the first tier. The wood was spongy, but held. The second creaked as she placed her weight on it. The third seemed more solid, as did the fourth.

She descended into the semi-darkness, holding onto the wooden handrail so she wouldn't fall. She couldn't see the bottom. She couldn't see anything, except a few steps ahead of her.

The stairs never turned, and her legs grew tired, but still the steps continued. Sweat broke on her brow, but did the air seem to be getting *cooler?* At some point, she started counting steps, but quit after one hundred when she noticed that the light was glowing brighter. Finally, she could see the landing at the bottom of the steps, illuminated by a single bulb and a pull chain. At that point, the steps made a right angle. She couldn't see what lay beyond the landing, but when she got closer, she noticed the ambient light getting brighter still.

She turned right, walked down three additional steps, and found herself in what appeared to be the spacious lobby of a well-appointed law office.

A receptionist looked up from her desk.

"We've been expecting you," she said, rising and coming around to the front. "Let me show you to the conference room."

Assumpta followed the attractive woman into a very long hallway. On both sides of the hallway to the left, glass walls let Assumpta peer into each office. *No goofing off here,* she thought. Steel and chrome, black leather, and polished wood made up identical work spaces. Beautiful men and women in fashionable business suits sat behind desks in each room, some talking on the phone, others reading reports or perusing files, most typed away at their keyboards. The hallway stretched on and on into darkness.

To the right, where the receptionist led, the view was the same— glass-fronted offices on either side of the hall. But they passed only ten offices, much more sumptuous and busy than the others, before they came to the end and two tall and imposing wooden doors. The conference room.

The receptionist opened one of the doors and gestured for Assumpta to take a seat around a table that could have held twenty or more people.

"Coffee? Water?" the woman asked.

"No, thank you." Assumpta sat and put her purse on the floor at her feet. Did eating and drinking in Hell bind you there for a specific time period, as Brona suggested? She wasn't taking any chances.

The table was cool to the touch, mahogany polished to a brilliant sheen and inlaid with something darker around the edge. *Gorgeous.* One end of the room held a refreshment bar with coffee, water, and snacks. The opposite wall of the room was paneled to match the table.

A moment later, an attractive man—*demon*, she reminded herself—walked into the room. He wore a gray suit, navy tie, cufflinks. His blond hair looked artfully wind-blown above his congenial blue eyes. He was tan. *Excellent look, if you want to masquerade as an attorney,* she thought.

He looked rich enough to prove he was successful—but not rich enough to denote he gouged his clients. She bet most people found the beach-boy look charming.

"Assumpta!" he said, coming toward her, hand outstretched. He winked, then grinned, a million-dollar smile. "At last we meet. I feel like I already know you."

Automatically, she put her hand out to his and immediately regretted it. Before she could jerk it back, he'd taken it in his own and gripped it firmly, placing his left hand on top and patting it. "I'm The Big Guy. I'm glad you could make it."

He released her hand and made himself comfortable at the head of the table.

"You can have a drink, you know," he said, still smiling. He looked so friendly, she could almost believe the fantasy he wove for her down here. But she'd seen the true visage of a demon from Hell, and knew everything she saw here was a lie.

"You're not Persephone," he continued. "Eating or drinking won't require you to spend a portion of your eternity here."

Assumpta smiled. "Just a rumor?"

He chuckled. "We deal in rumor and innuendo. Part of the business." He gestured to the room. "Do you like what you see?"

"It's certainly not what I expected."

"All that fire and brimstone gives us a bad name," he said. "It's not like that at all down here."

"Oh, no? What's it like?"

"However we want." He snapped his fingers and the law offices became a sandy beach. They sat at an open bar, in the shade of the palm-frond roof, a view of the clear, brilliant sea in front of them. A tanned waiter poured them pink frozen drinks from a blender and garnished them with fresh fruit and paper umbrellas. The temperature was noticeably warmer. "See? Anything we like. In an instant."

He snapped his fingers again and they were back in the law offices. The fancy drinks remained on the table in front of them. Again, the temperature was cool.

Assumpta felt a slight vertigo from the abrupt change of scenery and back. She wanted a sip of the drink, but she dared not. Just to be rude, she was sure, The Big Guy took a long swallow of his, setting the glass back on the table with a slight thump. He pulled a pineapple wedge off the rim and popped it into his mouth, chewing with an appreciative smile.

She ignored the temptation to drink and said, "I'm sure it's not like this for everyone."

He grinned. "Got me. No, these are just the *corporate offices,* if you will. This is how the *management* enjoys Hell. The souls who are down here for punishment...let's just say Dante wasn't far off the mark. None of them are enjoying themselves."

He took another sip of the drink and put the glass down. It didn't look as if he'd touched it; it remained full to the brim, and the pineapple was back on the edge.

"You know," he said. "It takes a brave soul to casually walk into Hell."

"I didn't have a choice. You own my mark; I want it gone. Since you weren't coming top-side anytime soon, I needed to come to you."

"Yeah, I've been having too much fun watching my lieutenants try to woo you. It's been high comedy." He snapped his fingers and two panels opened on the wall behind him, sliding left and right to reveal a bank of high definition television screens, all apparently tuned to the *Assumpta Channel*.

One screen showed Kenny showing up at Enoch Pratt Library to confront her. Two showed her struggling with the fake Dr. Barnes in the Tattoo Parlor. Two more showed her riding the bus, and her *conversation* with Dan. When they got to the part where he burned his hand on her religious medals, The Big Guy laughed uproariously, slapped his thigh, and turned back to Assumpta.

She kept her face sober. "So you should know by now that I have a few tricks up my sleeve, and at least one ability that most people don't: a talent that apparently gets me a key to the lock on the door of Hell."

"Not to mention the help of a certain released soul…" He drummed his fingers on the table. "I've got to hand it to Jak, I didn't think he could do it. A lesser *man* might not have been able to."

"Jak didn't help me out here."

"You came all on your own?" The Big Guy peered around the room, as if searching for something.

Assumpta nodded, suddenly unsure of why he wanted to verify that. Did The Big Guy think Jak had come with her? Couldn't he tell?

"So you're really here on your own."

*Yeah, he did think that. And he thinks Jak is still a spirit.* "Why don't you know that already?"

"Omniscience is not our gig."

"And that upsets you."

He lost his ingratiating grin. "Damn right, it upsets me. It's not fair we don't get the same advantage as the other guy."

"The Good Guy?"

"That's open to interpretation," he said.

"Look," said Assumpta, "I'm not here to debate religion, or who's good and who's bad, or which side is better than which. I've got a problem that, apparently, only you can solve, and that's what I'm here to discuss. So, let's get this over with so I can get out of here."

It didn't matter that the place looked like the local attorney's office: it still gave her the creeps. And the longer she was down here, the worse she felt—not quite nauseated—but ill nonetheless.

Was it a trick of her mind, or did she actually suffer from sort of malaise because she was in Hell? Perhaps there was a miasma in the air that made her sick. It didn't matter, really. She just wanted out. She lifted a hand to brush a stray hair away from her face and realized it was shaking.

"You want the mark gone."

"Yes."

The Big Guy said, "I don't know. I rather enjoy having you in my power."

"I'm not in your power," Assumpta said through gritted teeth.

He nodded, then took a long sip of the still-full drink in front of him. "You're partly right. Currently, I can't command you to do anything. But if you die with the mark on, you're mine in Hell for eternity. You'll have to do everything I say. If you want the mark gone, you'll have to give in to me. I like lording that over you. Over anyone, actually, but over you is especially fine, you being a church-going girl and all. I really like that."

"There must be something I can do to get rid of this mark."

He looked pensive for a moment. "Well, there is something you could do for me…"

"And if I do it, you'll erase the mark?"

"It's only a small thing," he said. "But doing so might make me more inclined to *think* about removing it."

She crossed her arms over her chest. "I'm smarter than that. You want something, then I definitely get something in return."

"All right." He leaned forward. "I need a bottle of holy water and another of blessed salt. For that, I'm willing to offer you protection of sorts. Dan won't visit you again if you can procure these items for me."

Assumpta sat up straight in her chair. What could he possibly want with holy water and blessed salt? He couldn't use them, couldn't even touch them without burning himself. Would he use them to torture his own demons for some perceived infraction within the ranks?

"What do you want them for?" she asked.

"You don't need to know that."

"I'd like to know. I could take some comfort in knowing you wouldn't use it for nefarious purposes."

He dropped the salesman act. His smile disappeared. No more Mr. Nice Guy. "I'm not here to soothe your heart. Justify it any way you want to make yourself feel better. I really don't care. But the deal stands: water and salt for the removal of Dan's unwanted attentions. Take it or leave it."

"Leave it," she said, rising from her chair.

"Let's not be hasty." The Big Guy rose, too, all smiles again. "Surely we can come to some agreement here."

She nodded. "I want the mark gone."

"No can do." He crossed his arms on his chest, raising one hand to rub at his chin. "No more visits from Dan or *Dr. Barnes.*"

"No more visits from any of your lackeys," Assumpta said.

A few seconds ticked by while she waited for him to think it over. Finally, he held out his hand. "Done. No more visits from any of them."

She nodded, ignoring the proffered hand—no telling what that would do to her, then sat down again. She bent and grabbed her purse from the floor. Better to get this over with now than to make a return trip. Turning over the salt and water in her handbag left her practically defenseless in Hell, but it beat not having to worry about demons turning up on the way home. The Big Guy wasn't going to harm her: he wanted something more from her, she was certain. She knew nothing would happen to her here.

*How strange was it to feel safer in Hell than in her own neighborhood?*

She rummaged through the purse and pulled out the small bottles she always carried with her and plunked them down on the table in front of him.

He pulled out a cell phone, swiped the screen, and held it to his ear. After a pause, he barked a few words into the phone in a language she didn't understand. Then he smiled at her, a cat-that-ate-the-canary smile, touched the screen again, and dropped the phone back into his suit jacket pocket.

Before she could even ask what that was about, the conference door opened and a tall man in a white lab coat strode into the room. He wore thick, nerdy glasses and rubber gloves.

"Are they those?" he asked, nodding to the bottles on the table.

The Big Guy nodded.

When the man in the lab coat came between them to take the jars, a patch of skin near his ear peeled away, showing purple-and-black mottled hide beneath. He bumped Assumpta's knee, and turned in her direction.

"Excuse me," he said, smiling at her. For an instant, his eyes glowed red and his incisors grew down to touch his bottom lip. And then he looked nerdy again.

Her heart thumped in her chest, reminding her that not everyone was of the same mind down here. The Big Guy might want to keep her safe, but why would anyone else want to?

Once he left, Assumpta stood. "I need to get out of here."

The Big Guy nodded. "Understandable."

"So, no more visits?"

He nodded. "That's right. Perhaps next time we meet, you could bring some of that precious holy oil you sometimes use."

"And you'll remove the mark?"

"No. I'll need something more substantial from you to remove the mark."

"What more could I possibly bring you that you couldn't get yourself?" *Well, probably more holy items.* If he started asking for relics, though, she knew she would carry his mark for the rest of her life. She couldn't do that. Oil and water and salt were cheap. No one would miss a few pounds or ounces here and there, but the price of relics was high, and she wouldn't risk jail, or worse, to feed whatever need he had.

"I was thinking more about you doing me a service, rather than bringing me anything."

"What?" She couldn't keep the bitterness out of her voice. This was where the last service had gotten her: demon-marked and visiting Hell. She didn't want to end up here full time, and that's just where she thought this was leading.

"You know…" He looked from side to side as if to make certain no one was near enough to hear. He lowered his voice. "Hell isn't all it's cracked up to be. Old Scratch's opinion that it's better to rule in Hell than serve in Heaven loses its luster after the first millennium or so. I'm not saying that I hate it here, just that I'm looking for a change of pace for a while."

"You want me to bust you out of Hell, too?" She put the strap of her purse over her shoulder and walked to the door, then stopped and looked back at him. "Since I'm demon-marked, can't you come visit any time you want?"

"Sure, I can come visit you, but I'm bound by a certain radius of your mark. If I wanted to spend that time with you—" he gave her a leer that sent a chill down her spine "—I wouldn't find it so onerous. But when I'm on your plane, I want to roam free. I want nothing to bind me."

So, in order to lose her mark, she'd have to set him free on Earth. She couldn't live with herself if she did that.

"I'll think about it," she said. *There has to be another way to get rid of this mark!*

"Well, think fast," he said. "I'm getting anxious. Remember, the longer you take to make up your mind, the longer you're fair game for any passing demon."

"What about the deal we just made?"

He smiled disingenuously. "I promised no more visits by my guys. I can't stop the riffraff."

"Great," she muttered.

She grabbed the handle of the door and pushed.

"Wait," he said. "You'll need this for the escalator."

Assumpta turned back. He stood and dipped a hand into his jacket pocket and pulled out a gold coin, which he flipped through the air to her.

"The escalator?"

"It would be *hell* to walk back up all those steps." Smiling, he put both hands in his pants pockets and rocked back on his heels. "The coin has my name on it, so you'll know who to call when you're ready."

She looked down at the coin. Indeed, one side was printed with a name across the center. She rubbed her thumb across the raised calligraphy font. She turned it over. On the obverse was his silhouette. She didn't know whether to be irritated by his hubris or simply amused.

"But if I use this on the escalator, how will I remember your name?"

"Oh, you can't lose the coin. If you spend it, or misplace it in any way, it will come back to you."

"Right, like a bad penny." She nodded. "And how do I find this escalator?"

"Back where you came in."

Assumpta shook her head and left the conference room. She passed the receptionist's station, unmanned currently, and came to the stairway she'd walked down. Only, instead of a stairway, it was an escalator. A turnstile blocked the entrance. Beside it was a metal box on a post with the words "Exit Pass" stenciled on the front. A thin slot was carved into the metal beneath it.

She thumbed her coin into the slot and heard the turnstile click. After pushing her way past the stiff mechanism she stepped onto the moving tread. She gripped the rubber handrail and held on tightly. The escalator moved upward much faster than she had walked down.

The lighting was the same, but the air seemed to move better than it had on the stairs. And she certainly felt better than she had earlier. She wasn't feeling the sickening miasma she had felt then.

Curious about the stairway-cum-escalator, she turned around and looked down. Immediately, the escalator stopped. The turnstile was missing at the bottom. Instead, she saw the single light bulb hanging from a cord. The mechanical treads looked exactly like a staircase. The hand rail she grasped was made of wood.

Taking a deep breath, she turned around again, facing the top. The escalator began moving again. It deposited her on a small landing in front of the gray service door she'd entered to get here.

She reached for the handle, then heard the sound of a coin hitting the floor. It flipped round and round in a small circle next to her left foot. She bent to pick up the gold coin with The Big Guy's face.

# CHAPTER 26

**G**REG LOUNGED ON THE SOFA WITH HIS LAPTOP, enjoying the peace with everyone else out of the house. Across from him, a small fire burned in the hearth.

He paged through recent photos from an archeological dig in Virginia, wondering if he shouldn't have gone back to work there. He'd been away for months. The urn they'd found there—the one he'd brought to Baltimore to be x-rayed before opening—had led him to his friendship with Assumpta. He'd just felt so damned guilty after being trusted with it.

He'd broken the urn *en route* from Virginia to Baltimore, releasing several malevolent spirits. He had sought Assumpta's help to find them and return them to the prison of the urn, but the task had been impossible from the start. He and Assumpta had wound up cursed by demons, eventually fighting and killing one.

Jak had been imprisoned in the urn as well. Who knew Assumpta would have come to care for the spirit? And now he was here in the flesh. How could he compete with that?

The screen on his laptop flickered, then a lightning bolt flared up from the bottom edge, and the screen went blank. A cool breeze filtered through his hair.

He slammed the lid down on the laptop and moved it to the side table, looking all around the room. His heart thudded dully in his chest. Something was here, and whatever it was had just tried to announce its presence without scaring him. Much.

"I know you're here," he said. "Show yourself."

Vesta materialized on the love seat across from him, lounging with her feet up and crossed at the ankles, her arms behind her head.

"Hello, honey," she said, her voice sugary-sweet. "We're finally alone."

"I thought you were off with Jak, checking on something." His heart slowed back to normal. *Vesta was one of the friendly ghosts. Maybe friendlier than he'd thought.*

She stood and shrugged one slender shoulder, then walked to the bookcase, looking at the primitive art showcased there, Greg's collection of earth mother sculptures with their bountiful figures. Vesta lifted a hand and caressed one statue's large, rounded belly. "I got bored with it all, so I came back here. It's their party, not mine. Besides, you and I haven't had an opportunity to talk."

Greg grabbed a pillow and leaned on it, making himself comfortable. When a woman said she wanted to talk, it meant things were going to take a while. He supposed it wouldn't be any different with a ghost.

"You have a lot of artifacts," she said, turning back to him.

"Just a few."

"Shouldn't they be in museums?"

"These aren't so important," he said. *Where was this going?*

"You must have paid a lot of money for them." Now he really wanted to know what her point was.

"I can afford it," he said. "Do you have a need for money?"

She laughed, a gentle titter behind one raised hand. Still smiling, she said, "Of course not. But a girl can't help being attracted to a man of means." She walked to the sofa, raised one knee to rest on the black leather, and slid onto the cushion, kneeling beside him so they were face-to-face. He hadn't felt the barest shift of weight when she sat down, but then, he hadn't expected to.

He leaned a little away from her.

"You scared, sugar?"

"Just trying to figure out what you're playing at." No sense beating around the bush at this point.

"Isn't it obvious? I'm just being…" She paused. "Friendly."

He laughed a derogatory chuckle. "Any friendlier and you'll be in my lap."

"Would that be so bad?"

"You're a ghost."

"Just like a man," she declared, "stating the obvious." She fanned herself, then unbuttoned the top button of her nearly translucent blouse. "Have you read through my diary?"

"I've started to," he said, glad the conversation had moved back onto a neutral track. "You were very detailed in your notes. You made some startling discoveries."

She nodded. "And they should be published. I'd like you to do that. Imagine how famous you'll be. You'll earn a lot more money."

"How I came into possession of your diary would take a lot of explaining," he said, turning over her phrases in his mind. "And you may have some relatives who'll claim the diary—"

"They can have it," Vesta said, putting her hands down on the sofa and sliding sinuously toward him. She laid a hand on his chest. He felt the slightest of touches, the barest weight, where her arm rested upon him. "Once we've revealed the hidden chamber to the world, they can publish it if they like. You'll still receive the accolades for having found the hidden room. I'll be famous. And so will you."

She looked into his eyes with serious intent and slid closer.

He moved away from her. "Are you trying to seduce me?"

She sat up again, still sitting close, an impish smile on her face. "Is it working?"

"Which part?" asked Greg, a sardonic smile on his face. "The fame, the money, or yourself?"

She laughed out loud this time, full and exuberant, flinging her head back and exposing her throat.

He found her quite attractive, for a ghost.

She looked back at him, eyes twinkling, then scootched forward again, leaning in close enough to kiss, and became solid. Cheek to cheek, she said, "I guess every bit of it, but I'd really enjoy a good romp right now. How about you?"

His eyes widened. "I can feel you."

"Mm-hhm." She kissed his neck, then ran her tongue down the side of it until she reached the crease at his shoulder. She kissed him again there, and raised her hand to his arm, grasping a solid muscle. She purred and sidled closer.

"Whoa!" he said, pushing her away. He didn't think sex was possible with a ghost. "Aren't you moving a little fast for having just met me?"

"I'm out of time, sweetheart, and you're not getting any younger. What's to stop us?"

"The fact that you're a ghost?"

"Do I *feel* like a ghost, sweet'ums?"

Greg felt the nearness of her, felt the weight of her body on his, and shook his head. "You don't feel at all like a ghost." And it wasn't just her weight, he thought. He noticed that she felt warm, not cold as he thought a ghost should have. Her hair tickled his nose as she slid one knee over his hips and straddled him.

*What's the harm?* he thought. *We're two willing adults.*

He slid his hands over her hips and up her spine, then pulled her toward him. She bent to him, kissing him with a passion that he hadn't felt from a woman in a long time.

She pushed against his chest and sat up. "Watch this," she whispered, closing her eyes. Her ghostly clothes faded from sight, and she was naked in his lap. She opened her eyes, and smiled. "I love being able to do that."

"And I love that you can." Greg pulled her into his arms.

# CHAPTER 27

**A**SSUMPTA OPENED THE DOOR TO FIND GREG AND Vesta hot and sweaty on the couch. She could only see the back of Greg's head, but Vesta's ghostly breasts bounced up and down in full view.

Vesta caught Assumpta's eye, then winked luridly before she disappeared.

"No!" Greg shouted. He beat one clenched fist against the sofa cushion.

"You really need to take these things into the bedroom now that you've got a roommate," Assumpta said.

"Whoa!" Greg turned his head to face her, coloring. He lifted his hips and pulled his pants up.

Assumpta turned away, even though she could see nothing with his back to her. She heard the faint zip of the zipper and the clink of his belt. Then he stood.

"I'm sorry about that," he said.

"No worries." She turned back, pasting a smile on her face, hoping she didn't look as sick as she felt. Her friend Caroline was wrong, very wrong, about the situation between her and Greg. Greg did not care about Assumpta *in that way.*

And even if Caroline weren't wrong, Assumpta didn't think she wanted to explore a relationship with a guy who fucked a strange woman—a ghost!—at the drop of a hat. Wait, did that make her hypocritical? She did sleep with Jak...but she had had feelings for Jak—still did— and it did take her a long time to come to grips with sleeping with him. Hell, it took her a long time to *decide* to sleep with him.

And she had no claim on Greg; he was free to sleep with whomever he wanted to at the moment. She tried for a light tone, smiling. "See, it's time I moved out. I'm cramping your style."

"Look," Greg said, running a hand through his already rumpled hair, "don't let this one little incident make you go running. We can make this work."

She wondered: did he mean, we can make *us* work?

"You should really be consoling Vesta right now," Assumpta said. "It's not every day a woman gets walked in on during such an intimate act. This is probably especially true for a woman from the past. She might be suffering a case of the vapors, or something."

He sighed. "She doesn't mean anything to me, Assumpta."

Well, that cleared things up. If she entered into a relationship with Greg, would she be hearing this excuse from him sometime in the future?

"She could be listening to you right this second, Greg. Did you give that a thought? She might not be happy to know how little you feel about her."

He cursed.

"I'll work it out with her," he said. "But you're the one I'm worried about."

She nodded. "I'm not ready to talk. Not now. I've got a lot of thinking to do."

"Don't come to any hasty conclusions," he said. His eyes begged her. "Please."

"I've got work to do." Assumpta headed into her room.

"Assumpta—"

"Later."

# CHAPTER 28

ASSUMPTA PUT ON A POT OF COFFEE AND STARTED some green pepper frying in the pan while she waited for Greg in the kitchen. They hadn't left things very well last night, but maybe they could hash it out over breakfast, though she wasn't certain what they could hash out.

She still had a thing for Jak, and she needed to talk to him about it. Was he going to stick around after this "mission" was done? He seemed to indicate that his body was on loan. Could they build a relationship on that? If he lost his physical form, what could they have together?

She couldn't start anything with Greg—whom she liked, but didn't love, though there was some definite attraction there. Not unless, or until, Jak was completely out of the picture. Greg was free to have relationships with whomever he wanted, including ghosts, if that's what he chose. Were they close enough for her to warn Greg about the pitfalls of relationships between couples who didn't share the same substance, or perhaps no substance at all?

She wasn't sure. But Greg wasn't afraid of voicing his opinion of Jak, so she guessed Vesta was fair game to her. Did that make them better than friends if they felt they could rag on each other's significant other? *Was* Vesta Greg's significant other?

*Crap*, she didn't know what to think.

Greg walked in, eyes bloodshot, back hunched. He looked as though he might throw up.

"Hangover?" she asked.

"No," he said, sounding surprised. He covered a yawn and reached for a mug, tossing in an ice cube and filling it to the brim. "Just dead tired."

"Late night?"

He took a large swig of coffee, then shook his head while swallowing. "No. After we had words, I just went to bed."

"Maybe you're coming down with something." Assumpta crossed the room and put the back of her hand to his forehead. "You don't have a fever."

"I'm not sick. Just tired." He drank more coffee. "About last night…"

She lifted a hand to forestall him. This was awkward. But why did she feel embarrassed? She wasn't the one who'd been caught in the act. "Let's forget about it," she said, suddenly too shy to bring it up. "We're not a couple. What you do is your own business. I'm sorry I crashed." She smiled, hoping it was more cheerful than grimace-like. It *felt* as fake as she knew it was. "Next time, put a sock on the doorknob, okay?"

"But that's not what I want." He ran a hand through his bed head and sighed.

*Don't. Don't. Don't,* she thought. If he actually said the word, they'd have to confront the situation. She wasn't ready for that. She held up a hand.

"I realize that you don't want to talk about this, but we really should," he said.

"Not now, we don't."

"I need to know if there could be something between us," he said. "I don't want you to move out. I want you to be with me."

*Damn, damn, damn. He'd said it.* "Could we have something in the future?" she asked, trying to buy a little bit of time. "I'm not sure. We'd have to explore it. Am I interested in exploring? Possibly. But I need to know what's going on with Jak. I can't move forward with someone else as long as there's a chance there."

Despite his fatigue, Greg gave her a stubborn look. "But—"

"No buts! If you want an answer right this second, then it's *no.* There can be nothing between us."

He slammed his coffee cup down in the sink and turned and left the kitchen.

Assumpta watched him go, stupefied. She thought she would have felt better, getting everything out into the open.

Why didn't she feel more relieved?

# CHAPTER 29

ASSUMPTA SAT AT HER FAVORITE TABLE IN THE back corner of Charm City Brewery, sipping her coffee and watching as patrons came in empty handed and left with steaming cups of joe, slices of cheesecake, or sandwiches and small bags of Old Bay seasoned potato chips. Chips sounded like a great idea right about now, she thought, her stomach rumbling. But splurging on the coffee meant she'd have to walk home tonight instead of taking the bus. She just didn't have the cash to spare for chips.

*Typical.*

She refused to take any more money from Greg—she'd done her job for him when she helped rout the demons he'd released when he broke the urn found at his archeological dig site. So, without that income, she was back to saving her pennies.

Caroline walked through the door, and Assumpta waved to get her attention.

Her friend smiled and waved back, then made a beeline for the table.

"Always sitting in the rear, girlfriend," Caroline said, bending to hug Assumpta. Caroline's multitude of braids and beads slid across her shoulders and draped over Assumpta with a clack. She pressed her mocha cheek against Assumpta's pale one.

"The better to watch my back, my dear." Assumpta smiled, and her stomach grumbled again.

"Oh, good, you're hungry," Caroline said. "Let's eat a late lunch."

"Nothing for me."

"Seriously?" Caroline offered her a sharp look. "You're still living with that rich guy, and you don't have two dimes to rub together?"

"It's not like that, and you know it."

"I know he was paying you a lot of money." Caroline sat down and offered Assumpta her full attention.

Assumpta fought the urge to get mad. Caroline had grown up poor and had money issues she really needed to get over. "Why do you assume he was paying me a lot of money?"

Caroline gave her a knowing look, and ticked her points off on her fingers. "One, he lives in one of the priciest high-rises in the city. Two, he had demon issues. Three, people pay big bucks to get rid of things that bother them—like roaches and rats. Demons? Really evil. So Greg must have paid you a huge amount of money to get rid of them—unless you're stupid and you didn't take his money." Caroline grinned, her whole face lighting up. She dropped her hands to the table. "I know you're not stupid. So he must have paid you well."

Assumpta couldn't fault her reasoning. It was sound. And she couldn't help smiling over Caroline's compliment. "You're right. He did pay me fairly well, but I've spent it all."

Caroline looked incredulous. "Nobody can go through that much money that fast and have nothing to show for it."

"I'll have something to show for it in a few years. I pre-paid my college tuition."

Caroline rolled her eyes. "But you've got no money now!"

"Exactly." Assumpta picked up her coffee and blew across the top of it to cool it, then took a tiny sip. "If I have don't have any money, my dad can't beg me for more."

"I hope that dad of yours burns in—"

"And I won't be tempted to spend it foolishly." Assumpta looked pointedly at the ruby ring on Caroline's left hand. Caroline wasn't dating anyone seriously, so she'd had to purchase it herself.

Caroline smiled. "Oh, this little thing? It's part of my good news. Let me get a sandwich and I'll tell you all about it. And get out that notebook you're always carrying. I need you to run some numbers for me."

Assumpta pulled out her notebook and pen, wondering how numerology worked into the picture here. Caroline wasn't always such a big proponent of it, even if she did send customers her way on occasion.

"Here." Caroline laid a chicken-salad sandwich on pumpernickel in front of Assumpta, along with some of her favorite chips. "I asked them to put some Old Bay on your sandwich, just the way you like."

"Thanks, Caroline. You didn't have to."

"Shut up. I'm feeling generous." She smiled to soften her words. "We can't have a proper discussion if your stomach's gonna keep interrupting."

Assumpta smiled and popped a chip into her mouth, savoring the salty flavor, punctuated by celery and cracked pepper. "Yum." She sucked all the salt and spices off before swallowing. "So, what's the good news?"

"I'm getting married!"

"Congratulations! Anyone I know?" Assumpta plastered a smile on her face, but inside she had a sinking feeling. It was great that Caroline was happy, but she absolutely could not afford to buy a bridesmaid's gown. *Good lord.* She hoped Caroline wasn't planning a destination wedding. And, God forgive her, she knew she was making this about her and not Caroline, but the timing just couldn't be worse.

"His name is Adrian Darcy. He says he knows you."

Assumpta tried to put a face with the name. "Doesn't sound familiar. But maybe I'll know him when I see him. When will that be?"

"If you can hang out long enough, this afternoon. I asked him to meet us here after work."

Assumpta checked her watch. "Sounds like a plan." After another sip of coffee, she said, "Look, don't think I'm trying to rain on your parade or anything, but this seems awfully sudden. I know we haven't talked in a while—" *Because you're always mad at me for something—*

"It is sudden," Caroline said, smiling again. "I'm being swept off my feet. But he's perfect. *We're* perfect. And it just feels right."

"Then why the numerology?"

"Because I want to pick a perfect date for the wedding. And if I can learn a little more about my husband-to-be at the same time, then why not?"

"You could just get to know your man the old-fashioned way."

"I know that," Caroline said, her voice deepening with sincerity. "It's just—I really like this guy. I don't want to mess it up."

Assumpta nodded. "What's his middle name?"

"I don't think he has one," Caroline said.

Assumpta wrote *Adrian Darcy* in block letters across the top of the page and then wrote the numbers corresponding to each letter beneath. Then she started adding. Numerology wasn't an exact science, and needed to be interpreted based on a lot of factors, but she could provide some generalities to Caroline based on the outcome. Once she'd met Adrian, she could fill in some pertinent details.

"Okay, here we go," she said, underlining the final number. "Adrian's life number is an eight. People with a life number of eight are usually full of energy and ambition. They have serious goals and tend to be wealthy."

"Sounds like my guy."

"But they can also be stubborn, too, and excessive. And status means everything to them."

"And there you go pissing in my Wheaties," Caroline said. Her smile faltered. "I'm not going to let you do it. And I'm not going to get mad at you for trying. I'm too happy about this."

"I'm not trying to bring you down. Just trying to let you know that there are two sides to everyone."

"Yes, you are trying to bring me down," said Caroline. "You think this is too sudden. But I am head-over-heels in love with Adrian and he loves me back." She took a deep breath, then gave Assumpta an accusatory look. "You're just unhappy that Greg hasn't asked you to marry him. Is that why you're so determined to move out?"

"Let's not make this about me," Assumpta said, switching gears and kicking herself for not leaving well enough alone. "This is about you and your fiancé, and getting married on the best day possible. When's his birthday? We'll work those numbers and see if we can't find the perfect wedding date."

Caroline still looked petulant, but she said, "June 6, 1986."

Assumpta frowned when she wrote down 6 - 6 - 1 - 9 - 8 - 6. *Three sixes. It could mean nothing, plenty of people have three sixes in their birth dates. But it didn't feel right.*

"Is something wrong?"

"I just forgot to mention that sometimes people with life numbers of eight are clumsy." Assumpta looked up from adding the numbers. She put a teasing lilt in her voice. "Is Adrian all thumbs? Or maybe he has two left feet?"

Caroline smiled, taking the bait. *Good,* thought Assumpta. She didn't need another argument with Caroline about this. But things really weren't looking good with Adrian's numbers. How do you explain to your intermittent best friend that there really isn't a good day to set a wedding with a guy unfortunate enough to be born under two such unlucky circumstances? That would turn Caroline into an off-again friend forever, she was certain.

"Left feet," Caroline said. "But at least he's got rhythm. I'll have him dancing yet."

"Just in time for the wedding."

"Exactly," Caroline agreed. "So when are the best dates?"

Assumpta reached into her voluminous purse for a calendar when she felt the mark between her shoulder blades start to itch. She looked up, her eyes trained on the door as it opened.

Caroline turned to look. "Oh, good! Adrian's early." She waved him over.

Sweat broke out on Assumpta's brow. *Oh, this isn't good, not good at all,* she thought, as The Big Guy walked over and put his arm around Caroline. He dropped a kiss on the top of her head and turned to Assumpta.

"Oh, my God," she said, resisting the urge to cross herself. That would have sent Caroline off on another tizzy.

"See, love," The Big Guy said to Caroline, "I told you she would recognize me when she saw me."

# CHAPTER 30

ASSUMPTA FELT THE BLOOD DRAIN OUT OF HER face. Her back continued to itch as the sweat ran down between her shoulder blades. *Think fast*, she thought.

Caroline said, "You look like you've seen a ghost. Are you all right?"

"Not a ghost," Assumpta assured her, staring at The Big Guy. She could never refer to him as Adrian. "Something much worse."

"What?" Caroline's concern turned to anger. "Don't be dissing my fiancé."

No good was going to come of this, Assumpta knew. Right now, it looked like she was going to lose Caroline for good: either by making her so angry she wouldn't speak to Assumpta again, or by putting her life in danger from The Big Guy. And if by some slim chance Assumpta could banish The Big Guy from her life and Caroline's without letting Caroline know, Caroline would certainly blame her anyway for his departure, and she would *still* have lost her friend. If ever she faced a no-win situation, this was it.

*So what was the best move?*

"You'll have to forgive me, Caroline," Assumpta said, turning her attention to her friend and pasting a brilliant smile on her face. "The Adrian Darcy I knew made it loud and clear that he wasn't the

marrying type. I can't help it if I'm a bit protective of my best friend."
She said more quietly, "Tigers don't change their stripes."

"Well, you were never my type, Assumpta," The Big Guy said. "But
I think you'll agree that it's true what they say about the right woman
having the power to change a man." He smiled down on Caroline as if
he meant every word he said.

*What was his game?*

"You never dated anyone more than once," Assumpta said. "If I
remember correctly, you said you didn't like the moss growing under
your feet. You were a free spirit."

He'd said nothing of the sort, of course. Call it poetic license, but
outing The Big Guy as a demon to her friend would get her all kinds
of nowhere. Caroline would never believe her, and it would send her
running full-steam-ahead into his arms. Assumpta couldn't have that.

Caroline crossed her arms over her chest and hit Assumpta with
one of her full-on stares. She could stop a Diamond Taxi with that
look. "You're starting to sound a little jealous, 'Sumpta. Did the two of
you date or something?"

"No." *Tread lightly*, she thought. "I just want you to be happy,
Caroline. Please don't blame me for wanting the best for you."

The Big Guy dropped his arm around Caroline's shoulders and
squeezed. The tension drained out of Caroline, replaced by a smile.
Caroline reached for Assumpta to give her a hug, too. "I know you
don't mean any harm. Just take it at face value that Adrian's changed
from the way you knew him. I'm so happy. I want you to be happy for
me, too."

Assumpta had to fight to keep the smile on her face. This was
all so wrong! The Big Guy must have Caroline under some spell or
something, a light one, because she'd shown a small bit of her old self
when she'd gotten mad at Assumpta a moment ago. But Assumpta had
never seen any man—*anyone*—charm Caroline out of a snit. Ever. Did
he do it by touching her?

She had a worse thought: *maybe Caroline was actually that much
in love?*

"So when's a good day to get married?" Caroline reminded her.

What could she say? There would never be a good day for these two to be married. You couldn't find happy when a demon is involved. But she wrote Caroline's birthday beside The Big Guy's and did a little calculation for Caroline's benefit. Then she said, "November 20th or December 16th look really good."

"But that's only a few weeks away!" Caroline said. "I couldn't do that. We—" She turned to The Big Guy. "Could we invite people that fast? But a hall, we couldn't. We can—"

"I meant next year," Assumpta said.

Caroline turned back to her friend, deflated. "I don't want to wait that long."

"Neither do I, dear," The Big Guy said. He bent to kiss Caroline on the top of her silky black braids. "Especially if waiting makes you so unhappy." He winked at Assumpta.

It took everything she had not to physically strike him. She said, "How long have you guys known each other?" She tried to put a teasing lilt in her voice. "You know what they say about anticipation?"

"Oh, you don't have to worry about that, Assumpta." Caroline was blushing.

*Oh, no.* If Adrian were as *gifted* in the sexual arena as even the stone minions of her last brush with evil, then Caroline was in serious trouble.

"It's not like we're *not* going to get married," she said. And she leaned toward Assumpta with a conspiratorial whisper. "We're already trying to have kids."

*Oh, God.* Assumpta looked at Caroline more closely and thought back over their conversation. Caroline's happiness—almost giddiness— her determination not to let anything get her down... *Had she gained weight? Oh, no, could Caroline already be pregnant?*

Assumpta forced a smile and made a pointed look at the clock on the wall. "That's so wonderful! I want to hear all about it, but I've got to go." She picked up her pen and notebook and shoved them into her purse. She could feel her smile fading. She needed to get out of here before she screamed. "I'll run some more numbers at home and give you a call."

"Okay," said Caroline, still wreathed in smiles. "I know we've kept you long enough waiting on Adrian." She moved closer to Assumpta and whispered, "Maybe we can double date one day soon: me and Adrian, you and Greg. It'll be fun."

"It's not like that between me and Greg."

"But it could be," Caroline said, her eyes twinkling. "Think about it."

Assumpta nodded. "I've got to go," she repeated. "Bye!" She air-kissed Caroline's cheek and waved limply to The Big Guy before escaping.

# CHAPTER 31

A LITTLE LATER, ASSUMPTA WANDERED INTO THE living room to find Jak deep in conversation with someone she couldn't hear. *Strange*, she thought. It was like listening to someone else talking on the phone.

Jak's ghostly Roman friends huddled together at the far window, their watery shapes barely visible in the sunbeams shining through. She squinted, counting them by their much brighter auras. No, Jak wasn't talking to one of them. *Vesta? No. The conversation seemed far too serious for that.* Then who? She set her purse down on a chair in the foyer and stepped around the waist-high bookshelf to the living room. Waving to the ghosts, she sat on the black leather couch, pulling her feet up under her, and waited for a lull in Jak's conversation before she spoke.

"Hi, Jak. We've got to talk. Who's your friend?" She nodded to the corner he seemed focused on, then let her eyes drift out of focus. The brightness of the aura hit her like a lightning bolt, its brilliant, golden yellow nearly blinding her. She wiped a tear from her right eye, and blinked furiously to stop the others from falling.

"Good afternoon, Assumpta. Meet Saint Michael." He nodded toward the corner. "Michael, Assumpta."

"T*he* Saint Michael? The Archangel?" When there was still no response from the corner, she gave up and turned to Jak. "I don't see a thing." Yet who else could it be with that kind of aura? She was in the presence of one of God's messengers. How should she act? What should she do?

"Will you show yourself?" Jak asked the corner. After a pause, he turned back to Assumpta. "He'd prefer not to."

"You see him," Assumpta said.

"Of course, I'm working with him. I'm on a mission."

"From God. I know," said Assumpta. "Like in *The Blues Brothers*. It's not funny in real life." Jak gave her a puzzled look. Suddenly, she was annoyed.

She turned to where she thought Saint Michael might be standing. "This game would be a lot easier to play if the people on my side of the war played by rules I understood. Seeing each other while we converse—unless we're on the telephone—is not too much to ask, I think." She looked upward. "Did you hear that, God?"

She waited a moment longer, then, crossing her arms across her chest, she said, "My best friend is joyfully humping the demon who owns my mark, and I think she's pregnant. Can someone tell me what happens when demons and humans make babies? Please don't tell me they'll be beautiful."

"Actually," said Saint Michael, popping into view, "God forbids demons to mate with humans—but human/demon spawn do tend to be preternaturally beautiful."

*As...are...angels*, she thought, his words dying on her as she slid off the sofa onto her knees. She really was in the presence of Saint Michael, the Archangel. She fought the urge to cross herself, her eyes drawn to the glowing halo floating a few inches above his head, the front of it dipping rakishly low.

"Get off your knees," he said tiredly. He turned to Jak. "Do you see what I mean? Now you know why I didn't want to show myself. Give me the visage of Samael any day. I vastly prefer fear to adoration.

People get over their fear so much more quickly, and it's a lot less of a nuisance."

Jak shrugged.

Assumpta stared at Saint Michael. She couldn't seem to take her eyes away from his beautiful face. She loved the way his dark hair curled to his shoulders. Must he wear his armor, even now? It seemed out of place in such a relaxed atmosphere, but she had to admit, he wore it well. *Michael, the Archangel, is hot,* she thought. And then a sick feeling settled in her stomach. Was there some kind of rule about not appreciating the sight of one of God's holy messengers? Was it blasphemy of some sort? Was thinking him hot *lustful?* Now, *that* was a sin.

*No,* she thought, taking in the whole of him, *I'm simply enjoying his beauty—from his halo to the golden tips of his pearly white wings nearly touching the floor.*

Michael turned his complete attention to Assumpta and smiled wickedly. She felt herself smiling back. She didn't want to turn away. He was beautiful.

In an instant, his flesh melted away, and he was a skeleton—*Samael*—with flames burning in his eyes and insects crawling in the cage of his ribs. He said, "Feel like bending a knee to me now?" in the discordant voice of all the souls he had reft.

"Oh! Ahhhh!" Assumpta yelled, surprised. She fell back. Jak chuckled.

She scooted onto the sofa, away from Saint Michael, no longer feeling the fascination of his beauty.

Michael, still in the visage of Samael, moved to the hearth and snapped his fingers. A fire appeared in the grate. He sat in the love seat diagonally across from Jak and Assumpta. His bones grew flesh and hair and features, and he was once again beautiful Saint Michael.

"What just happened?" Assumpta's heart had stopped its reckless beating, and she felt calm enough to ask.

"You've just met Saint Michael in his preferred guise of Samael," Jak said.

"The Grim Reaper?"

"Close enough," said Jak.

She nodded, still a little befuddled.

Saint Michael cleared his throat, drawing Assumpta's attention. "What do you mean," he said to Assumpta, his voice low and modulated, "that your friend is pregnant by a demon?" It seemed to Assumpta that he tried to control a lot of anger behind his question.

"Just what I said." Assumpta swallowed. His anger aside, she could get used to basking in the holy light he emitted. She squinted her eyes and saw again the hot, yellow aura—that reserved for truly holy souls—enveloping him. "Well," she amended, "I think Caroline's pregnant. Or at least, she's very soon to be. Caroline is seeing a demon high-up in the political structure of Hell, and they're actively trying to make a baby." She paused for affect. "If I had to guess, I'd think that's his plan: to make babies with as many women as possible—starting with my best friend, of course, because that's the lowest thing he could do."

Jak whistled long and low between his teeth. "It's ingenious, really. In as little as fifteen years, he could have an entire army of children ready to do his bidding."

Saint Michael said, "But the consequences—"

"—don't matter when you're already damned." Jak tossed another log onto the fire.

"Caroline's glowing," said Assumpta. "I'd say she's already pregnant. Of course, it could just be the first blush of love."

"I have to go," said Saint Michael. He lifted his chin to the ceiling, closed his eyes, and vanished.

# CHAPTER 32

**A**SSUMPTA PICKED UP THE PHONE AND CALLED Caroline for the third time. She had to warn her.

*Ring.*

*Ring.*

*Ring.*

*Ring.*

*Click.* The other line picked up.

"Don't hang up this time!" she said. "Caroline, I care about you."

The silence on the other end of the phone unnerved her, but at least her friend wasn't hanging up. "Caroline, I'm not trying to ruin your happiness. Please believe me. But—"

"How touching," came the deep, deep voice on the other end of the line.

"Who is this?"

"You know very well who it is, Assumpta."

"Leave Caroline alone! She has no experience with creatures like you!"

The Big Guy chuckled. "I know. That's what makes this so damned easy."

The phone went dead in her ear.

# CHAPTER 33

**A**SSUMPTA KNOCKED ON CAROLINE'S DOOR, reveling in the mid-morning sunshine warming her as she waited on the stoop. She rubbed her hands together to make them warm.

She hadn't called before she took the bus over. She didn't want to get hung up on again or be forbidden from coming over. Or have to talk to The Big Guy. Canton was a fair distance by bus from Roland Park, and she'd hate to have wasted the effort. Yet the trip was necessary.

She had a feeling this was not going to go well. A woman was going to choose her man over her girlfriend—especially her on-again, off-again girlfriend—any day of the week. Still, she felt an obligation to try. Assumpta had known Caroline for a lot of years, and she couldn't ignore the situation.

She just wished she had more to offer Caroline than knowledge. She knew she had her facts straight, but she had no concrete proof to offer Caroline that her lover was, in fact, a demon.

How do you even broach that subject? *Caroline, I've been to Hell and back. I've seen this guy's true colors. He's not human; he's a demon. And, he owns my soul.*

He owns my soul. Did that sound too much like she had a thing for the guy? She couldn't admit that. Caroline would be all over it, accusing her of trying to steal her man. In the past, she'd seen Caroline turn on women for just such an imagined infraction.

She knocked again.

When no one answered after a moment longer, she turned and walked down the two marble steps to the sidewalk.

Then, she heard the door open behind her.

"What do you want?" Caroline growled.

Assumpta turned to face her. Caroline stepped out of the house, folded her arms across her chest, and leaned one hip on the wrought-iron railing.

"I want to help you."

It was the wrong thing to say.

Caroline's face tightened into a hard mask of anger. "What makes you think I need help? I am *not* one of your projects."

"No, you're not," Assumpta said. "You're my friend, and I care about you. I don't want to see you get hurt."

"You mean you don't want to see *you* get hurt. You're just jealous that I've got a man who wants to marry me. What have you got?"

Assumpta knew Caroline didn't mean to come off sounding like a bitch—she was under The Big Guy's thrall, and all she could think about was marrying him and having babies. He was practically making Caroline say these things. "I've—"

Caroline wasn't finished. "And what do you know about men that makes you some kind of authority? You're living with, *living with—*" Her voice got all hoarse and tears leaked from the corners of her eyes.

Assumpta found herself tearing up at Caroline's emotion. It was hard to keep strong in the wake of such feelings—feelings she was fairly certain were real. Caroline sounded almost jealous that she was living with Greg. But Assumpta knew that wasn't the case, or at least it hadn't been, until *Adrian* had come along.

Caroline swallowed, seeming to collect herself, and said more quietly, "You are living with a good man, a *rich* man, who wants nothing more than to marry you and make babies, and you're waiting for some fantasy to come rescue you. Grow up. You know nothing about men. Go away and learn something. Then maybe we can talk again."

Caroline stepped inside the house and slammed the door.

Assumpta felt numb inside. Stunned. She'd wanted to help, but she'd just made things worse. Slowly, she turned away and walked to the corner to catch the bus that would take her back to Greg's apartment. *There's nothing like a good friend letting you know how she* really *feels,* thought Assumpta. Even if those feelings were trumped up by the demon she was dating.

Where did Caroline get all that nonsense about Greg wanting to marry her? Had Greg poured out his heart to her? Or was she making it all up?

Maybe Caroline just *thought* she knew how Greg was feeling. Maybe she inferred something more in the relationship just because Assumpta and Greg lived in the same apartment. She wouldn't be the first person—or demon—to leap to such a conclusion. The Big Guy couldn't know what was going on in Greg's house. He was guessing, and just passing those guesses on to Caroline.

Assumpta knew he liked her, but if his feelings were that strong—Vesta notwithstanding—she had to get out of the apartment much sooner than she'd planned. Like, today, or as soon as possible.

# CHAPTER 34

"WHERE'S JAK?"

Greg walked into the kitchen where Assumpta sat nursing a beer. *Her third, from the looks of it*, he thought.

"What do you care?"

"I don't," Greg said, "but he's usually tied to your hip this time of day." He paused. "If Jak's not around, maybe it's time for us to talk."

"I can't imagine what there might be for us to talk about." She looked up from her beer. "I'll be moving out this weekend, by the way. I can't take this anymore."

"*You* can't take this anymore?" He went to the fridge and grabbed a beer for himself, stopping to wrench the cap off with a bottle opener before pulling a chair out across from Assumpta. "How do you think I feel?" He raised his voice. "I finally meet the girl of my dreams…"

Assumpta interrupted him with laughter. "Those must have been some dreams. I never pictured you for a paranormal nerd."

He slammed his beer bottle down on the table. "V*esta* is not the girl of my dreams."

"Well, surely you aren't talking about me," Assumpta said.

Their eyes met. There was a strained silence for two beats of Greg's heart, then he said, softly, "Who else is there?"

Assumpta lowered her eyes.

"Greg, we come from two different worlds." She picked at the label of her beer, where the condensation had licked away at the glue and it had come undone. "I'm just a novelty. You came to me when you needed help and I gave you what you needed. You're just confused."

"I'm not confused."

"Think about it. You found yourself cursed by minions of evil: life in jeopardy, soul in peril, and no idea how to extricate yourself from the predicament. By sheer happenstance, you know a person who points you in my direction. It takes time—time in which we get to know each other, for certain—but we remove the peril from your life and save your soul. Perhaps you feel a little beholden, you're certainly astonished, as nothing in your previous life has prepared you for this kind of experience. You might even feel that you can't bear to let me go. Certainly it's fear of finding yourself in a similar situation without backup. But how often could you possibly get yourself cursed? And you know the way to keep your soul from jeopardy. So, I say, yes—you're a little mixed up right now. But you'll get over it." She raised the bottle to her lips and, tilting her head back, chugged the remainder of the beer.

She looked a little swimmy, thought Greg. *That was some speech.*

Was she such a lightweight she couldn't handle a couple of beers? *She could be, come to think of it,* he thought. He'd never seen her drink a beer—or anything alcoholic, for that matter—since she'd moved in with him.

*Why was she drinking now?*

"I'm not confused," Greg reiterated. "If I were confused, would I have gotten you this?"

He pushed back from the table and went to the cookie jar on the far counter. He opened it, pulled out a small black box, and returned to the table. He laid it in front of Assumpta before he sat down.

"I bought this for you the day Jak showed up. Open it."

She hesitated, then reached for it, and flipped the top open. A large, square-cut diamond ring lay nestled in its depths.

She snapped it shut and pushed it back toward Greg.

"That's…"

"An engagement ring." He pushed it back toward her. "Do you like it?"

She opened the box again and stared at the ring for a full five seconds before she snapped it shut again and pushed it back toward him. "It's stunning."

"I looked for the most beautiful ring I could find," Greg said. "I wanted it to match the beauty of the woman I love."

Assumpta sucked in a breath, not liking where this conversation was going. "We've never talked of love."

"We've never had the chance, until now. I'm opening the conversation. Do you love the ring, Assumpta?"

It was an absurd question, and she found herself getting surly. Was it the beer? *Definitely not*, she thought. *It's Greg, and he's being an ass.* She took a deep breath and calmed herself before she said anything she'd regret. "Yes, I love the ring. It's gorgeous. But that doesn't mean I'm *in* love with you. It doesn't mean that I love you at all."

"Agreed," said Greg. "But would you concede it might be possible, that under the right circumstances, you *could* love me?"

Yeah, she could concede that, but she wouldn't. It would only give him false hope to tell him that if she'd met him first they might have had a chance. He was a nice guy, but her heart belonged to someone else.

She stood up, banging the chair against the wall. "What's wrong with you? Do you think the deliberate use of confounding logic will trick me into loving you? Quit playing games."

She slammed down her bottle and left the room.

# CHAPTER 35

GREG DREAMT OF ASSUMPTA, HER LONG, AUBURN hair trailing down her back, with just a few strands hanging in front to cover the tips of her breasts. He lay on his back, his hands resting on her bare hips and her thighs gripping his waist as she sat astride his belly. He could feel the heat of her breasts as she bent forward to nip his chin with tiny love bites, then slide her tongue down the side of his neck to the crease on his shoulder.

He wrapped his arms around her, sliding his hands up to her shoulders and pressing her tightly to him as her lips found his own. She nibbled, kissed, and licked his lips, darting her tongue into his parted mouth to taste him, then darting out again, giggling. He could taste her smile, the warm breaths of air she exhaled, tickling as she worked her kisses from his lips to his torso.

Moving his hands to the back of her head, he gently urged her upward again. He was done with the teasing. His lips found hers, his tongue parted them with a firm thrust, and he entered her mouth, coaxing her tongue into a duel.

He felt her shift upon him, her right hand trailing down his chest, over his waist and down to his hip. She brushed a palm across his cock. Immediately, he felt a heaviness as it grew, felt a twinge in his balls as she wrapped her hand around him and squeezed gently.

When she moved again, she straddled his hips and sat on his cock, sliding all the way down in one slick, almost tortuous, slide. *God*, she felt so good.

He let her take the lead, rising and falling in a gentle rhythm. Groaning, he felt the sweet, velvet pulse of her hot core slip up and down his cock, driving him crazy. He wrapped his hands in her hair and pulled her close.

She put her lips near his ear, kissed his neck, then said, "You like that, sugar, don't you?"

*That doesn't sound at all like Assumpta*, he thought.

She squeezed her thighs against his hips and clenched her inner muscles, tightening around his cock.

And just for a moment, it hurt. *A lot*.

Greg woke.

He opened his eyes to find Vesta staring him right in the face. In the darkness, her eyes looked hard and sharp, completely unlike Assumpta's warm brown ones. Smiling wickedly, Vesta gripped the tip of her tongue between bared teeth and raised her eyebrows in further invitation.

"No!" he shouted, thrusting his hips to heave her off of him. He didn't need Assumpta to catch them at this again. He'd made up his mind: he wanted Assumpta.

"Not quite yet," she said, "I haven't come." She grabbed his shoulders and held on while he bucked and heaved to dislodge her.

"But I don't want this." He lifted his hands to grab her and push her sinuous body away from him. His hands went through her, and he grasped nothing.

She laughed. "I'm a ghost, remember?"

And yet, different, he thought, if she could feel solid to him sometimes and not be solid at others.

He heaved sideways, attempting to roll off the bed. Maybe if he landed on his belly, he might be able to dislodge her. But when he tried, he found himself unable to move more than a few inches. She had some kind of electrical hold on his muscles. He should have been able to roll himself over, but he couldn't.

Lifting his knees, he slid his legs up until he could plant his heels firmly on the mattress. He bucked with all his strength, lifting his hips sharply—but again, moved only by a few inches.

She laughed and continued to move on top of him, running her hands up and down his chest, squeezing him passionately. How could he feel her touches, her heat, when she lacked enough substance for him to grab her and get her off of him? He was simultaneously excited and repulsed.

"Yes!" Vesta shouted. She convulsed upon him, her back arching in apparent ecstasy.

A moan escaped Greg. He might not want her, but his body wasn't complaining.

She leaned forward, grinding down upon his erection, seeking his lips, but Greg turned away from her kiss. She laughed, a throaty, triumphant arpeggio soft and dark near his ear. "It doesn't work that way, sweetling. Once I've had you, you're mine until I suck you dry. But don't worry, I fuck like a demon." She laughed again. "When you realize how wonderful it's going to be between us, you're not going to care, I promise."

She wriggled her hips, and he could feel himself still hard and heavy, caught within her heat. "Let me go," he said between clenched teeth.

"Soon enough, but first, let's have another ride." She gripped him hard around the waist with her knees, rising and falling to impale herself over and over on his cock.

Greg gripped the sheets, clenching his fingers so hard they hurt. But, oh God—she was right—it felt so good. Her tight little pussy clenched his cock with every heave and thrust. He couldn't fight this for long. The more he tried to fight, the better it felt. Wouldn't it be more advantageous to go along and enjoy the ride until it was over? Maybe, if he stopped fighting, it would be over more quickly.

*No*, he couldn't reconcile giving in to her desires.

"Touch me." She reached for his wrists, pulling them to her breasts. He fought her hands, gripping the sheets, but she was too strong. "Touch me," she said again. "Giving me pleasure increases your own."

He uncurled his fingers and pressed them against her breasts. He cupped them in his palms, smoothing the sides of them with his fingers, running his thumbs over her prominent nipples.

Vesta leaned into his hands, sighing, whispering coaxing words as caressed her. His cock felt over sensitized. And she was right again: the more he touched her, the better her touches felt. He could learn to enjoy this, he thought. *No*, he thought again. *Assumpta...*

Vesta sank down on his cock, her movements becoming slow and languid.

"Hurry this up, damn you," said Greg.

She climaxed again, with a deep shuddering sigh, and this time, he climaxed, too. Vesta milked his cock with deep muscular contractions. He could feel himself tire, exhaustion overtaking him. *Assumpta...* he thought. *Assumpta...Vesta...*

He heard Vesta's seductive laugh in his ear one last time before he drifted off to sleep.

# CHAPTER 36

THE BUS RIDE BACK TO THE COLLEGE SATURDAY afternoon was uneventful.

Assumpta put her things away in her locker and grabbed her lab coat, then made her way to the chemistry lab to review some of the first-year's naked-egg experiments that she was babysitting for a professor over the weekend. *Lazy prof*, she thought, glad she was in the honors program. She'd performed this experiment in grade school with her mom in the kitchen. The professor should have assigned it for homework and saved something bigger for class.

She opened the fume hood, took a big whiff of fifty or so beakers filled with vinegar, each with a single egg floating in them, and wrinkled her nose. Over the course of the weekend, the vinegar would eat the shell off the egg, leaving a rubbery sphere floating in the beaker. That's when the real fun began.

Some of the eggs were starting to show some yolk, and as she suspected, all was well. Not a rotten egg in the bunch. Annoying to have to watch over, but she couldn't complain. She was getting a few hour's pay just to keep an eye on things. There was no real work involved, so how could she argue with that?

Having done her duty, she slipped out of the lab and into the tiny, attached office she shared with three other honors chemistry students and logged onto the Internet.

She typed *how to call a demon* into the search engine and waited for the results to appear. She had The Big Guy's coin to call him, but what if it was a one-shot deal? She wanted options, just in case she needed him again. And if she used the coin, was she beholden to him in some manner? Perhaps *he* was bound to certain rules if she used the coin...just like all the visiting demons were bound to certain rules because of her demon mark.

If only she knew his name. Names were powerful. If she knew it, she could have him here faster than she could snap her fingers. There had to be another way to get him to come forward without using the coin so she could keep the coin for a rainy day. Once she figured that out, she'd talk with Jo about setting up some protections and wards: something to keep herself safely guarded, and to keep The Big Guy confined until she sent him back to Hell. But first she needed more information on how the coin, and objects like it, worked. If she used the coin, could he come and go as he pleased? That wouldn't be good.

"You could just whistle," said a sultry male voice over her shoulder, just as her mark started to itch.

"Oh!" She pushed the wheeled chair backwards and swung around. The demon had already moved a few feet away, avoiding her backward rush. Her heart beat wildly in her chest. It didn't matter how many demons came to visit, she couldn't get past this initial heart-thumping fright. That was probably a good thing, right? It kept her on her guard.

She'd never seen this demon before. "What do you want?" she asked.

"I was just offering some advice," he said, leaning casually against the desk by the window. "You don't need elaborate spells to call a demon. Just think it, and one of us is certain to show up."

He smiled, teeth white and shiny against skin that looked Spanish or Greek, though his accent suggested the latter. His wavy dark hair touched the collar of his white shirt in a feathered style reminiscent of the 1980s. Assumpta found him attractive—or would have, if she didn't know his appearance was nothing but a sham.

"I need to call a specific demon."

"Because only one will satisfy your needs?" His dark eyes smoldered. Before she could blink, he was pressed against her, kneeling beside her chair. His warm body touched hers as intimately as Jak's had. He kissed her, sliding his tongue into her mouth when she gasped. The odor of sulfur rose between them.

She raised her palms to his chest and pushed, pressing the holy medals dangling from her fingers against the thin fabric of his shirt. The demon howled, and released her. She scooted away, watching as the burns on his chest healed and the shirt become whole again as the demon brushed the ashes from it.

"We had a deal!" Assumpta wiped a hand across her mouth. "The Big Guy promised he wouldn't send any more of his demons around." She felt like spitting, just to get the taste out of her mouth. "Why are you here?"

"I'm not one of The Big Guy's lieutenants. I don't have to follow his dictates," the demon said. He glanced around the room, surveying it with disdain, as if he were above it, above servitude in general. "You might say, I have my own agenda."

"And that is?"

"Helping you."

She laughed, forgetting her fear and disgust with the pure absurdity of his statement. "I can't see how that might have gotten to the top of your *to do* list," she said.

"Helping you helps me." He shrugged, grinning, and put his hands in his pockets. She caught herself smiling back at him, realizing just how devastating his smile was.

He said, "Why don't you tell me *why* you want to call a specific demon."

Assumpta wondered, *what's the harm in telling him?* Maybe she could learn a thing or two with this conversation. Would it matter that whatever she learned from a demon would be used to help her accomplish her goals? Would it matter if by doing so, she helped a demon in return? She took a deep breath, buying some time to think about it. She could always go to confession afterward—well, not *immediately* afterward, but after she got rid of her mark. And if she never got rid of the mark, well, she was damned anyway. *Why not?* she decided.

"I've got something this particular demon wants," she said, "and while I'm fairly certain I could *whistle him up*, with the right know-how, I also want to make certain I'm protected and that I don't unleash some wily demon on the world. I need to get this right."

"Oh, that's easy," the Greek Adonis said. He leaned forward and whispered something in her ear.

The plan sounded reasonable. "Why should I trust you?" Assumpta asked.

"You shouldn't. But great battles are never won by the faint of heart." He lifted a hand to blow on his knuckles, then rubbed them on his chest right above the place where he'd have a heart, if he were human.

She looked intently at him, watching while she turned the idea over in her head. Finally, she said, "What's in it for you?"

"Nothing, at the moment."

"And in the future?"

"Let's just say that The Big Guy's loss is my gain, shall we?"

She crossed her arms on her chest. "Control of the demons in the mid-Atlantic area."

He nodded. "Among other things." He gave her that devastating look. "Do you think you'll do it?"

She thought for a long moment before she nodded *yes*.

# CHAPTER 37

**T**HE BIG GUY HAD REQUESTED HOLY OIL, TOO Assumpta remembered. If she gave it to him, would he remove the mark? He hadn't promised her that, but he did promise *something*.

Well, he could damn well come get it himself, she thought, pushing Greg's black leather love seat against the wall and rolling up the area rug. She was not walking down a million flights of stairs back into Hell just to make a delivery. If The Big Guy wanted it so badly, he'd have to come to her.

She drew a chalk circle on the floor in front of the fireplace, then surrounded it with holy salt, making certain not to leave any portion of the circumference broken. She didn't want The Big Guy getting out of the ring. She poured holy water into a small bowl and dipped her finger in it, then drew a circle around the salt, being careful not to touch any and dissolve the barrier. For good measure, she dipped a sprig of rosemary into the water and sprinkled holy water all around the room. Rosemary was for remembrance, but it was also for power—and protection. And she needed all the protection and power she could get.

With a pocket compass, she found magnetic north, hoping the variation wouldn't affect her mission, and placed a white candle at that location, just outside the salt-ring perimeter. Assumpta placed three more at south, west and, east.

She took the small bottle of holy oil off her altar and placed it three-quarters of the way between the center of the circle and the southernmost point. She assumed the demon would materialize exactly in the center, and didn't want him to knock it over when he appeared. Nor did she want to place it too close to the outer edge of the circle, because she didn't want to be that close to him when he reached for it. She stepped back and lit all the candles, then returned to the southern point of the circle and knelt. She called on Saint Michael for protection.

She prayed the traditional prayer for Saint Michael, then added a personal plea, since she'd met him. "Saint Michael, please protect me in this endeavor. I really need your help."

She paused, thinking she should probably say a quick prayer to the man upstairs as well. "Lord, I've called upon your servant Michael to protect me here. I'm begging for your protection as well. I can't do this alone. I need you to have my back." She paused, wondering if her language should be more formal to a God who seemed to require pomp and ritual in order to be praised. "Lord, I'm probably going to Hell for that thought," she muttered. "While you're at it, can you send me some help, some sign…point me in the right direction to remove this demon mark. Your will allowed it to be done, show me that your will can allow it to be undone." *Without me having to give up my life to these demons,* she thought.

She closed her eyes and took a deep breath. "Amen," she finally whispered. "Here goes."

She pulled the papers she'd printed off the Internet out of her pocket and unfolded them. She read the Latin words haltingly, unfamiliar with their rhythm and cadence. And then she waited.

A few seconds passed, then a whorl of black smoke eddied up from the center of the circle. It swirled to the ceiling in a thin, unbroken line. More smoke appeared at the floor, twisting, revolving into a vortex that pulled the smoke from the ceiling down into itself. With an audible pop, it all disappeared and The Big Guy stood in its place. He looked quite pleased.

Nudging the bottle of oil with his toe, he asked, "The oil?"

"Yes."

"Excellent." He looked around the room, at the circle, the candles. "You didn't have to go to all this trouble," he said. "Reading the name from my coin would have been sufficient."

"I wanted a little more protection than that," Assumpta said.

He nodded. "Understandable, but unnecessary, as well as inadequate."

She frowned. "Inadequate?"

He pulled a pair of rubber gloves from his pocket and snapped them on, precise as a surgeon. A plastic bag followed. Bending, he retrieved the oil, placed it in the plastic bag, and pocketed it. Then, he walked to the very edge of the circle, the toe of his wing-tipped shoes not quite touching the blessed salt Assumpta had laid around the chalk for additional protection.

"You didn't think you could keep me here, did you?"

She frowned. What was she missing?

"I don't see how you can escape. I drew the circle correctly. It's warded."

"And you've called on Saint Michael, too. Nice touch." He nodded toward one corner of the room.

Assumpta turned to look, but saw nothing.

"You see, had you used the coin, I would have answered your call, but I still would have been trapped in Hell. I would have some minor power here, some minor power over you, but I would have had to return to Hell."

He toed the salt, pushing it away from the circle. Then he wiggled his foot back and forth, grinding more of the salt—and much of the chalk—away, making a space wide enough for him to walk through.

Assumpta felt the color drain from her face. A sick feeling rose in her throat.

"But when you draw a circle and summon a demon, you bring him to your plane. So, here I am *out of Hell* and in your little neighborhood. Lucky me."

"You shouldn't be able to touch the salt," Assumpta said.

"It *does* hurt," said the Big Guy, still smiling. An eddy of smoke rose up from his shoe as if to prove his words. "But I won't be here long enough for it to be an issue."

Assumpta stepped away from the circle.

"Dear God," she said softly. "What have I done?"

"Don't be so hard on yourself," The Big Guy said, stepping out of the circle. "I maneuvered you into this. It's not your fault. I knew you wouldn't fall for the coin trick, so I planned you'd do things this way." He walked to the fireplace and studied a framed photo on the mantle. Then, he turned back to her.

She gulped, her mouth suddenly dry. "But you shouldn't have gotten past the chalk or the warded candles.

"My magic is stronger than your religion," he said.

"Saint Michael, protect me," she whispered.

"Oh, he is." The Big Guy bared his fangs at her. And for the briefest of seconds, he dropped his mask, showing his hideous face: purple-and-black bubbled skin, horns on his head, teeth like razors. And then it was gone. He was once again the attractive attorney. "If Saint Michael wasn't here, I'd have killed you the moment you freed me from the pit."

"But I've done nothing to you. Why would you want to kill me?"

"On principle." He chuckled. "You're so weak it took nothing to break your wards. Or maybe for sport, who knows? Maybe it's just my nature and I like the taste of blood." He smiled his smarmy lawyer's smile. "Just remember, Michael won't always be there to protect you."

# CHAPTER 38

ASSUMPTA SMELLED SULFUR BEFORE THE MARK ON her back started to tingle. She looked up from the beaker, half expecting the The Big Guy to materialize in front of her. But she didn't see anything and her back continued to itch.

*Goddamnit! I can't get anything done without demons interfering. At this rate, I'll never graduate.*

Where could it be? The lab door was closed, so it had probably materialized right in front of her. It was either very small or keeping itself invisible. *Could demons do that?* She hadn't found one yet who was invisible. *Great.* Just another thing for her to have to worry about.

She looked down—there it was, running along the baseboard of the lab wall. Nasty little thing, dripping slime and leaving a trail on the neat floor. *What could it want in her lab?*

She set down the beaker and walked to the cleanup station for a broom. At least with the molded tile baseboard, there would be no mouse hole for it to bolt into. This thing was as good as squashed.

She lifted the broom to swat the sneaky little demon and felt a searing pain between her shoulder blades. "Ow!"

Tears welled in her eyes.

"That's not the way to treat a fellow demon," boomed a voice behind her. She whirled, lowering the broom with one hand and pushing the protective goggles she wore up into her hair with the other. Assumpta wiped away the moisture at her eyes. She could hardly see the demon through the tears, though she could tell he was tall and disguised as a human. Thank God for small favors; she hated their true appearance.

Had the point of the little demon been to take her off-guard? She gripped the broom more tightly in case she needed to fend him off. But she thought that might not be necessary. If he'd wanted to hurt her, he would have done it already. *Right?*

"I'm not a fellow demon," she said, her eyes finally clearing. The pain in her back was subsiding. *What was that about?*

"Ah, but you could be." His eyes glittered with an unholy passion, making a lie of the debonair appearance he cultivated, from the crisp collar of his pleated tuxedo shirt—open at the throat—to the tips of his shiny leather shoes. She was certain the missing jacket was meant to make him look relaxed, rather than like James Bond: on a mission. "Think of all the perks," he continued, smiling, as if aware of her appraisal. "The ability to flit from here to there in the blink of an eye, mystical powers, amazing strength—"

"Inability to step foot in a church, loss of humanity, unbelievable ugliness beneath that fake human appearance, forfeiture of my soul—"

"Well, that's a given, honey." He raised one eyebrow in a sardonic quirk. "You're marked. Your soul has already been *appropriated*...it's just a matter of time." He smiled, and his teeth glistened, toothpaste-commercial white.

"And until such time, I'll be certain to take every opportunity I can to get it back."

"And I'm here to offer you just such an opportunity."

Assumpta leaned the broom against the black laminate counter. "So you're the genius that *owns* my soul?"

"Not at all. I—"

"Then I don't see that we've got anything to talk about," she said, turning away.

It took guts to turn her back on a demon, but she had to show some strength. She needed to come to the bargaining table with some kind of advantage, and if showing the latest demon plaintiff that she wasn't afraid of him was all she had, well, she needed to make that plain from the start.

He materialized in front of her, a look of annoyance on his face. He was so close, she could almost taste the sulfur beneath the heavy application of men's cologne that filled her nostrils. That totally detracted from his good looks.

"You seem to think I have nothing to offer."

"No more than the rest of your kind do." She shrugged, and leaned a hip against the eye-wash station. The tilt of her hips pulled the long muscles in her back, igniting the pain between her shoulders again. She felt a trickle of something run down her spine, and hoped it was sweat. She'd never get bloodstains out of her lab coat.

"The others were sycophants and wannabees," he said, waving a hand. "All clearly lacking the power that I possess."

"And do you have more power than the demon who's marked me?"

He paused. "Perhaps not, but I have something more valuable."

"And what would that be?"

"Knowledge."

A laugh bubbled out of her. *Knowledge*. That's just what Jak had bargained with. And she'd had to *fuck* Jak to get it. What would a demon require?

"And just how does a demon impart knowledge?" she asked.

He gave her a puzzled look. "Why, I tell you, of course."

*So mundane*, she thought, considering the offer. A little knowledge went a long way in some cases, but how could she know if he had anything useful or not? Could she gain that knowledge and keep him dangling on a string? Maybe, but she wasn't certain she wanted to bet her soul on it.

She said, "I simply need to cede my mark to you in exchange for your knowledge?"

He nodded. "I have a contract right here…" He patted his rear end with his left hand. The inconvenience of forgoing a jacket, she presumed.

"And how am I to be protected by the current owner of the mark when he comes looking to collect?"

"He won't even know the deed is done," the demon said smiling. He snapped his fingers, presumably to prevent the indignity of yanking the contract from his rear pocket like a schoolboy. The folded document appeared between his fingers. He unfurled it with a flick of his wrist. "Sign right here. I'll need a drop of your blood."

"I haven't consented to anything yet," Assumpta said. "I have a hard time believing that the mark's owner doesn't keep some kind of tab on me with this mark on my back." She folded her arms across her chest. "Once it disappears, isn't his homing beacon likely to go dark? Won't he come looking?"

The demon colored. "You're right. He'll know right away—"

"And he'll be angry."

"Yes, but it won't be you he'll be angry with. It will be me, and all will be well."

"You've already said you don't have enough power to take him. What makes you think that after he's done ripping you to pieces, he won't do the same to me?" Assumpta looked him straight in the eye. "There's something you're not telling me. Why risk his wrath?"

"There is no risk," the demon said. "Your soul is one of the most sought-after in Hell. A soul as pure as yours—"

She laughed. With her distinct questioning of the faith she'd been raised in, her recent tendency to curse God, and her dabbling in pagan ritual…how could her soul be so pure?

The demon quickly lost his aplomb. "Laugh if you want, but it's true! The Archangel Michael watches over you. You have been chosen for great things by…*Him*. It's precisely your lack of conceit—your doubts—that bespeak your worth."

"My doubts? Lots of people have doubt. There's got to be more to it than that."

He smiled, a condescending look with barely restrained frustration.

"Certainly many people have doubts, but you have explored yours, and taken action. You helped poor Jak."

"Does everyone know about my helping Jak?"

He made that smile again. "Anyone who keeps their eye on things in Hell, anyone who craves power." He seemed to think about that, and then nodded. "Just about everyone, yes." He paused. "Your action led you to the attention of God, who you seem to treat with far less reverence than the rest of us. How refreshing is that?" Now, his smile was pure evil.

She put up a hand to stop his next words. "And what do you gain by my signing?"

He let out a deep sigh, as if disgusted that he'd lost the upper hand in the conversation. "My power grows by the number of souls I voluntarily collect. If I obtain your signature, not only do I gain prestige and power, I weaken the one who owns your mark because he took your soul through trickery and stealth." He looked her straight in the eyes. "I'll have the power to defeat him if he tries to win back your mark. You have nothing to fear."

"Let me see the contract."

He handed it to her.

The stiff, cream-colored paper felt heavy in her hands and smelled faintly of sulfur. The words were in English, but the font was archaic and uneven, as if the document had been handwritten by a scribe. It was beautiful.

She started reading from the top, watching him surreptitiously as he wandered around the lab, permitting her to read the contract without his overbearing presence. "Don't touch anything."

"Certainly," he agreed.

The contract seemed straightforward, and she was tempted to sign when she got to the bottom. She picked up a ballpoint pen, and clicked the top of it with her thumb. But there was one clause that bothered her. She scanned to the top of the page to read it again, and the words began to swim in front of her eyes.

"Why are the words moving around on the page?" she asked.

"Dammit!" He stood in front of her instantly, and tore the contract out of her hands. "Trouble-making son of a vituperous whoremonger." He looked at the page. "Just sign it," he said. "You read to the bottom, right?"

"Yes, but there was one troubling clause…"

"Which? I'll explain it, and we can get on with this deal."

"The one which states…" *Well, that's funny*, she thought. "I can't remember. In fact, I can't remember what any of the document says." She straightened her shoulders. The pain bothered her even less this time. "I won't sign this."

He snarled. "God-damned fucking hell spawn—may he burst into flames borne from all that's holy!" Assumpta took a step back away from the demon. His human façade faded with his anger, revealing the beast beneath. Red eyes blazed. A ropey vein pulsed across his high, bony forehead, just beneath a pair of black, twisted horns jutting forward.

He squeezed his fist and the contract burst into flames. "He won't get away with this, I assure you."

Assumpta breathed a sigh of relief as she realized this demon's anger was not directed at her. Still, she saw no reason to prolong the interview. "Perhaps you need to confront him face-to-face."

"I will," he said, softly, his human façade once more in place, "and then we can continue our business. Until then." He nodded once, and disappeared.

"Not likely." She pulled her goggles from her hair, tossed them onto the lab table and stripped out of her lab coat—grateful to see no bloodstain on the back of it. She wouldn't get any more work done today. She locked up the lab, wishing for once in her life she could be like her father and drown her fears in alcohol.

# CHAPTER 39

**B**ACK IN HER ROOM, ASSUMPTA REMEMBERED THE tuxedo-clad demon had mentioned that he had knowledge that could help her against the demon who held her mark. What did he know? Right now, she'd settle for knowing about a really good weapon. If she killed off the demon who owned her mark, wouldn't that be as good as losing the mark itself?

After all, if he were dead, there would be no one to claim her soul.

But demons lied. It was part and parcel of their makeup. Who was to say that the tuxedo demon really had any *useful* knowledge?

Still, she felt left with a nagging possibility that he might know something. Even a small bit of knowledge could help her, right?

She retrieved her pendulum and the paper with the alphabet drawn on it, then made herself comfortable on the bed cross-legged. She dangled the pendulum and asked, "Has Jak returned to me in spirit form?"

The pendulum swayed back and forth, then, as it gained momentum, began a tight counterclockwise circle, signaling *no*. Assumpta stopped it and asked, "Am I working with a ghost in Enoch Pratt Library?"

As soon as the pendulum responded affirmatively, Assumpta stopped it, satisfied that she had reached spirits who would answer correctly for her. Lord help her if she ever stumbled across a malicious group.

She ran her fingers down the cord and asked, "Does my recent demonic visitor actually have knowledge about my mark's owner?"

There was a slight pause before the teardrop began to sway. It picked up momentum, then started a clockwise circle.

"Yes," Assumpta said quietly. "What does he know that I don't?" She suspended the pendulum over the lettered paper.

The pendulum hiccupped and swung wildly on its path before settling in a back-and-forth motion over a series of letters.

"G," Assumpta said.

The pendulum continued on its path. Not G.

"H," she guessed.

H was correct. The pendulum deviated.

"A," she said before it found its next path. But the arc didn't fall far enough to reach the letters on the bottom side of the paper. "E," she guessed.

The pendulum jumped again, signifying E was correct, and swung past the forty-five degree mark of the semicircle of letters.

"P, Q, R, S," she said, pausing between each letter.

It signaled for S. Then moved, but only slightly from the S angle.

"H. E. S," Assumpta said, trying to formulate words. "Hesp, hest...H, E, S...R?"

The pendulum moved again.

"He's!" Assumpta said. "He's R..."

The pendulum moved along what she called the "A" path. When a word needed a vowel and it swung nearly left to right over the protractor-shaped paper, she knew it signaled *A*.

"He's ra—"

The path turned sharply upward along the arc.

"G," she said. But there was no deviation by the pendulum.

"H?" The path was similar to the first.

"J," she said, thinking it a low possibility. The pendulum continued to swing.

"K." Assumpta knew that wasn't it. K was too unusual. It was also too far away from the pendulum's swing. Another vowel? She finally settled on I. I," she said aloud.

The teardrop moved again.

"He's rai...raid, raiding...raining...raisin." The pendulum jumped.

She frowned. "That doesn't make sense, *he's raisin.*"

The pendulum started on a clockwise path. "He's raisin," she repeated, still confused. "He's raisin."

The pendulum continued to turn.

Assumpta's eyes opened wide. "He's raising!" she said. "He's raising...what's he raising?"

The pendulum leaped and started a back-and-forth motion over the A path.

"A."

It moved past the forty-five degree mark again. "S," she said, then, "T, P...R."

It moved again. A and R were correct.

"O," she guessed. It continued to swing. "N."

It remained on the same trajectory. Both O and N were wrong.

Her arm was getting tired, holding the pendulum over the paper. How she hated anything other than yes-or-no questions. "M," she guessed, when the pendulum failed to deviate after her *N*.

The pendulum jumped. M was correct.

"He's raising an arm..." *Oh, dear lord*, she thought. "Y." She said it, knowing it was true before the pendulum answered. But she had to be certain.

"He's raising an army."

The pendulum hiccupped, then started moving in a clockwise circle.

*Dear God*, she thought. The earth would soon be overrun by demons.

"Thank you," she said, sending out the brief prayer to the souls who'd relinquished the information.

Then, her heart started beating with terror as the magnitude of the knowledge bore down on her. She almost wished she hadn't pried.

Ignorance would have gone a long way to soothe her troubled mind. She knew there was an army coming, but she didn't know a tinker's damn about how to stop it.

She raised the pendulum again. "How do I stop the army?"

The pendulum hung slack. Assumpta's hand started shaking, and she felt fear like a leaden weight on her chest. "Who can I ask? Jak? Michael?" She waited. "Father Tony?"

The pendulum simply hung there, unmoving. Apparently, it didn't know anything about stopping an army, either.

# CHAPTER 40

**W**AS SHE COMING?
Despite the nearly overwhelming fatigue he'd been feeling lately, Greg lay awake in his bed, wondering if Vesta would come again tonight. She'd been right: he loved her visits. He couldn't get enough of her. She was more woman than anyone he'd ever met.

She materialized by the nightstand, close enough for him to feel the temperature in the room drop a few degrees, but far enough away that he could see her womanly outline silhouetted in the window.

He hoped she thought he was sleeping; he didn't want to ruin the little masquerade she played. You'd think a woman like her, a *ghost* like her, would realize the difference between a sleeping man and one playing possum. Maybe there was enough humanity left in her that she couldn't.

Vesta slid between the sheets. She ran a soft hand up his thigh, grabbed his hardening cock, and with a few deft twists of her hand, made him rock-solid in her palm. She pushed the sheets off and straddled him, taking him inside her molten core in one dexterous plunge.

She was hot and slick and oh, so, tight. Greg couldn't suppress a groan.

Vesta leaned forward onto her hands and knees, keeping a steady, grinding rhythm on his cock and teased his mouth with little bites, then soothed them with kisses. "You didn't think you'd fool me with your pretense of sleep. Did you?"

Greg lifted his knees and slid his hands to her waist, feeling out her cadence, and matched it with the lifting of his hips. The slapping of their bodies together heightened his pleasure.

He pulled her tightly to him, slowing their pace. If he wasn't careful, he was going to come, and she didn't like it when he came too fast. Truth be told, he didn't either. He liked it to last and last and *last*. If he satisfied her the first time, then maybe she wouldn't be so insistent that they fuck all night long. After the third or fourth time, he found that it was more work than pleasure. Still, he loved fucking her.

And when she left him in the wee hours of the morning, he was more sated than he'd ever been in his life, and exhausted enough to sleep through to next week. *Ghosts must just have more stamina than people*, he thought.

Where was she drawing all that energy from?

"I've lost you," she growled in his ear. The hot, pebbled tips of her breasts rubbed against his chest, and he slid his hands up to capture the swaying globes. He squeezed hard, just as she liked, then thumbed the nipples before sucking one into his mouth and biting down. She loved that, too, arching into his mouth as if she wanted the pain to go on forever. He could only imagine she liked it rough because she lacked a physical body and it took that much more for her to feel the sensation. Although, she felt real enough to him.

"Harder," she groaned, the words coming deep from her throat. She ground her hips down on his, tightening her muscles and squeezing his cock.

"Ohmygod," he said, releasing her breasts and letting his hands fall back on the bed.

"Don't stop!" She slapped his thigh and leaned forward on him, shoving her breasts in his mouth.

He licked the sensitized tips, then sucked them into his mouth, scraping his teeth over her engorged nipples.

She rewarded him by squeezing her thighs together tightly, her inner muscles clenching his cock while she bucked wildly.

He came in one explosive gush, all the muscles in his body clenching. His hips rose off the bed, forcing himself higher into her quim.

"Yes!" he heard her scream, felt her tighten even more around his cock, to an almost painful degree.

His breath came out in raspy gasps, fast and shallow as if he'd been running a marathon. He opened his eyes to see a smile of satisfaction on her lips. He smiled back. Not once in their short relationship had he managed to fulfill her as much as that smile seemed to indicate.

"That was good," she purred, leaning down to kiss him.

*Thank God*, he thought, *maybe I can get some rest.*

Greg lifted a hand to her jaw, opened his mouth wide to let her in, and suckled her tongue. He slid his other hand to her shoulder, rubbing, caressing, letting his heart slow down, catching his breath.

"Let's do it again," she said, and he froze, suppressing a groan.

"Tomorrow," he whispered.

"Now." Vesta unseated herself and grabbed him once more in her fist. She pumped her hand up and down, slick with the juice of both of them, until he grew hard again, then seated herself on top.

"Move," she commanded, and he nodded, because he could not tell her *no*.

# CHAPTER 41

As USUAL, THE SMELL OF FRIED CRABCAKES COMING from Bertha's Restaurant reached Assumpta almost as soon as she got off the bus in historic Fells Point. Her mouth watered, anticipating the taste of Maryland blue crab and McCormick's famous Old Bay Seasoning.

Too bad she wouldn't be staying for dinner. Actually, she wouldn't be staying long at all if Caroline wasn't around.

Whenever they'd had two dimes to rub together, they'd shoot down to Bertha's for a crab cake or an order of mussels, which the restaurant was famous for. But Caroline always liked to bring her dates here, too. With luck, Assumpta would find Caroline and The Big Guy having an early dinner. She'd confront them, show Caroline what was going on, and, hopefully leave with Caroline in tow. She felt certain she could break The Big Guy's hold on her friend if she could just make Caroline *see* what was going on. Here, Caroline couldn't hang up the phone. And she'd stand her ground and just shout at Caroline if she had to, but she hoped it wouldn't come to that.

A jazz trio played on the small stage in the back, and the bar was already crowded two-deep at the rail, all the chairs taken. She and Caroline had a favorite booth around the back. She squeezed her way around the crowd at the door and turned to the left to try there first.

*Bingo*, she thought, spying them in the corner alcove. The two small tables that flanked it were empty. *Caroline looks so happy*, she thought. *I hate to ruin this.*

Deep in conversation, The Big Guy and Caroline didn't look up from the table until she'd pulled out a chair and sat down next to Caroline.

"What are you doing here?" Caroline asked.

"I'll only stay a minute," Assumpta said.

"You need to leave. *Now*," Caroline hissed, "before I call a waiter and have them bounce you out of here."

"Please, just give me a minute."

"Let her talk," The Big Guy said. "A few words can't hurt." He smiled, looking every bit the confident suitor. "We'll clear this little misunderstanding up, and then your friend—"

"Former friend," Caroline said with a shake of her head, the beads on the ends of her many tiny braids clacking together like wind chimes.

"And then *Assumpta*," he amended, "can go home satisfied and we can finish our date in peace."

Tight lips pressed together in a firm line, Caroline nodded to Assumpta. "Okay. But then I want you gone."

Assumpta knew she should have gotten right to the point, but she couldn't help herself. She looked at Caroline, "Do you think when this is over, that you and I can salvage our relationship?"

"No way, no how," she said. "Any woman thinks she can come between me and my man is no friend of mine."

"But what if I could prove to you that Adrian is *not* a man?"

Caroline burst out laughing. "Oh, I can assure you that Adrian is more man than any man I've ever known." She winked at The Big Guy.

If Assumpta weren't so worried about her friend, she might have been sick at the lovey-dovey gesture.

"Darlin'," Adrian said to Assumpta, "this is going to be harder than you thought. But I'm willing to let you have a go. Try me."

"Bear with me," Assumpta said to Caroline, and reached into her purse for her bottle of holy water and blessed salt. The painful touch of either should force The Big Guy to drop his human persona—even for just a moment—and prove to Caroline what he was. She hoped he'd be strong enough to control it, however, and not burst into his full-fledged demon self in such a crowded location. She didn't think she could handle him. "This will only take a second." Assumpta sat the bottles on the table beside each other, like a matched set of salt and pepper shakers, the painted gold cross on the holy water bottle gleaming.

Caroline turned on her with an incredulous look. "Are you kidding me?"

"It's the best means I have to show his hand," Assumpta said.

"Do it, darlin'," Adrian said. "Give me all you've got."

Assumpta paused. His eagerness made her uneasy. "The holy water and salt will burn through your skin. Aren't you the slightest bit afraid?"

The waiter arrived, forestalling his answer, and placed a bowl of garlic mussels in front of Caroline and a crab cake sandwich with fries in front of The Big Guy.

"Will you be joining the party?" the waiter asked Assumpta.

"She was just leaving," Caroline uttered from behind clenched teeth.

"Okaaaay, then," he said, clearly uncomfortable. "Is there anything else I can get for the two of you?"

"Not right now, sport," The Big Guy said, "Why don't you run along?"

The waiter got glassy-eyed, then nodded and left.

"Let me make this easy on you," The Big Guy said to Assumpta, reaching for her salt. He opened the jar and sprinkled it liberally on his French fries. Then he picked up a handful and shoved them into his mouth, chewing appreciatively.

"You shouldn't be able to do that," she said. "You shouldn't be able to touch the jar!"

He smiled, uncapped the bottle of holy water, and took a huge gulp, washing down the hot, steaming fries.

Her eyes widened. How *could this be happening? How else was she to show Caroline?*

"Let me touch you with my medals." Assumpta raised her palms to show The Big Guy the medals dangling there.

He lost his smile, and tipped his chair back away from her.

"What?" Caroline asked.

Assumpta saw the look on her face and thought quickly. "Never mind. You've got me," she said, holding out her right hand for The Big Guy to shake. "I give up. Friends?"

Caroline said harshly, "No, not friends. Not after all of this." She looked at The Big Guy. "Don't you dare shake her hand." Caroline scraped her chair back and stood. "I'm going to the ladies' room," she announced, then said to Assumpta, "When I get back, I want you gone."

When Caroline was out of earshot, The Big Guy said, "See, dearie, I told you it was going to be a hard thing to prove."

"How are you doing it?" she asked. "You should have been writhing in pain the moment the salt touched your mouth."

"That little donation of salt and water you made during your visit to my domain? We were able to create an antidote—a vaccine, if you will. You've given me the means to immunity on your plane."

"Holy Mother of God." She stood so fast she knocked the chair over. Defenseless against his power, she fled the bar, with the sound of The Big Guy roaring with laughter behind her.

# CHAPTER 42

"JAK, I HAVE TO GET TO CLASS, BUT I DON'T WANT TO leave Greg," Assumpta said. "There's something wrong with him."

Greg lay on his back on the sofa, a hand thrown over his eyes. He looked pale.

"I'm afraid he might have to go to the hospital," she added.

"I'm fine, just tired." Greg sighed heavily. "Really tired."

"You've been really tired for days," Assumpta said. "And you've been getting more sleep than usual. There's something wrong. You look green—maybe you're anemic."

"It's not anemia, it's fatigue."

Jak said, "Well, he seems well enough to argue."

"His aura doesn't look good," Assumpta said. "It's all brown and murky around the edges, but a weird kind of happy glow in the middle. It's like he's got a disease that he's happy about."

Jak frowned and approached the sofa. He pulled a chair closer and sat. "Have you had any weird dreams lately, Greg?"

"What does that—"

Jak held up his hand to halt Assumpta's words. "Greg?"

Greg smiled and moved his arm, revealing his overly bloodshot eyes. Assumpta gasped. Greg said, "I *have* been having some really terrific dreams lately."

"Amorous dreams?" Jak asked.

Assumpta wondered what Jak was getting at. Didn't everyone have a sexy dream every now and then?

"H*ot* would be more like it," Greg said. "I think I'm falling in love." He lifted his head off the couch pillow and looked at Jak. "Is it possible to fall in love with a dream girl? When I'm sleeping, it's like I never want to wake up. She's...*awesome*."

"Are you sure it's a dream?" Jak asked.

Greg lowered his head back to the pillow, looking suddenly confused. "Well, of course it's a dream," he said. "This kind of stuff doesn't happen in real life. People can't really have sex with ghosts."

Assumpta wanted to argue that he was wrong about that, but decided not to. Greg was more important than scoring a few conversational points.

Jak prompted, "Who's your dream girl?"

But Assumpta already knew the answer. "Vesta."

Jak looked up at her, startled. "Where is Vesta? I haven't seen her in a while."

"I see her every night," Greg interjected.

"I've seen more of her than I needed to," Assumpta said, "but come to think of it, she's been rather absent lately." She gave Jak a hopeful look. "Maybe she's gone? This is the worst of it?"

Jak shook his head. "I don't think so. She's not gone—she's hiding. She knew we'd catch on to her sooner or later. She's not done with Greg, and she doesn't want to be found until she is."

"Done with him?"

"She won't leave until she sucks out his remaining energy. Bleeds him dry, so to speak." Jak looked her right in the eye. "She's not going to leave him until he's dead. Then she'll move on to the next unsuspecting soul."

"That sounds like some kind of vampire," Assumpta said.

"Not vampire. Succubus."

"A sex demon? I thought Vesta was a ghost." Well, that explained the little tête-à-tête she'd walked in on a few days ago. Vesta hadn't looked the least bit repentant at having been caught in the act. "She's going to kill him?"

"Succubi aren't always demons. But, death is usually the outcome—it's what they do. They feed off the energy of others in order to maintain their own existence." He looked downcast. "This is my fault. I brought Vesta here, and Greg's been spending a lot of time with her since they have a common interest. I'm sorry I didn't put it together until now."

"Hello?" Greg said. "I'm right here. I can hear everything you're saying. Vesta isn't going to kill me. She loves me. She is *not* a vampire. She doesn't suck my blood. But she's excellent at sucking my—"

"Let's get him to the hospital," Assumpta said.

"The hospital can't do anything about this," said Jak, taking a closer look at Greg. "We need intervention. Father Tony."

"Father Tony?"

"He'll have to perform an exorcism."

"He's not going to like that," Assumpta said. "He may not want to do it."

"Then I truly believe Greg will die."

Assumpta looked to Greg. He appeared to have fallen asleep, a look of ecstasy on his face.

"I'll give Father Tony a call."

# CHAPTER 43

ASSUMPTA PHONED FATHER TONY'S DIRECT LINE.
"Hello?"

"It's Assumpta," she said. "I need your help."

"Well, *hello* to you, too." Assumpta could hear the laughter in his voice.

"Sorry." She ran a hand through her hair, pushing it out of her face. "It's just that the help I need is urgent."

"I'm just teasing," said Father Tony. "You know I'm always here for you."

She caught herself nodding, knowing that was true. "Right." She paused. How could she say this without it coming out all wrong? She couldn't think of a good way to do it. *Here goes*, she thought. "Father, can you swing by the apartment? I think I need you need to perform an exorcism."

She heard the squeak of his desk chair through the phone as he sat up. She imagined him pulling his glasses off and rubbing the bridge of his nose. He asked tiredly, "Assumpta, what are you mixed up in this time?"

"It's not me. It's Greg." This was true for the current circumstances, but she knew she sinned by omission. There was so much more she wasn't telling him. "He's been possessed by a ghost who has him under her power."

"Well, at least it's not more demons."

Assumpta wasn't certain if that was supposed to be a joke or not. "I'm serious, Father."

"I'm sorry. I know you wouldn't come to me if you didn't have cause. The problem is, I can't help you. I know how to perform an exorcism, but I'm not allowed to. I need a dispensation from the bishop before I can perform one. And before the bishop will agree, he'll require that Greg be examined by a psychologist or other doctor to see if he is merely unwell." Father Tony paused. "It could be that your friend is simply suffering from a mental or physical illness."

*Of course, blame the victim*, she thought.

"I don't think we have that long, Father."

"What do you mean?"

She captured a curl of her hair and wound it around her finger while she spoke. "Jak's looked at him. He's certain Greg's been possessed by a succubus. He believes she will kill Greg in the next day or so, maybe even within a few hours, now that we've discovered what she's up to."

There was silence on the other end of the phone.

"Father?"

"I'm here, child. I'm just trying to think of the best course of action."

"I don't want Greg to die."

"Then take him to a hospital."

"Jak assures me that a hospital cannot help him now. Even if they stabilize Greg or whatever, the succubus will just go to him there and finish what she's started. How can you turn your back on a sheep you brought into the fold?"

Father Tony had baptized Greg a few months ago. Assumpta wasn't above a little emotional blackmail if it did the trick.

Father Tony sighed. "Assumpta, I could be excommunicated. The church takes this very seriously."

"But he will die."

"You don't know that."

"Father, if you won't perform the exorcism, then I will."

"You can't!" She heard the squeak again, and a bump, as though Father Tony had stood up too fast and slammed the chair against the wall. "Someone who is not trained stands the risk of being possessed himself. Or freeing the demon to perform other mischief."

*Oh.* Well, she was already guilty of that sin. She would have to confess it—once she was able to confess again—*if* she would ever be able to confess again. She took a deep breath, knowing she had to twist his arm or have to do this herself. "I know you can get into serious trouble if you do this, but I can't let my good friend die while I stand by and do nothing. If you don't come, I'll perform the exorcism myself."

# CHAPTER 44

GREG LAY ON THE SOFA, AS IF SLEEPING. WHEN Father Tony came near, his head rolled left to right on the pillow. He slid one leg to the floor and pumped his hips in a slow, shallow rhythm.

"He looks terrible," Father Tony whispered to Assumpta. "How long has he been this way? It doesn't look like he's eaten in over a week."

"He hasn't," Assumpta said, "Though I've seen him drink a beer. I think the ghost knows he'll die if he doesn't eat, but will die sooner if he doesn't drink. She's keeping him alive—at least for the time being—so she can suck all the energy she can out of him before she moves on."

"Ghost?" Father Tony said. "We're not dealing with demons this time?"

Assumpta shook her head.

"I'm not certain how an exorcism would work in this case, Assumpta. Are you certain it's a spirit?"

Jak turned to her with raised eyebrows. She considered it, then shook her head. "It may not be a ghost, but it's certainly not a demon. If it were, my mark would be going nuts. Vesta was living here quite a while before she took over Greg. I would have known."

"Living here?"

"Haunting this apartment." Assumpta shrugged. "We're talking semantics. Can we just agree that a supernatural being has taken over Greg, and he needs your help to get loose of her?"

Father Tony met her eyes with a determined stare, but she refused to say more. "Okay. We'll do it your way for now," he said. He put a hand to Greg's shoulder and shook him, "Greg, son, can you hear me?"

Greg's eyelids fluttered, then opened and turned, unfocused, to Father Tony. Then they closed again, and his head lay still on the pillow, although it was thrown back a little farther than before. His hips continued rocking.

Father Tony shook Greg hard, "Greg? Greg, can you hear me?"

This time, Greg didn't acknowledge the priest.

Father Tony put his hand on Greg's forehead. "He feels warm—feverish, Assumpta. Have you tried getting him to a doctor? You should call an ambulance."

"It's not a doctor he needs, Father."

Father Tony sighed, and opened his bag. "I'm not supposed to perform an exorcism without permission from the church. There are channels to go through, rigorous testing to be done. I could get into serious trouble."

"I wouldn't ask if I didn't think it were absolutely necessary."

"You didn't ask," he said, pulling out a prayer book, a bottle of holy water, and a smaller container that Assumpta knew contained chrism—blessed oil.

*Ouch*, she thought, pushing a hand through her already wilted hair. "You're right. I'm sorry—it's just that I was so worried about Greg."

Father Tony put a hand to her shoulder and gave it a quick squeeze. "Already forgiven. I know you care about Greg—so do I. And I'm here to help—but we're going to do this my way." He donned a white surplice—a waist-length tunic with wide sleeves—then reached for his purple stole. He kissed it and placed it around his neck, the long ends reaching almost to the floor.

"Your way?"

"No exorcism," he said.

"But—"

"Trust me, Assumpta. I cannot perform an exorcism without permission from the Bishop. Even if I am willing to risk excommunication, without the bishop's consent the rite will lack the backing of the Church and I will not have power or authority to cast out demons. The exorcism *will* fail."

"But—"

"But I can perform a Deliverance." Father Tony approached Greg and stood at the end of the sofa near his head. "It is prayer designed to weaken and cut the bonds of demonic influence. It's similar to exorcism, but I won't be putting anyone's mortal soul in danger, and I've the full backing of the church."

Assumpta was disappointed. She wanted the best for Greg, and the best, she thought, would be an exorcism. She believed that, even if Father Tony didn't. Still, she had a priest in the room, and he was willing to help the best way he knew. She couldn't fault that. "Let's get started, Father."

He nodded. "You'll recognize some of the prayers, Assumpta. Respond in the appropriate places. The more people we have praying for Greg, the better."

"Okay."

He crossed himself and began, "Lord have Mercy."

"Lord have Mercy," Assumpta echoed.

"Christ have Mercy," he said.

"Christ have Mercy." Jak joined in this time.

"Lord have Mercy," Father Tony said one final time.

"Lord have Mercy."

"God, the Father in Heaven. Have mercy on us. God, the Son, Redeemer of the world. Have mercy on us. God, the Holy Spirit. Have mercy on us. Holy Trinity, one God. Have mercy on us." He paused, glancing briefly at Assumpta and Jak. "Holy Mary, pray for us..."

"Pray for us," Assumpta and Jak intoned.

The mark on Assumpta's back started to flutter and itch. *Why?* she thought. *It's not like I'm praying for absolution.*

"Holy Mother of God, Holy Virgin of virgins, Saint Michael, Saint Gabriel..."

After each invocation of all the angels and saints, the patriarchs and prophets, apostles and evangelists, bishops and confessors, naming many of them by name, Assumpta and Jak responded, "Pray for us."

The flutter and itch of Assumpta's mark didn't get any worse. *Well, the praying bothers it, but doesn't cause it to burst into flames,* she thought. *Thank goodness!* She could continue helping without fear of that.

Father Tony said the Lord's Prayer and then Psalm 53, "God, by Your name save me, and by Your might defend my cause. For haughty men have risen up against me, and fierce men seek my life; they set not God before their eyes. Turn back the evil upon my foes; in your faithfulness destroy them. Freely will I offer You sacrifice; I will praise Your name, Lord, for its goodness..."

Just as he finished the psalm, the room grew dim.

Father Tony looked up from his prayer-book, wide-eyed.

Assumpta looked around, straining to see Vesta. The temperature started to climb. Father Tony wiped the sheen from his forehead with the sleeve of his surplice, then retrieved a small, silver crucifix from his bag and placed it on Greg's forehead.

Greg started to writhe, his mouth opening and closing, but his eyes squeezed tightly shut.

Father Tony made the sign of the cross over Greg's head and chest and said, "I command you in the name of the Lord, unclean spirit, whoever you are, along with all your minions now attacking this servant of God, by the mysteries of the incarnation, passion, resurrection, and ascension of our Lord Jesus Christ, by the descent of the Holy Spirit, by the coming of our Lord for judgment, that you tell me by some sign your name."

Greg continued to writhe.

Father Tony laid his hands on Greg's shoulders. "They shall lay their hands upon the sick and all will be well with them. May Jesus, Son of Mary, Lord and Savior of the world, through the merits and intercession of His holy apostles Peter and Paul and all His saints, show you favor and mercy. Tell me your name."

*"Leave us alone."*

The words were spoken in a high pitch, like the beating of a thousand flies' wings—a discordant whine of a multitude of voices speaking the same words together.

Father Tony looked around. "Who said that?" He turned to Assumpta. She shrugged. He said, "I command you, in the name of Christ Jesus, to tell me who you are."

*"Remove the cross; we cannot take it."* Greg mouthed the words, but the voice was not his own. Then, "Ahhhh!" he cried in his own voice, his body convulsing as if someone had jumped into his lap.

Vesta appeared, nude, coalescing into the room from nothingness to appearing nearly solid. She straddled Greg's hips and ground her own against his. Her breasts swayed with each rocking motion of her hips.

"Leave us alone, Father," she said, reaching for the cross on Greg's forehead and slapping it to the floor. "I've got a job to do here, and as soon as it's done, we'll all go away."

Father Tony acted as though the batting of the crucifix across the room was old hat. He calmly retrieved it.

*"Us?"* Jak asked. He narrowed his eyes at the couple on the couch. "How many are there of you?"

Vesta looked up at Jak with an ecstatic expression. "As many as it took to enable my purpose."

Father Tony dipped the cross in holy water and once more laid it on Greg's forehead. He held it there with his hand. Vesta flinched, bending away from the cross, but remaining seated in Greg's lap. "Take it off, take it off, take it off!" she shouted, her eyes dark, her face contorted.

Father Tony spoke quickly: "I adjure you, ancient serpents, by the judge of the living and the dead, by your Creator, by Him who has the power to consign you to Hell, to depart forthwith in fear from this servant of God, Gregory Claude, who seeks refuge in the fold of the Church. I adjure you again, for it is the power of Christ that compels you, who brought you low by His cross. Tremble before Him. Make no resistance nor delay in departing from this man. It is God Himself who commands you; the majestic Christ who commands you. God the Father commands you; God the Son commands you; God the Holy Spirit commands you."

The high-pitched voices screamed, the buzzing growing louder, Greg's and Vesta's mouths opening synchronously, the thousands of voices echoing discordantly, *"Noooo!"*

"Depart, transgressor. Depart, seducer, full of lies and cunning, foe of virtue, persecutor of the innocent. Give place, abominable creature, give way, you monster, give way to Christ, in whom you found none of your works. He has cast you forth into the outer darkness, where everlasting ruin awaits you. To what purpose do you brazenly refuse? For you are guilty before almighty God, whose laws you have transgressed. You are guilty before His Son, our Lord Jesus Christ, whom you presumed to tempt, whom you dared to nail to the cross. You are guilty before the whole human race, to whom you proffered by your enticements the poisoned cup of death."

Vesta continued to writhe in Greg's lap, bending away from the cross, seemingly ignoring the words. Greg's eyes were tightly shut; his face strained, almost contorted in pain.

Father Tony stepped closer to Greg. "I command you in the name of Christ, you heinous monster, to depart from this man, to depart from the Church of God. It is futile to resist His will. The longer you delay, the heavier your punishment shall be; for He who rules the living and the dead is coming to judge the world by fire."

The voices came again, the whine growing louder, *"We cannot take it...we are telling Him to have mercy on us! Have mercy on us, Jesus!"*

Father Tony gasped and took a step back. "Where did you learn that?" he shouted. "Where?"

*"We are telling* Him, *have mercy! Come to us with mercy!"*

"I command you, in the name of Christ, to tell me where you learned that!" The temperature in the room suddenly rose again. The sheen on Father Tony's forehead evaporated in an instant, replaced by droplets running down his face. "Where did you learn to beg for mercy?"

*"We learned from this man,"* the voices said from Greg's mouth. *"He always says, 'Have mercy on me,' so we are saying it. Maybe He will have mercy on us, too. He should have mercy on us! But He has mercy on this man...not on us... Fucker!"*

"That is because you have to suffer!" Father Tony said.

Vesta laughed, her voice singular again, and seductive. She leered at Father Tony, then winked. "I don't have to suffer. I'm here for the pleasure, for the payoff," she said, and reached down between her thighs to unzip the fly on Greg's jeans. She opened his pants and reached for the erection straining against the denim. She pushed his briefs aside, then gripped his throbbing cock in her fist and pumped up and down.

"There will be no fornication here tonight," the priest said. He stepped forward and pushed at Vesta's shoulders, but his hands went right through her.

She tilted her head back and laughed. "Of course there will be."

*"Yes...yes! Fornication."* The multiple voices seemed to come from everywhere in the room this time. *"Do the job and we can all be gone. The pain grows inside us. He shows us no mercy... Ahhhh! Get it done."*

Wide-eyed, Father Tony glanced around the room. He crossed himself, then made the sign of the cross in the air in front of Vesta. She leaned away, but only for the seconds it took him to make the gesture.

Then, Vesta raised her hips and moved forward, sitting down on Greg's erection with a look of sublime passion on her face. Her eyes closed, her head fell back and she raised and lowered herself in languid motion. Greg's hands found her hips, seeming to urge her on.

"Yesssss..." Greg whispered in his own voice. He seemed to find more strength to meet her demands, and the coitus grew more aggressive.

Father Tony reached for the chrism, dipped his thumb into the oil, then made the sign of the cross on Greg's forehead. Quietly, he began praying in Latin, several times making the sign of the cross over Greg and in front of Vesta, who recoiled, but didn't stray from her purpose

"*It pierces, it burns,*" cried the voices, thundering louder and louder. "*You hurt us. Where is His mercy? It's fire—ahhhh!*"

Father Tony flinched, still keeping one hand on the crucifix on Greg's forehead. Assumpta put her hands to her ears. The glass in one of Greg's artifact cases shattered, and Jak bent away from it, covering his eyes.

"You lost the grace of His mercy eons ago," said Father Tony.

The voices screamed again, "*It burns, it burns our pride. He puts the nail in us, the nail they hammered into Him…*" It screamed again.

"You are defeated."

"*We are totally defeated with His power. He destroys us. He says, 'You are cursed. Depart. You will leave my son…'*"

"Not. Until. I'm. Done," said Vesta, her choppy voice echoing the motion of her hips. She leaned forward, hands on Greg's shoulders, and moved up and down more rapidly.

Father Tony averted his eyes.

"*It's over! It's over! We know the power that You put in your children. We have experienced it. You have proved to us that we have no power against Your children.*"

"Because He is the Lord of Lords and the King of Kings," said Father Tony. "That is His name."

"*Yessss! We cannot stand up to Him or His children. He is too much for us. Ahhhh!*" The screams echoed around the apartment, kicking up a wind and blowing loose things about. The pictures on the walls rattled, and two books tumbled off the bookshelf. "*We are done. We have not the power to do anything more.*"

"Even if you are set free?" Father Tony asked.

"*It makes no difference, considering the place we go to.*"

"Where are you going?"

*"To Gehenna."*

Assumpta turned to Jak, "Gehenna?" she whispered.

"Hell," he said.

*"Throw us down to earth so that we may go under—we are cursed, defeated, worthy of all humiliation."*

"Not yet. Not yet. Not yet." Vesta rocked against Greg.

"Because He is strong, you will descend, straight to Gehenna," Father Tony said.

*"We will descend, we will."* They screamed again, then the voices trailed off into wails and then sobs.

"You are going to where you belong. Why are you crying?"

*"We are humiliated. All our pride is gone."*

"We thank God for that," said Father Tony. "We thank God."

Screams again.

More wind.

*"We have been humiliated..."*

Screams.

*"Get it over with... Ahhhh!"*

"It is over?" Father Tony asked.

*"Yessss!"*

"Yes!" Vesta shouted, throwing her head back and grinding her hips on Greg's. He convulsed, his entire body tensing as he thrust his hips with such force it would have toppled a human woman.

"You will depart!" Father Tony said.

*"We will depart of him: burnt, strangled, slaughtered, and dead. Humiliated and despised...and all that you want us to say."*

"Say it," Father Tony said, "Promise: 'I do covenant—I the sorcerer, and all my armies, and enemies and helpers—before the Lord of Glory, and the Virgin Mother of the Light, and the Holy Angels, and the martyrs, and the saints and the pope—'"

"Yes," they wept. *"We will depart from him, and take all our sorcery with us, and all sickness, and not leave anything behind. We so covenant."*

"In the name of the Lord of Glory, I command all of you to depart."

"*Ahhhh!*"

"In the name of the Lord of Glory, I command all of you to depart."

More screams.

"In the name of the Lord, depart."

Screams.

"In the name of the Lord, depart."

Louder screams.

"In the name of the Lord, *depart.*"

Vesta disappeared.

A dozen black shadows, very much like the ones Assumpta had seen in the store room at Jo's Turning Wheel—wailing still—peeled themselves away from Greg and rushed to the front door. They collapsed and slid under the crack, leaving the apartment silent.

Father Tony made the sign of the cross over Greg's head and prayed for several moments in Latin. After concluding his final prayer, he walked to the loveseat across from Greg, pulled a handkerchief from his pocket and wiped his brow with a shaking hand. He sat, collapsing into the back of the sofa, clearly wrung out from the experience.

"Will Greg be all right?" Assumpta asked quietly.

"Yes, but he'll probably be spiritually drained for a while. Perhaps depressed. He needs rest."

Jak disappeared into the kitchen, and came back shortly with a bottle of cold water for each of them. Assumpta accepted hers gratefully, sitting down next to Father Tony. Her own hands were steady as she twisted off the cap, but then, she'd had more exposure to demons than the priest. Lord help her if she ever became complacent about it. She said, "You can't tell me that wasn't an exorcism."

Father Tony took a long drink from the bottle, then laid it against his forehead. "No. I certainly can't."

# CHAPTER 45

AFTER FATHER TONY LEFT, ASSUMPTA WENT TO HER room and started unpacking boxes.

Jak knocked on the doorframe, and entered. "What are you doing?"

"What does it look like?" She knew that sounded peevish, but she couldn't help it. She was mad at herself.

This time, it had been her who had put Greg in danger. Jak might have brought Vesta with him when he came, but surely it was Assumpta who'd called the shades that had corrupted Vesta when she'd worked magic with Jo at the Turning Wheel. It hadn't been her intention, but her desire to protect herself must have rallied The Big Guy. He'd sent the shade-like minions to do his work for him.

But had they really corrupted Vesta or had the ghost been evil all along? She might never know. Either way, what she and Jo did, had brought the shades.

She didn't blame Jo. She blamed herself for not seeing that when she sought to protect herself, the demons increased their attack, and that meant going after the people she loved.

*Loved?* Did she love Greg? Of course, she did. Family love. Brotherly love.

Jak sat down on the edge of the bed and looked around at the open boxes. "It looks like you're not moving out."

"I can't. Not now." She pulled a small stack of books from a box and put them back on the shelf below the window.

"Because of Greg?"

"You saw him. He needs someone to take care of him."

"And that person has to be you? He's rich. He can buy the best of anyone to take care of him." Jak punched a pillow. "Besides, the crisis is over. Father Tony got rid of the demons."

"They couldn't have been demons. They didn't make my mark itch like hell. They must have been some kind of evil ghosts. Shades, maybe? They had no form."

"Father Tony got rid of whatever they are. Now Greg just needs to rest."

"I can stay a little longer while he recuperates." She turned a box of clothing over onto the bed and started sorting.

Jak picked up a blue sock and dug for a mate. "Are you staying because you feel guilty? Because, if you do, that's not a good reason." He stacked the socks and reached for another pair.

"I'm staying because he needs me. He helped me when I was down and out. I can stay a while longer and help him."

"What about us?"

"What *us*?" Assumpta stopped sorting the clothing and gave Jak her full attention. "There isn't any *us*."

"Of course there's an *us*. We've been intimate. Staying here with Greg out of pity, or a misguided sense of duty, is just wrong. You should be with me. Move in with me."

Assumpta sat down on the bed, her head nearly spinning. She guessed she shouldn't be offended by the Neanderthal attitude regarding intimacy; he was a child of the 50s, after all: the *350s*. She couldn't educate him on today's social mores, women's suffrage, or bra burning overnight. Although...wouldn't he have been keeping up on these things? He'd told her he had—maybe he just couldn't follow *everything* while trapped in the urn. She tried a different tack: "You bring up an interesting point," she said. "Where have you been staying?"

He shrugged. "God provides."

"In the park? On a bench? You expect me to live like that?"

"We can get an apartment. Maybe something a little smaller than what Greg has here." He looked around the room. "We could find a place close, if that's what you want, so you can be near Greg. We should all remain friends." He gave her a piercing look. "Sometimes friends can be closer than family."

She laughed. "If you believe that, then you know why I've got to stay. Besides, we couldn't afford to live anywhere near here. I certainly don't have any money. I'll be lucky to find something in the dangerous part of town on what I can afford."

"How much do you need?" Jak asked, reaching for his leather jacket. He slipped his hand into the inside pocket and pulled out a wad of cash. He peeled five hundred-dollar bills off the top. The top bill remaining on the stack was a hundred, too. "Do you need more than this?"

"Where did you get all this money?"

He smiled. "God provides."

"Did you steal it?"

"You think so little of me that you think I'd steal?" he asked, the smile falling from his face. "I won it on the lottery."

"God told you to play the lottery?"

"Of course not. You gave me the idea when you told your dad that's how you got the money to pay him back."

She gave him an outraged look. "I never told my father I won the lottery."

"Well, you said enough to make him believe that you did."

She silently counted to ten. "That doesn't explain how God hooked you up with the lottery."

"Well, I knew I needed some cash, so I prayed to God and asked what numbers to play."

"And he told you?"

"Not in so many words."

Assumpta's head was beginning to hurt. "Explain, please."

"I prayed to God and asked him for help with money. A job was out of the question, because I can't work full time and take care of you. So, it had to be something legal—and moral."

"Some people would disagree with your idea of morality."

"I'm trying to explain." He looked annoyed.

"Go on."

"You mentioned the lottery, and it seemed like a good idea. I explained what I wanted from God, and told him if he agreed—"

"Thy will be done?"

His face tightened in anger. "Precisely. I asked him to give me some help in choosing the numbers. So, after my prayer, I began looking for numbers all around me."

"How does that work?"

He thought for a minute. "We went to lunch that day and the bill came to $16.18. The cashier asked if you had eighteen cents change. I chose the number eighteen. If she hadn't mentioned exact change, I would have played sixteen and eighteen. Greg played an album on the stereo and it kept replaying track nine. I played a nine. Those are the kinds of signs I looked for from God."

She looked at him disbelievingly. "I think you just got lucky."

"I have won money each time I have listed the numbers God has given me."

"Just how much money have you won?"

"It was only twenty-five thousand dollars the last time."

"*Twenty-five thousand dollars*? The *last* time?"

"That's not a lot of money when you consider things," Jak said. "Rent, clothing, food, bus rides…"

Assumpta stopped listening. "If you have all this money, why are you sleeping on park benches?"

"Because I haven't needed anything else until now."

"I don't know, Jak," she said, feeling suddenly exhausted. "I don't think I can leave, not until Greg's feeling better, and maybe not until my mark is gone." She looked him in the eye. "I need peace. I don't think I should make any more changes until my life is a little more on an even keel."

# CHAPTER 46

"I FINALLY FIGURED OUT WHAT YOUR GHOST BUDDIES have been up to, Jakkie," Brona said, after materializing in the Poe room.

"They are here to fight when the time comes," Jak said. "They're just waiting to be told when and where."

"Fight?" Assumpta asked. "As in, fight demons?"

"Of course."

"Then why haven't I gotten any help?" Assumpta hissed.

"You have!" Jak said. "Whenever Michael has not been around to protect you."

"Saint Michael hasn't always been with me?"

Jak flushed. "I assumed you realized that. It's not like he tells you when he comes and goes."

Assumpta could feel her face getting hot, as if her temperature were skyrocketing—or her blood pressure. It was one thing to tangle with demons when you're fairly certain you've got a major deity's protector at your back, even if you can't see him—and another to act all big and bad when the only thing protecting you is a small group of two-thousand-year-old ghosts. "You think your ghosts could protect me?"

"They're warriors!"

"They're ghosts! How can they possibly fight the power of a demon?"

"Oh, I can help with that one, dear," Brona said. "There'd be a hell of a fight. Chances are, with Jak's five friends against a demon, the only outcome would be the destruction of the demon. They have solid mass against the demons, and they're trained in hand-to-hand combat."

"See?" Jak said. "You've got nothing to worry about."

Assumpta crossed her arms on her chest. "You still haven't explained why they haven't fought off the demons who have attacked me."

"Because they weren't the ones protecting you when it happened," Jak said.

"Saint Michael *let* me be attacked?"

"More like was commanded to," Brona said. Jak gave Brona a hard look. She shrugged, the look on her face unapologetic.

"So God gives me a holy protector—who isn't allowed to defend me. This is the same god who also refused to get rid of my demon mark." Assumpta stared at the floor, stunned. "So what's the point of it all, anyway?"

"He wouldn't let you die," Jak said.

"Small consolation. Officially, I'm on my own against these things—unless I'm going to die—then someone will lend me a hand."

Brona moved toward her. "If I've got this right," she said gently, her Irish brogue a little thicker, "it's because—"

"It doesn't matter," Assumpta said, straightening up with some resolve. "I see where I stand." She thought, it probably would not have mattered if the ghosts had been the ones protecting her when she was attacked, either. They were more than likely commanded not to help as well. Here she was on a mission from God—still not funny in real life—without much in the way of perks to get things done. Even Moses had a staff. But wait—she had her holy medals and her friends. And friends were worth far more than power. It would do.

"Assumpta—"

"Drop it, Jak."

"But—"

"Drop it. Tell me how the ghosts are going to help us out in the final battle."

"They're warriors, hale and fit, with tremendous knowledge and experience they gained on the battlefields of Rome."

"But that didn't teach them to fight wily demons."

"Trust me on this, Assumpta."

"I'm going to have to." She turned back to Brona. "So, what have the ghosts been doing when they're not guarding me?"

Brona smiled. "Looking for another entrance into Hell—and they've found one."

"We have an entrance," Assumpta said.

"You know about the entrance The Big Guy *wants* you to know about," Brona said. "You can be certain it's guarded day and night."

"And it's restricted," Jak said. "You can only get to it when the mall is open." He shoved his hands into his pockets. "The ghosts are right. We need another way in if we're going to surprise The Big Guy."

"Who said anything about surprise?" Assumpta asked.

"It's common in warfare. If The Big Guy is growing an army, we need every advantage we can get."

"Follow me to the map room." Brona said. "I had your ghostly legion point out the location on the map to me last night."

She turned from the Poe room and headed down a hallway.

Jak and Assumpta followed her into the nearby room.

Assumpta looked around, hoping they wouldn't bump into anyone. Would she and Jak look like they were talking to themselves? Or would Brona be visible to just anyone?

The map room was empty of people.

Brona led them to a wide, chest-high cabinet, and pulled open a drawer about halfway down. The inch-deep drawer held several flat maps Assumpta guessed to be about four feet wide by three feet tall. Brona pulled out a map, laid it on the top of the flat cabinet, and closed the drawer. They huddled around to inspect the drawing.

"I wonder why they didn't tell me they were doing this," Jak said.

Brona suggested, "Perhaps they were looking for a way to help. I got the impression that while you offered them a chance to do so in Rome, you haven't really given them much to do."

"That's—"

"Take it up with your friends, Jak," Brona said, holding up a hand. "Let me show you what I've learned." She leaned over the map. "This was drawn in 1850 when Baltimore started laying cast iron pipe as part of its water and sewer system." She ran a finger down one side of the map, and pointed to a thick line. "This is the sewer pipe running beneath Eastern Avenue. This conduit is one of the largest in the city, over fifty-four inches in diameter. You could drive a small car through this pipe-way. Well, it turns out that over here—" Brona slid her hand all the way across the map.

The lights dimmed, and the bulb in the lamp hanging over the map cabinet burst in a shower of sparks. The mark between Assumpta's shoulder blades itched; she looked around the room.

"We can't have this." The demon appeared next to the cabinet.

"Pournelle," Assumpta said, recognizing the dapper demon whose business card burned up in her hand the first time. "You're not supposed to visit me anymore."

"Not so."

"But The Big Guy promised—"

"I'm not one his lackeys, and yet, I'm here to make your situation worse." He ran a finger down Eastern Avenue on the map, just as Brona had done. A thin line of fire trailed behind his finger.

*He certainly enjoys his fire tricks*, Assumpta thought.

They backed away from the cabinet as the entire map went up in flames, the heat of it scorching Assumpta's face.

The map was a lost cause, but maybe she could do something else. Assumpta reached for the holy salt in her purse and threw a handful at Pournelle. It hit him full-square in the chest, though some bounced off onto the map, extinguishing part of the flame.

Several grains struck him in the face. His dark skin sizzled and popped where it touched, and Assumpta could smell the strong scent of sulfur.

"Dammit!" he yelled, brushing at his chest. The layers of his three-piece suit blocked most of the salt, allowing Pournelle to brush it away. But some burned through to the skin of his chest. Deep red blood, nearly black, welled from each spot where the salt touched his flesh. His large hands took the brunt of it, the lighter skin peeling away from the palms and smearing his suit with the dark demon blood.

"I didn't think that would actually work," Assumpta said, reaching for the holy water bottle.

"Thankfully, not all of us are privileged to enjoy Adrian's inoculations against blessed items."

"Thankfully?"

Pournelle gave her a look that told her he'd said too much.

Assumpta wondered, what had gone wrong with the inoculations? They seemed to work just fine for The Big Guy when he'd consumed the blessed salt and holy water at Bertha's. She said, "What do you want from me?"

He gave her a surprised look. "Oh, I want nothing from you now. We could have made a deal weeks ago, but you refused me. Things have gotten much worse since then." His look turned mocking. "Didn't I tell you they would?"

He made a circular motion with his right arm and snapped his hand toward the map cabinet. The entire structure burst into flames. "I wouldn't want to be you right now," he said, then winked out.

The ballast in the overhead fluorescent light exploded, plunging the room into darkness, except for the flames continuing to lick their way across the map cabinet.

# CHAPTER 47

**F**IRE ALARMS ERUPTED THROUGHOUT THE LIBRARY. "We'd better get out of here," Assumpta said, grabbing Jak's hand. She felt certain he had no idea the ramifications of the siren. Brona could take care of herself. She pulled Jak into the dimly lit corridor, grateful for the emergency lighting, and headed toward the stairs.

"What's going on?" Jak shouted above the din. "Where are we going?"

"Outside!"

Patrons mobbed the door. Jak and Assumpta joined the crowd and made their way through the exit.

A hand clasped her wrist as she left the building. "Trying to sneak out with the crowd, eh?" A Baltimore City Police officer pulled her to the side. "Where do you think you're going?"

"I don't understand," Assumpta said.

"Remove your hands," Jak told the policeman.

The officer pulled his billy club from his waist belt and laid it against Jak's chest. "Back off, unless you want to be arrested, too."

"Arrested?" Assumpta said. She felt the cool touch of metal on both her wrists and heard the click of the handcuffs tightening. They weighed more than she'd imagined.

Jak moved closer. Assumpta shook him off. "Go away, Jak. You don't need to get mixed up in this."

"What is it she's supposed to have done?" Jak asked.

"An eyewitness said she's the one who set the fire," the officer told him.

"I didn't!" Assumpta said, as the policeman pulled her by the elbow to the marked sedan.

"I can vouch for her," Jak said. "She was with me the entire time. I swear to you she didn't start the fire."

"Maybe you helped her," the cop said. "Do I need to take you down to the precinct, too?"

"Officer!" Brona walked toward the police car with an authoritative gait, her library ID swinging from the bead-chain around her neck. She was not quite solid. Assumpta could just make out the texture of the building's brickwork visible through the smooth skin on her face. Her lack of mass was less evident if you gazed at her clothing. "Officer! Did you catch the miscreant?"

"Yes, ma'am," he said, tugging on Assumpta. "Right here. I was just about to take her down to the station."

"This isn't the arsonist!" Brona looked outraged. "I saw him myself! A black man, about six feet tall, dressed impeccably. I would have never guessed."

"But that's the eyewi—" The officer reddened.

He released Assumpta.

"I see that he's taken you in, as well," Brona said. "I told you I wouldn't have believed it if I hadn't seen him do it. Ms. O'Connor and I were walking into the map room when we saw him light the match. He's introduced himself as Pournelle and often masquerades as an employee."

"Pournelle *what*?" The officer took out a notebook and started writing.

"I have no idea," Brona said. "He's never mentioned another name."

Assumpta gave her a sideways look, then said to the policeman. "Are we free to go now?"

"Yes ma'am," the officer said. "Sorry for the trouble." He nodded politely and stepped back.

She rubbed her wrists. "No harm done."

The officer turned and walked off.

Assumpta looked to Brona. "I guess we'll have to come back later to discuss the project we were working on."

"No need," Brona said, taking Assumpta's elbow and pulling her out of earshot of the police officer and a few lingering bystanders. Jak followed. "I had an opportunity to review the maps last night. You'll find what you're looking for in the 2700 block of Eastern Avenue. It borders Patterson Park."

"And that's it?"

"It's the information you've been waiting for, yes?" Brona said. "Find the entrance, challenge The Big Guy. Win or lose, your fate is in your own hands now."

"But he knows we know about the second entrance," Jak said. "We won't be able to surprise him."

Brona nodded. "There is that. But at least you'll be able to choose your time instead of being forced to adhere to the mall's timetable—or The Big Guy's."

Assumpta looked at Jak. "Are we ready to do this?"

He gazed steadily into her eyes and said boldly, "I have always been ready. The question is, are you?"

He might as well have asked her, *Are you ready to die?* She was pretty certain the answer to that was *no*. And yet, she couldn't avoid this fight. The demon mark had to go, and the only way to get rid of it that she knew of, was to kill The Big Guy. As long as that was the case, Brona was correct: she could at least pick the time of the fight.

Assumpta took a deep breath. "Am I ready? Almost."

# CHAPTER 48

**W**HEN DO YOU WANT TO DO THIS?" JAK ASKED AS they walked to the bus stop. It was cold, and their breath came out in white puffs as they talked.

"Tomorrow night," Assumpta said.

"One more day shouldn't make a difference, but why wait so long?" Jak fiddled with the buckle on his leather jacket.

"There are a few things I want to take care of first," Assumpta said. "I can't get everything done by this evening."

He gave her a questioning look.

She sighed and held up her hand, ticking the options off on her fingers. "I want to go to church and pray. Take communion. Write a note to my mom."

"You're afraid you're going to die." He acted surprised.

"Not afraid, exactly," Assumpta said. "Just being pragmatic about the situation. My death is a distinct possibility. Even if I don't die, per se, there's the fear that I'll be trapped in Hell for eternity. For my mom, that's probably the same thing as me dying. She'd never see me again. You can bet that once they trap me in Hell, they'll never give me an opportunity to escape." She moved her hand to touch the wad of holy medals through her shirt.

Jack nodded. There was a long pause, then he said, "I'm not afraid of The Big Guy. I'm afraid of what comes next."

Assumpta gave him a puzzled look. "I don't understand."

Jack said, "He's like a Roman emperor: everyone under his authority does his bidding, but they're all gunning for his job behind his back. If we slay The Big Guy, we'll have to face whomever comes behind him in order to get out of Hell. The Big Guy's defeat doesn't guarantee our escape."

Assumpta drew in a large breath, frowning. "Maybe we can't ever win, because eventually we'll have to face something we can't overcome. Maybe this is just a suicide mission."

Jak seemed to consider what she said. "I feel that, too. Yet, a part of me doesn't think this is a no-win situation. Saint Michael has been your protector, and he answers only to God—who, I don't believe, would put you through all this just to snap away your life at the end."

"God doesn't think like we mortals do," Assumpta said. "Perhaps He would put me through all this, only to let me die, because Heaven is a reward, right? Perhaps God will take my life and feel like He's doing me some huge favor. Heaven trumps Hell, no?"

He gave her a long look. "Not necessarily."

"You've got to be kidding me."

"You already know that there are thousands of souls—thousands in Baltimore alone—that would rather remain in limbo than make the journey to Heaven. For them, Earth—despite the drawbacks of being a roaming spirit—is the better place to be. Heaven requires obedience to God. And for some, that's a deal-breaker."

"And those that think that way choose Hell?" She brushed a few strands of hair out of her eyes.

"Of course they do. For certain there are demons out there wreaking havoc on the human world, or killing us, or trying to win souls—because that's all what they wish to do. They thrive on chaos and inflicting pain. And there are others that wind up in Hell because they were tricked, or did something stupid, or were just in the wrong place at the wrong time. But there are others, like Satan, who would rather rule in Hell, than be just another worshiper in Heaven."

"God demands worship? Even in Heaven?"

"To be honest, I don't know the answer to that. I can only guess. I'm almost certain he'd demand respect and obedience. You can't blame Him. You'd want your houseguests to be respectful, wouldn't you?"

She blinked at him, as if seeing him for the first time. "You'd rather be in limbo, wouldn't you?"

"I'm not sure," he said, looking away. "I was a soldier in the Roman army until my death. I followed my leader, did as I was told, and it was a good life. But it always left me yearning for more—despite the respect I felt for him—respect he *earned*. Does God deserve respect?"

"I guess that depends on what you base your respect on."

"See? You have your doubts, too."

"Of course I do," Assumpta said. "I voice them daily. Father Tony despairs of me. He wants me to simply *trust in the Lord*." She brushed the hair out of her eyes. "But it's hard to trust in what you can't see, you know?"

He nodded. "I do know. But you've seen it," he said. "You've met Saint Michael. You know he's a messenger sent by the Lord to protect you. *I'm* here to protect you, also sent by the Lord. How much more proof does a person need?"

His words felt like a poleax to her midsection. Had she missed something? "How can you tell me to believe and to trust when you can't believe and trust in Him yourself?"

Jak gave her a wry look. "It's not the believing and the trusting I have a problem with. My being here right now wouldn't have been possible without His help. And yet, I don't want to be beholden to a god that demands so much. I yearn for Mars and Ceres and Venus—the Gods I grew up with. Samael—Saint Michael—assures me they are one and the same, and so I was quick to agree to serve Him in order to help you. And now—" He looked to his feet. "When this battle is over, I will be judged, and found either unworthy, or worthy, to enter

Heaven. But I'm not certain I desire to be welcomed there. That leaves me a place in limbo, or worse, Hell."

"Even if it means never seeming me again?" Assumpta walked under the Plexiglas bus shelter and sat down on the bench to wait.

"Oh, you're sure you're going to get to Heaven?" he asked, a smile on his face.

She smiled back, glad that he was trying to lighten the mood, but she couldn't let him. "Not if you won't be there. I'll see you in limbo."

# CHAPTER 49

**W**AKE UP."

The voice was soft, feminine, *Southern*. A presence at the door of the bedroom. The voice barely registered to Assumpta, who lay exhausted, deep in slumber.

"Wake up," the voice insisted, louder, drawing nearer to the bed on cloud feet.

Assumpta rolled onto her belly and burrowed deeper under the covers.

"Wake up!"

Something cold and damp touched Assumpta on the back of the neck and she shrieked, ripped from her deep sleep and rising to her knees. She looked around the darkened room.

"Greg?" She knew it wasn't Greg. *But who else could it be in his apartment?*

Vesta moved into Assumpta's field of vision, smiling, her eyes hard, a look of triumph on her face.

She'd changed her clothing into something diaphanous rather than the prim, buttoned-up style of the 1800s. Assumpta wondered, *How does a ghost go changing clothes? Does she mug another ghost?*

"What are you doing here?" Assumpta brushed the hair out of her eyes. The digital clock read four a.m. *God, it's way too early for this*, she thought.

"I'm just here for a tiny visit. I wanted to show you something, then I'll be on my way." She did a little twirl in front of Assumpta, the ends of her dress flaring out as she spun, her feet so transparent as to be nonexistent.

*Creepy.*

The gown looked straight out of a trailer-trash wedding catalog, and showed off Vesta's lush breasts and—

"Oh, my God!" Assumpta shouted.

Vesta winked the moment Assumpta realized and then popped out of sight, but not before Assumpta registered the baby bump—and how far along in pregnancy Vesta looked. It was either one huge baby, or she'd be dropping that load any day now.

*Good Lord!* Assumpta thought, sinking to the bed as a wave of foreboding crashed over her. She'd assumed that it would take The Big Guy at least fifteen years to raise an army of demon spawn. Apparently it took only weeks if he enlisted ghosts to do the job. But what kind of creature would it be?

# CHAPTER 50

THE POE ROOM AT ENOCH PRATT LIBRARY WAS LIKE a war summit—a ghostly one. The light above the scarred table flickered and waned, and occasionally buzzed, before brightening again and starting the cycle over. Though eight people crowded the small room, only two were alive.

Jak and Assumpta, as well as Brona and one of the Roman soldiers accompanying Jak, huddled around a hand-drawn map. The other soldiers stood guard around the room. They were visible to Assumpta now, though not as solid-looking as Brona. Still, it was nice to be able to see them, instead of deciphering their locations through their auras.

"I pulled this together from what I remembered of the blueprints Pournelle managed to set afire," Brona said, "and a street map drawn roughly in the same time period. I filled in some of the gaps with the help of your friends, Jak." She nodded at the ghost who'd joined them at the table. Assumpta smiled her thanks to him. Though not as corporeal as Brona, he—like his brothers-in-arms—was remarkably more substantial than he'd been when he'd arrived. She'd bet money Brona had been teaching them a trick or two.

Assumpta picked up a pencil. "Here's what we'll do," she said, turning to Jak and touching the drawing with the pencil's eraser. "You gather the troops—the ghosts and Saint Michael—and meet me at the corner of the 2700 block of Eastern Avenue, *here.*" She tapped the paper. "Do you think you can find it?"

Jak nodded. "Of course." He sat back in his chair, grinning as he crossed his arms over his chest. "What's the rest of your plan?"

Assumpta paused. She hadn't given it much thought—other than to gather everyone at the location of the Eastern Avenue entrance of Hell, bringing the largest weapons they had, and then storm the castle, so to speak.

Brona chuckled, her eyes dancing. "He's got you there, dearie."

"What did *you* have in mind?" Assumpta said.

"I'm glad you asked," Jak said, smiling. "I do have a bit of experience at this, you know." He uncrossed his arms and tugged the pencil out of Assumpta's hand.

She gave him a look she hoped would imply she was joking. "But your experience is *so* old. Roman tactics are obsolete these days."

He cocked an eyebrow. "I'll have you know," he said, "your U.S. Army still studies legion battles—proud of that, I watched them practice, countless times, from within in the urn. Further, I and my troops were victorious in every conflict we fought. We—"

"I was teasing." She grasped his elbow, moving closer to him as they looked at the map. "Tell me your plan."

He looked down at the map, then indicated a manhole cover near the Pulaski Monument in Patterson Park. "We should let the ghosts enter here first," Jak said, "and flush out any demons who might be waiting to ambush us. The ghosts might be worthless against humans—" He turned to the ghostly soldier at his side. "No offense." The soldier shrugged as if to say, "*It is what it is.*" Jak continued, "But in Hell—or against demons anywhere— the ghosts are as solid as you or I. That makes them as formidable as any human soldier you could call upon, and probably more so."

Assumpta nodded. "Then what?"

"After the ghosts clear the path in for us, we enter the sewer and travel single file until we reach the perimeter of Hell." Jak dragged the pencil down the felt-tip line that Brona had sketched. "I'll lead with two soldiers behind me, then you—for your protection, so no arguing—then the remainder of the ghosts. Saint Michael will be last, protecting our rear."

"But how do we find The Big Guy?"

Jak shrugged. "I'm hoping we'll cause enough ruckus that he comes to us. We'll be ready. But hope, as we said in the glory days of Rome, is not a strategy."

"I think military people still say that," Assumpta said. "Maybe Saint Michael will have some ideas. Can you confer with him?" Jak nodded, and she looked at her watch. "If I hurry, I can make confession and early Mass tonight—"

"You can't confess," Jak said. "Your mark—"

"I can confess. I just can't be absolved. I know it seems like a moot point, but I want to face death with a clear conscience. I'll ask Father Tony to pray for my soul if I don't return. It's not the same, but it will have to do." Assumpta pulled out her wad of holy medals and held them tightly in her hand. "I'll also ask him to bless my Saint Benedict medallion."

"I thought it was already blessed," Brona said.

Assumpta shrugged. "I've learned not to trust the advertisement." She thought back to when she had been cursed by stone gargoyles— which were really demonic minions in disguise. She couldn't touch anything holy without literally being burned. She discovered the hard way that the salt Holy Rosary had brought pre-blessed for the May Fair had turned out to be plain ordinary table salt. "I'm not taking any chances. I should have asked Father Paschel to bless it when he helped me choose, but my mind was elsewhere." She turned to Jak. "We'll meet at 8:30 p.m. It should be dark enough by then that we won't draw too much attention."

"Don't we need to talk about your weapons?" Jak said.

"I can only hope that Saint Michael can bring one for me as well. If he can't, I'll be stuck using only my wits."

"Hope is not—"

"I know."

# CHAPTER 51

**A**SSUMPTA AND JO GOT OFF THE BUS AT THE General Pulaski stop, a few hundred yards from where they believed the entrance to Hell lay, disguised as a manhole cover. Assumpta carried a paper shopping bag containing candles and various spell components. Jo had her large cauldron and a basket of additional supplies.

In her pocket, Assumpta carried the gold coin The Big Guy had given her a few weeks ago. If she couldn't escape through this exit later, she might have to use his infamous turnstile.

As they neared the manhole cover Brona had identified from city maps, five ghosts dressed in full Roman armor materialized beside them.

Assumpta stopped. "Where are Jak and Saint Michael?" They shrugged their ignorance, but took up a guarding stance around her.

She felt panic rising. "Isn't Jak coming? What about Saint Michael?" She turned in a circle addressing them all. This time, there were nods, though their faces remained as stoic as ever.

She let out a deep breath, not realizing she'd been holding it, and marched toward the manhole cover. As long as she knew Jak and Saint Michael were coming, they could get started. "Spread out, boys, we need some room." She and Jo knelt by the metal plate, and the soldiers took up a five-pointed stance around them.

"I didn't know your Caspers would be so hunky," Jo said, rummaging in her basket.

"Caspers?"

"Friendly ghosts," said Jo.

Assumpta smiled. Trust Jo to break the tension. "And they're all cut from Jak's mold." She set her paper shopping bag on the pavement and extracted four pillar candles.

Jo chuckled. She pulled a small cloth-wrapped bundle from her basket and set it on the ground by her knee. She reached for another bundle, and laid it next to the first, and then another, lining up all the bundles in a neat row.

Jo was a last minute addition to their plan, and Assumpta was glad she was here to help. Once Brona had suggested warding this access point to Hell, Jo's inclusion made total sense. Assumpta knew she'd made a mess of keeping The Big Guy confined to the circle when she had called him to this plane and she needed Jo's help now to do things right—since her own skills were basically worthless with the demons now immune to blessed water, salt and oil. Jo knew other methods to fortify this passage.

The plan was to make the access point one-way only for demons, so that if she and Jak—and Saint Michael and the soldiers—were not successful in defeating The Big Guy, then at least no demons could exit here. There were other entrances and exits to Hell, of course. But it couldn't hurt to ward this one so that the demons wouldn't pour out after them like cockroaches from the kitchen drain when they made their escape.

Jo took chalk from one cloth-wrapped bundle and drew a circle around the manhole cover, leaving enough space for her and Assumpta to work comfortably inside. From the second bundle, she took a wide-mouthed jar of rosemary oil which she uncapped and set by her knee. The third bundle held rosemary springs. Jo rubbed them vigorously between her hands to release the pungent scent of rosemary into the air, then dipped the branches into the oil and drew a rosemary circle just outside the chalk one.

"For power," she said to Assumpta, handing her the branches.

Assumpta rubbed the rosemary briskly between her own palms, enjoying the heady fragrance while she coated her hands with oil.

When she was done, she put her pre-dressed pillar candles at the four compass points of the circle, adding a little of the rosemary oil to each, and lit them: north, south, east, and west.

She was reaching for other herbs when the manhole cover was pushed up and away from the entrance, and The Big Guy clambered up.

Jo gasped. She stepped out of the circle without breaking its lines, and pulled a dried sprig of rosemary from her basket. The ghosts stepped forward, crowding into the circle, each with his hand on his weapon.

*How effortless*, Assumpta thought, with a sinking feeling. *Will the rest of the battle be so easy for him? No,* she decided. *The Big Guy wasn't going to win, no matter what. She wouldn't let him.*

He stood just in front of the sewer, in the small space provided by the circle, arms crossed over his chest, while five additional demons, all dressed like gang members, followed him up from the depths. *They fit right in in Baltimore*, she thought, *a city that had once held the title of Murder Capital of the World.*

Each was armed, except for The Big Guy. *So arrogant.* He didn't think he was going to get dirty here.

"Are you going to let the others fight your battle?" Assumpta asked.

"I have no battle to fight."

"Of course you do," she said, not feeling at all confident. *Where is Jak? Saint Michael?* She hoped she could bluff her way through until they arrived.

Out of the corner of her eye she saw Jo light the dried rosemary sprig and toss it into her cauldron. The contents inside ignited, and Jo began chanting.

Assumpta pointed at The Big Guy's companions. "Are you so certain of their skill that you believe your own is unnecessary? Or, would you simply have them fight me on your behalf since you can't be bothered?"

"I merely offer them for my defense." He looked her up and down. "If I am not mistaken, it's *you* who has come to fight and kill."

"I have only come to retrieve my soul."

He laughed. "Is that what this is about? You still have it."

"But you've got a lien on it, and I aim to get that back."

"And you think you can do that by killing me?"

"I'd hoped it wouldn't come to that." She knew what it took to fight a powerful demon, and didn't relish the thought of having to do it again. It was messy and frightening—because there was always the chance that you wouldn't make it out of the duel alive. Also, since she was marked, she'd be eternally damned if she died trying. Her reluctance to enter Hell grew stronger. Could they manage this fight top-side? If all else failed, she prayed the coin was the way out.

Jak materialized behind her, so close, she could feel the heat coming off of his body.

"About time you showed up," she said quietly. "What kept you?"

"Gathering the reinforcements."

She squinted and looked for auras, seeing one at her left. A brilliant flame appeared suddenly, washing out the aura and nearly blinding her. And then she saw a knight, flaming sword in his hands, gleaming armor, and a thin band of gold floating inches over his head. *Saint Michael.*

Assumpta felt an urge to kneel, her knees weakening. She had to get over this feeling! Michael lifted his sword, staring with deadly intent at the demons, but he said to her, "Kneel not, the fight is at hand."

She nodded, feeling the strength return to her legs. To The Big Guy, she said, "Just give me my soul back and we'll call it quits. There's no need to fight this battle now or any other day."

He shook his head, smiling. "I can't yield the mark."

In a blink, they were all in Hell.

# CHAPTER 52

ASSUMPTA LOOKED OUT OF THE STONE BARS OF the cell they had been transferred to onto a clear, rocky horizon. It was a flat expanse of rock, broken only by rivers of lava that flowed along with occasional pops and spurts, bursting forth with steaming clods of molten stone. The liquid stone rocketed high in the air—sometimes disappearing into the dark expanse of the ceiling—then careened back down, hitting the river banks and sizzling and cooling into rough formations. Here and there, a tall hillock of rock dotted the stony field.

The air was almost too hot to breathe. It was hotter than a July day on the cracked asphalt of a Baltimore city neighborhood. Her clothes stuck to her. The skin on her face felt hot and dry, as if she were standing next to a roaring fire.

Assumpta could smell heated rock, the reek of unclean bodies, and something so foul she didn't want to put a name to it. The acrid smell of sulfur burned her nose. She felt like vomiting.

And in Hell, The Big Guy had legions of demons to back him up, she thought. There was no way they were getting out of here. What had she been thinking to challenge him?

The Big Guy had had the power to pull her down into Hell. He must have had it all along. Why had he toyed with her? And where was he now?

She looked around. The cell couldn't have been more than fifteen feet square. Any smaller, and they would have been on top of each other: her, Jak, Saint Michael, and the soldiers.

"Where's Jo?" she asked, looking around frantically for her friend.

"She was outside the warded circle when we were brought here," Jak said. "She's safe above."

It made sense. Assumpta smiled grimly. It was one less thing she had to worry about.

By unspoken agreement, the ghosts spread out to protect the three sides of the barred cage. The fourth side was a flat wall of rock, presumably from which the rest of the stone cell had been created.

She walked to the limit of the cage, studying the rock bars. Their cage appeared to be hewn from a single piece of stone—even the barred ceiling was part of it. Could the bars be broken? She toured the perimeter, testing the strength of the stone, kicking at the joints at the base, looking for a way out. The stone was too hot to touch for any length of time.

"We've got to get out of here," she said, almost to herself.

The ghosts looked to be waiting for orders, oblivious to the heat. Jak, too, tried the bars of the cell. He looked weary, like she imagined herself to look—wilted. But beneath the outer fatigue, he seemed anxious for something to happen. He paced the length of the cell, watchful.

Saint Michael appeared far worse in body and spirit than any of them. He sat on a stone large enough to be a bench, looking dejected. His flaming sword no longer alight, it lay dull and pitted as it rested against his thigh.

"There's no way out," Saint Michael answered.

The mark on her back was going crazy: itching and *crawling*. She could almost feel it dancing on her skin. *Oh, Lord*, she thought, *I'm in Hell, literally, surrounded by demons. Of course the mark is going nuts.*

And just as she thought that, the demons were upon them, screeching and howling outside the cage, poking their taloned hands through the bars, reaching for all of them, beating on the bars as if to break them down. Assumpta stepped back, closer to Saint Michael.

The ghosts moved forward, hacking and slashing, slicing off limbs that entered the cage, and thrusting their weapons through the bars to do as much damage as possible outside of it. Thick demon blood dripped to the stone floor and sizzled. Excited cries turned to howls of pain each time a soldier hit his mark.

Jak drew the switchblade Saint Michael had given him and pushed the button. In an instant, the switchblade flipped out, grew, and became a fiery spear. Just as quickly, the flames extinguished, the gleaming metal grew lusterless and looked as corroded as Saint Michael's sword. What is it about Hell that weakened their weapons?

Still, Jak hacked at the demons side-by-side with the ghosts, screaming something unintelligible under the din of the demon onslaught.

"Oh, Michael," Assumpta said, looking around at all of them. "I had no idea The Big Guy could pull us—any of us—into Hell." The tears that welled in her eyes dried as quickly as they came.

Michael fell to one knee, breathing harshly, his halo dipping over one eye. "The Big Guy should not have had the power to do so," he said, his gleaming armor turning dull. Head bowed, Saint Michael looked as though he would tumble to the ground.

Then he looked up; his gaze burned into hers. "You have something of his. You've got something he was able to focus on to bring you—you, and everything surrounding you—into his domain."

She swallowed, her mouth gritty and dry. She knew exactly what he hinted at.

"The coin." She reached into her pocket, pulling it out. The soft gold had warmed in her pocket and warped slightly.

"Destroy it," Michael whispered, the anger in his eyes turning to a determined gleam. "Destroy the coin and you will destroy him. We will be freed."

"Will destroying the coin remove the mark on my back?"

Michael turned his bleary eyes to look upon her. Did she imagine the contempt she saw there? Yet, even in his ravaged state, he was beautiful. She still felt a small compulsion to kneel. What would it be like in the presence of God, Himself?

"I don't know," Saint Michael admitted, hanging his head again.

"If I destroy the coin before the mark is gone, I run the risk of still being damned," she said. "I need to get rid of the mark first."

"If you die before you destroy the demon, you are damned anyway. God will remove your mark as he did for Jak."

"Can you guarantee that?"

Michael closed his eyes as if to concentrate on something. A minute later, he shook his head. "I cannot communicate with Him from here. I cannot tell you that He would do that for you. I cannot ask Him to remove it as I did for Jak." He took a deep breath of the sulfurous air, coughed, and said, "But He is all powerful and all good. He will remove the mark if you destroy but one of these evil creatures." Michael's gaze bored into hers, willing her to do as he suggested.

"Life is sacred," Assumpta argued, remembering her catechism classes. "If God had wanted them dead, He would have done it himself instead of just casting them out of Heaven." Assumpta gripped the gold coin tightly, feeling the soft edges curl into the palm of her hand. It softened more, exposed to the heat. "But letting them live may have been the wrong choice. He seems to have very little power here."

"Don't speak of Him so. He is all powerful!" Michael yelled above the din of the fight. "Destroy the foul demon and you will be rewarded."

"He is not all powerful," Assumpta hissed. "Look at you. Your power wanes in Hell. You can't even communicate with Him."

Saint Michael spoke quickly, fervently. "Destroy the coin and we will be freed. Free me, so I might continue His work. Free yourself, so you might see His goodness." He looked at her with pleading eyes. "Why do you not trust in the Lord?"

Assumpta wondered if Michael could hear himself speak. He sounded surprisingly like a zealot on a tear. Was Michael blinded by belief? He couldn't be, could he, having worked so long in service of the Lord? On the other hand, Michael had suddenly lost all that protection, and been cast into Hell—arguably the worst place for one of His creatures to find himself. Saint Michael had realized that in at least one place, God is not all powerful. And if God had no power in Hell, there might be other places where He had none.

*Michael was speaking from fear.*

And it wasn't that she didn't trust the Lord. She wasn't talking to the Lord here, she was talking to Saint Michael, who, for as much as he served the Lord, did not speak for Him. If the Lord wanted her to trust Him, Assumpta decided, she needed some face time. The Lord spoke directly to Moses. Why not her?

Why didn't God just help her?

Still clamping the coin tightly in her fist, she walked to the stone bars. "I still have your coin, Big Guy, and I'll trade it to you if you remove the mark on my back."

"No!" screamed Michael, lurching to his feet. "Do not give him the opportunity to take it from you. Destroy it, and you destroy him. We will be freed."

Assumpta pressed closer to the bars, dangerously close to the reach of some of the demons, away from Saint Michael.

Jak jerked back his spear and came between them, putting his arms around Assumpta, protecting her from the demons and Saint Michael's wrath. Saint Michael sank down again.

Silence fell as the horde of demons outside the cage disappeared.

The Big Guy was at the bars in an instant. He snapped his fingers and six demons appeared in their true form, purple-and-red mottled skin gleaming in the heat of the lava, horns protruding from their foreheads, clawed hands and feet ready to fight. They flanked him, three on each side, his own private guard.

"Give me the coin." The Big Guy held out a hand.

"Remove the mark."

"Coin first."

"Mark first," she said. "I have no reason to trust you. I'm not giving in."

"I have no reason to trust you," he said. "We're still at an impasse."

"You have every reason to trust me," Assumpta countered. "I'm church-going, backed by God's minions—"

"I am not a minion!" Michael was furious, rising slowly from his crouch to stand tall behind her.

"You have no idea the monstrous things done in His name," The Big Guy said. "So many of those people wind up down here." He spat on the ground, and the sputum sizzled away in a puff of steam. "Bringing up *His* name is not the way to win me over."

"Fair enough." She lifted the coin to her mouth, then bit into the soft metal. The Big Guy's suit tore across his chest, and the skin on the right side of his face peeled down in strips, revealing the purple-and-red mottled demon flesh beneath.

"No!" he yelled, slamming against the bars, reaching for her with clawed hands.

*Saint Michael was right*, Assumpta thought. *Why did I doubt him?*

Assumpta jumped back, pulling the coin out of her mouth long enough to demand, "Remove the mark."

In an instant, the bars of the jail were gone. The Big Guy snapped his fingers, and the demons were upon them.

# CHAPTER 53

*S*IX, ASSUMPTA THOUGHT. *ONLY SIX DEMONS TO worry about.*

The Roman soldiers, along with Jak and Saint Michael, formed a semicircle around her, facing away from her, their backs protected by what had been the back wall of their cell.

They leveled the points of their spears toward their attackers. Five were on them immediately, biting and clawing. The foul stench of them was even worse up close.

A scabrous demon with a single horn upon its forehead and veined, leathery wings took to the air. It flew low over the lava river, beating its wings in slow, even motions. A bubble burst in the lava stream, shooting steam and molten rock into the air. The flying demon rode the steam cloud up. It gained height, circled back, lifting clawed, bird-like feet, and—swooping between the pointed edges of both spear and sword—struck Assumpta in the chest, scratching her with its claws and knocking her to the ground. Screaming, she fell on her back, the wind knocked from her—her scream abruptly silenced—nearly scattering her circle of protectors.

The demon landed harmlessly to the side, skittering across the stone.

The nearest soldier raised his spear and gored it. The creature howled, but tore free and righted itself, then took to the air again, dodging the soldiers' spears and getting away.

Assumpta's protectors regrouped around her as she caught her breath and scrambled to her knees. Her chest hurt, but the scratches were minimal.

"Get the coin!" Assumpta heard The Big Guy yell.

The rest of the demons attacked. Only, it was more than six, *way more than six*, that attacked. In the blink of an eye, a legion of demon warriors swarmed around them. Assumpta tried to make herself as small as possible behind the wall of men protecting her.

The Roman soldiers—as solid as Jak—stepped forward in a checkerboard formation, two in front, three behind, still guarding Assumpta at the sides. Jak stepped forward to join the two and even the forward defenses.

"Stay behind us," Jak growled at Assumpta.

*Of course*, she thought. Did he think her stupid? Although she did feel guilty for not joining in the fight. But what could she do?

Jak swung his spear downward to knock away a small demon attempting to sneak between his legs. He skewered it, red-purple blood bursting from its chest to coat Jak's ankles and knees. It screamed, flapping tiny wings and arms, then it exploded, covering them all with gore.

"Hallelujah!" Saint Michael declared, a small smile brightening his face. "They might not look pretty, but our weapons still have some power in this realm."

Assumpta got to her feet in case she needed to run, but remained crouched. She dragged the coin against the rough-hewn cell floor, sawing it back and forth to file it down.

The Big Guy screamed. His suit flaked off in pieces as if he were being flayed. The human skin peeled like a banana, black blood welling to the surface where his flesh separated from his human form.

The demons surrounded the warriors' circle five deep or more, pressing forward with talons and claws, teeth and wings, trying to get to Assumpta. They varied in shape and size; some walked on two legs, some four. Large and small, flying and slithering, each came with a different advantage to break through their defenses.

Jak stabbed his spear through the spine of a demonic snake whose fangs curled once around its head like ram's horns. It squealed and curled up on itself, the muscled coils nearly pulling the spear from Jak's hands. He hurled the demon away before it could explode.

Seeing its chance, the creature behind the demon-snake stepped forward, swinging a heavily muscled arm at Jak's unprotected mid-section. Talons unfurled at the last moment, scraping across Jak's midriff, sinking through the black T-shirt and into tender flesh, gouging Jak from left hip to right.

"Agh!" he screamed.

"Jak!" Assumpta turned to him.

"Stay back," Jak grunted, falling to one knee. The demon swung again, but Jak blocked it with the haft of his spear.

Saint Michael and one of the Roman soldiers closed in front of Jak, protecting him from further harm. Saint Michael impaled the eager demon through the chest. The demon sprang back, but Saint Michael thrust forward to maintain contact. He shut his eyes, and the demon exploded, raining blood and gore over all of them.

The nearby demons stepped backward, and Saint Michael filled the breech. Demons backed away.

Jak stood, blood dripping from the tears on his belly, and took his place in the ranks just as the ghost soldier to his left fell. Demons swarmed the soldier, dragging him to the rough stone ground, howling and shrieking as they tore him to pieces. His screams of pain were the first sounds Assumpta had heard him utter.

Suddenly, his cries ceased, and a great white light exploded in the midst of the demons, flinging them back. The demons touched by the light screamed in pain and writhed on the ground, helpless. A wisp of white smoke rose upward and was collected by a golden beam dropping down from the ceiling, then disappearing upward into the darkness.

Assumpta crossed herself. *Father, Son, and Holy Ghost*, she thought, sending up a quick prayer for the soul of the fallen soldier.

Their semicircle tightened, pushed together by the press of the demons. Assumpta moved closer to the wall.

She continued to scrape the coin back and forth. The heat rising off the floor singed her knuckles. She could no longer see what was happening to The Big Guy, but could only assume that she continued to wear him down as she wore down the coin.

Something flickered to her left. The winged demon who'd struck her previously flapped its wings and shrieked at her, then swooped through the hole left by the fallen soldier. It pecked at her hands, drawing blood, trying to get at the coin. She grunted, making a fist around the eroded metal to protect it. Blood welled on the top of her right hand, and the wound burned as though doused with acid. Tears flooded her eyes.

Saint Michael lifted his dulled sword toward the creature. He swung, connecting with a glancing blow. Then, he took two steps to the side of the bird-demon and thrust his sword under its left wing. Black ichor gushed from the wound, dripping to the rocky ground and sizzling on impact. The demon squawked and backpedaled, pulling itself off the weapon, watching Saint Michael with worried eyes.

It continued to bleed, sizzling blood pooling next to it on the hewn stone, then running in rivulets across the uneven ground toward Assumpta. Finally, the demon fled, but another came forward to take its place.

The ichor reached Assumpta's feet and sizzled against her shoes, burning through the leather. She stood, scraping the toes of her shoes against the stone floor to get rid of the blood before it burned through to her socks, and backed away from the burning liquid toward the wall. Though she couldn't help feeling that it was a mistake to be this close to it. Where would they go if the demons pressed any harder?

She placed the coin against the wall, and started to shave it down again.

Almost three-quarters of it remained.

"Hurry!" Saint Michael swung his leaden sword at a small, three-headed demon trying to reach Assumpta.

"I'm going as fast as I can," Assumpta said. The heat was making the coin softer, and she was able to fold it in two. She rubbed two edges against the stone, wearing it down faster.

"Give me the coin!" The Big Guy yelled, pushing through the ranks of demons toward her. They deferred, giving way once they realized who he was.

No human part of him remained. Black gore and blood ran in streams from his face and chest. Something dark and curdled oozed from the broken horns protruding from his forehead. He wept red tears from bulging eyes, but his teeth looked shiny and razor sharp. She couldn't bear to look at him. "Remove the mark." Assumpta continued to saw the coin against the wall.

Michael said, "We can't hold them off for much longer."

The Big Guy made a gesture with his right hand, and suddenly, they were doubly surrounded by demons.

Assumpta screamed, the demon mark on her back tightening with the pressure of acknowledging so many demonic creatures. *But, damn it, it itches*, she thought. The itch was so insistent, it burned like fire. Between her back and the wound in her hand, the pain was nearly unbearable. Nearly. *We can make it through this*, she thought. They *would* make it through this.

A cry to her right signaled another of the ghosts overtaken by the barrage of the demons. The bright, white explosion came sooner than the last. Again, she crossed herself and said a quick prayer as the golden beam collected the wisp of smoke.

*There is no way Jak and Michael will be able to fend off this many demons*, she thought.

Suddenly, the ground between Assumpta and her protectors buckled and heaved. A split appeared and molten lava oozed from between the widening gap, creating another river—this one separating her from Jak and Michael. Assumpta pressed her back against the wall, scrubbing the coin against the rough stone even faster.

Sweat pricked on her scalp and poured down her face. The heat rising off the lava river was insufferable. If she moved any closer to it, she thought, it would melt the skin from her bones. The Big Guy laughed, his evil smile punctuated by torn and dangling flesh. Assumpta wondered if he'd caused the fissure to open, or if it were just a natural occurrence in Hell.

"I've got you now," he said, clearly in pain as cuts and rips continued to appear on his flesh. He spread his giant wings, testing them.

Assumpta scraped faster, and lacerations appeared in his wings.

"I love you," Jak said over the din. He didn't look at her, continuing to battle a muscular demon a foot taller than himself. "I want you to know that before I die."

"You are not going to die," she said, as the demon swiped with a fist and hit Jak on the shoulder. "The Big Guy is going to take this mark from my back, and then I'll give him his coin, and we'll go our separate ways."

"He's not going to give in," Jak said, swinging faster to keep up. "It's all about pride. That's why he's in Hell, and not in Heaven."

The Big Guy moved toward them, grimacing in pain, his bloodied smile wide and stiff. A short-handled trident appeared in his clawed and twisted hand, the center blade a good six inches longer—or more— than either of the other two points. And Assumpta knew he was going to kill Saint Michael and Jak before he came for her.

Michael stepped toward him. The Big Guy raised the triple-pointed dagger and thrust at him.

Assumpta looked around. What if she tossed the coin into molten lava river? Would it be destroyed? With her luck, the river would be some kind of demonic catch-all, and everything thrown into it was collected and returned to The Big Guy. She couldn't take the chance.

Jak stabbed an approaching demon in the foot, bending over to hold the spear to the ground, never losing grip even while the larger demon pummeled him in the head and shoulders.

"Come on, come on," she heard Jak mutter.

A moment later, the demon exploded in a shower of black flesh and purple blood. Jak tumbled backward, nearly into the lava stream. But he picked himself up and joined Saint Michael to battle The Big Guy.

Saint Michael swung his sword, and The Big Guy blocked it, caching the blade between the points of his trident. He twisted and ripped the weapon from Saint Michael, tossing it into the flowing lava.

Assumpta sucked in a breath. She continued to saw on the coin, watching as more cuts appeared on The Big Guy's body and bits of his flesh fell off.

Jak stepped forward and speared The Big Guy in the chest. He bellowed as he pulled the spear from between his ribs.

Assumpta shoved the coin into her mouth and chewed hard, ignoring the lingering taste of demon blood and whatever other foulness collected on the floor of Hell and onto the edges of the coin as she'd scraped it. Her lips burned, on fire from the acidic demon blood. Her mouth dried, puckering, as something wicked away the saliva as she chewed.

"Nooooo!" The Big Guy screamed, turning toward her.

Her teeth penetrated the soft metal, but it was worse than chewing the hardest piece of licorice or caramel. She forced it to the front of her mouth, trying to bite off tiny slivers with her front teeth. She swallowed, the edges sharp and bitter without saliva to soften them. She choked the pieces down, her throat scalded and lacerated. Assumpta wondered if the shards of coin would burn a hole through her esophagus and drip out the torn edges of her throat.

This time, the heat from Hell wasn't strong enough to dry her tears. She cried with the pain of it—coughing and gagging—finally swallowing most of the chewed segments.

The Big Guy fell to the ground, writhing, screaming, his demon form having less and less shape as she crunched the coin into bits. She chewed the last portion and swallowed. And The Big Guy was nothing more than a smoldering pile of rot and gore lying on the bank of the molten river.

The remaining demons disappeared, their shrieks and cries vanishing with them. All Assumpta could hear was the flow of the lava river and the occasional burst of steam and rain of molten rock.

Pain filled her belly and she fell to her knees, finding it difficult to breathe.

"Assumpta!" Jak yelled, moving to the edge of the lava river that separated them. But he was too far away and couldn't help her.

She and Jak and Saint Michael stared at each other. "What now?" she asked, gasping out the words.

The ghosts were gone. Then Jak and Saint Michael disappeared, and she was kneeling on the barren, hellish landscape all alone.

The pain in her stomach grew worse, searing, hot and intense.

Then, she was expelled from Hell.

Utter silence filled Patterson Park, except for the sounds of a few late crickets. A chill was in the air. Her labored breath came out in white puffs, and she still felt as though heat singed her skin and dried her face.

Her wet shirt stuck to her chest. Her jeans were soaked with blood and ichor from the floor of Hell. She smelled the odor of burning flesh and the acrid scent of sulfur.

She groaned, and sat down hard on the curb in front of the bas relief of General Casimir Pulaski, clutching her belly.

She realized that Saint Michael had been right about more than the coin. She doubted him—and she'd doubted God—and she was no better off than when she'd started, because up until the moment all the demons disappeared, she'd still felt the itch of the mark on her back.

Clutching her holy medals in her right fist, Assumpta laid her head on her knees, and cried.

# CHAPTER 54

**A** SSUMPTA!"
Assumpta woke with her head in the gutter, her cheek wet with something foul, and more than a taste of blood on her tongue. It was pitch dark, and someone was shoving something hard and flat into her mouth, muttering, "...evil are the things thou profferest, drink thou thy own poison." The words were feminine. The *something* tasted metallic.

*Saint Benedict medal,* Assumpta thought, remembering the inscription.

"Brona?" she asked around the medal, and coughed up blood. The pain in her belly had moved to her ribs and liver, but it had lost the potency of fire. It was simply *everywhere* now. She knew she was going to die.

"Swallow it," Brona said.

Assumpta spit it out. She felt slick, hot blood run down her chin. "Not another."

"You must." Brona shoved the medal past Assumpta's teeth again and covered her mouth with a cool, soft hand. "Please."

Assumpta was too tired to fight. She closed her eyes and swallowed, thankful the inexpensive medal had been smaller than the others. Blood eased it down, even still, sharp edges scraped the back of her throat.

The coin reached her stomach, and the burning ceased. She felt a coolness there, a calming of body—and spirit. Immediately, she felt better, though still exhausted. Assumpta pushed off the curb and stood. She felt a hand at her elbow, helping her up, and Brona suddenly appeared. Assumpta felt an inexplicable joy at seeing her—she could almost smile at the woman.

"Brona?" Assumpta looked her up and down. She had taken on color and substance and looked almost human. "How are you able to leave the library?"

"I'm free at last, thanks to you. I'm moving on."

"I did nothing." Assumpta dusted her pants off as best she could. The toes of her leather shoes were burned through and stained with demon blood. She still smelled sulfur.

"You let me help you. That was the key." Brona shook her head slowly, as if she could hardly believe the logic of it herself. "I'd been trapped in that library for so long, I'd forgotten that my place in life was to help other people. I'm afraid I'd gotten out of the habit of that just before I was killed. When I didn't take the opportunity to pass on when I first died, I guess someone *upstairs* decided to teach me a lesson." She smiled broadly. "Thanks to you, I was able to find my lost calling." She stepped forward and threw her arms around Assumpta. "God has sent you down a stony path, my young friend, but I'm fairly certain that He's given you shoes tough enough to deal with it. Just remember, you're not alone, and you've got at least one friend in Heaven. I'll be praying for you."

She stepped back, hand still on Assumpta's shoulder, and faded into a brilliant light.

# EPILOGUE

I
T'S BEEN SIX WEEKS," GREG SAID, USING A RUBBER
spatula to transfer plain scrambled eggs to a plate. He set it in
front of Assumpta. "Get over it."

*Easy for him to say*, she thought, giving him a baleful look.

"Eat."

She pushed the plate away. "I don't want to eat."

She wasn't hungry. She wasn't anything. She just *was*.

The toast popped. Greg buttered two slices of marbled rye and put
a slice on each of their plates. "You've got to eat. You're going to wither
away to nothing."

"I've been eating. I'm just not hungry right now," Assumpta said.
She nibbled on the edge of the toast, but put it back down on the plate.
It was tasteless, just like everything else in her life right now.

"He's not coming back," Greg said.

She knew that should have hurt. But it didn't. She'd stopped feeling
anything days ago, or was it weeks? Was he *trying* to make her angry?
Assumpta looked at Greg. He seemed more matter-of-fact than
accusing. "I know," she finally said.

And she did know. But it wasn't just Jak. It was a lot of things. She'd
been to Hell, *twice*, and killed off The Big Guy. Yet, she still had her
demon mark. God had removed Jak's mark. Why not hers? It seemed

like a massive failure on God's part. She'd killed a major demon—didn't that count for something? Apparently fighting His fight didn't guarantee a place in Heaven—because if it had, wouldn't God have removed her mark? She wasn't welcome in Heaven as long as she had it.

And yet…she kept replaying the battle in her head. No—not the actual battle—but before the battle, what Saint Michael had said about destroying the coin and freeing him to do His work. She felt like she'd failed some test. And that didn't sit right with her. If only she could figure that part out.

The only person who seemed to have benefited from all this was Brona.

Greg nodded, oblivious to the conversation in her head. "Then take some action. Move forward. You can't sit here and mope all day."

"I know that, too," she said, raising a hand to her limp, greasy hair. "I'll be out of your way in a few days."

He looked stricken. "That's not what I meant." He put down his fork and reached for her hand. "Assumpta, you don't have to leave. I never wanted you to. I just don't like seeing you like this." He paused. "You've accepted that Jak's not coming back. Yes, it's sad. He's been a big piece of your life. But you're still alive, and you need to act like it. Please, don't move out. Lean on me until you've found your feet again."

*Oh, Greg,* she thought. *If only I'd been attracted to you first.* "I have to go. It's better that way."

"Please don't."

She shook her head. "I'll stay until I can find a place," she said, looking around at all Greg's luxury. Staying would be so easy…for a while. He didn't realize it, but she'd be doing him a favor by leaving.

A knock sounded on the door.

"Could it?" Assumpta's eyes widened. Suddenly, she felt buoyant.

"It's *not* Jak," Greg said. "Don't get your hopes up."

"Who else could it be?" Assumpta jumped to her feet and jogged to the door. It was the most energy she'd had in weeks. She floated into the foyer. "Jak's the only person I know who can get past the door downstairs. Your security's too tight."

"It's not him," Greg said, rising. He followed her to the door.

Assumpta pulled the chain out of the slot and unlocked the deadbolt. She swung the door wide open.

Caroline stood there, crying her eyes out.

Assumpta's lighter-than-air feeling disappeared as quickly as it had come. The smile left her face, and she felt her own tears prick her eyes. She felt suddenly weary from it all. She wanted to slowly close the door in Caroline's face and hide away once more. "Caroline, are you all right?"

Caroline stepped forward and flung herself into Assumpta's arms.

"He's gone, Assumpta," Caroline cried. "He's gone, and he's not coming back."

Assumpta patted Caroline's back. She led her to the sofa. "I know, Caroline, I know."

"How do you know?" she asked.

"Because Jak's gone, too." She felt the tears burn behind her eyes as she admitted that.

Caroline stared at her. "But Jak didn't leave you alone and pregnant."

A Blue Collar proposition

A Charm City Darkness Novel

BY

Kelly A. Harmon

## Chapter 1

The demon mark on Assumpta's back itched, and she sat up straight in bed. The harsh glare of a streetlight shone right into her window, making her squint against the brightness. A tower of cardboard moving boxes generated deep shadows into which anything could hide.

"*Goddamnit!*" she shouted, looking around the room. She'd just managed to find the place yesterday, and move in, but she'd been so exhausted she hadn't taken the time to ward the doors and windows.

Ten-thirty p.m. according to the digital clock. She'd fallen into bed a mere half hour ago.

She reached for the holy water she put on the cardboard box serving as a night stand. Father Tony had *tsked* at her irreverence when he saw she used a mustard squirt bottle to hold it, but she refused to give it up until she found something that worked better, but was still compact enough to carry in her purse. She could hit a demon twelve feet away with a good squeeze and keep the water trained on it until its skin started peeling from its body. Sometimes, they exploded—if they hadn't been inoculated by the Big Guy.

Demons kept their distance when she showed them she could do that.

"Show yourself!" she shouted, her heart thumping wildly in her chest. She'd been to Hell and returned, fought two major demons already, but it didn't make her immune to the fear of them—especially when they showed up unannounced on her turf.

"It's just me," said a voice from the hallway. She heard footsteps, and then a head peeked around the doorframe and into the bedroom.

It was the demon, Kenny. He wore Navy Blue Docker pants and shirt and steel-toed boots. His black hair was brushed off his forehead and back, and just curly enough to cause a slight pompadour. All he needed was one of those old-fashioned lunch boxes to look like he was heading to work down at Sparrows Point. Too bad they'd closed the Baltimore steel mill ages ago.

She breathed a sigh of relief, but didn't put down the holy water. She knew this one: he'd been trapped in the urn with Jak for thousands of years, but liked to go around pretending he was from her time. Were the Dockers meant to make her feel akin to him? A demon of her class of people? The blue-collar demon had been trapped in Hell, apparently due more to bad choices than evil ones, but she still didn't trust it.

"What do you want?"

He stepped into the room and put his hands in his pockets, and shrugged. He certainly had the hang-dog look down pat.

"I want you to help me get out Hell," he said.

"Are you kidding me? This couldn't wait until tomorrow?"

She rubbed her forehead, then reached to the night stand for a chopstick she'd used to keep her long, wavy hair in a bun while she'd moved her few things in. She shoved it down the back of her shirt between her shoulder-blades and scratched the demon mark there. *Ah, sweet relief.* But only for a moment. It would continue to itch until the demon went away.

"You might have the place warded up by tomorrow," Kenny said. "I had to get while the getting was good."

"It's not like you can't accost me on any old street," she said, throwing the chopstick at him. "It wouldn't be the first time."

He disappeared and reappeared eighteen inches to the left, the chopstick passing by him. "I couldn't wait."

"Not even a few hours?"

"I hate Hell. It's awful."

"Not my fault."

"Well, it's not mine!"

"We've been over this ground before, Kenny. Now please—" She reached for her pillow and punched it a few times, then laid down. "Get the hell out. I can't help you."

"You've got power," he said. "You can get me out. With your help, and Jak's—"

"Jak's gone!" she snapped, sitting up in bed again. She felt the burn in her eyes and willed the tears not to fall. Her sinuses got all tight. *Jesus Christ.* She would not cry in front of a godforsaken demon.

He looked contrite.

"Sorry. What happened?"

She *so* did not want to discuss this with a demon. *Jak had been ...what? Some kind of fallen angel? A messenger from God?*

*Her lover.*

She'd rescued him from demon imprisonment, gotten herself demon-marked in the process, and fallen in love, despite him being ...*what?* Not a demon. Not a human. Certainly not a ghost. God himself had sent him back to Earth in human form to fight beside her when she challenged the high-ranking demon who owned her mark, and he'd been killed in the process.

Killed? She wasn't certain. But he'd disappeared after the fight— along with Saint Michael. Was he in Heaven now?

"I haven't heard from Jak in months." She gave Kenny an inquisitive look. "Why don't you know that? You guys seem to know everything else."

He shrugged. "I try not to pay attention to what goes on in Hell."

"What?" She threw the covers back and stood up. "You're a demon who resides in Hell. You see what goes on down there all the time." She threw the other chopstick at him, and he dodged it just as easily as the first. "You were the freakin' *message boy* for The Big Guy. How can you not know what's going on down there?"

"I just don't care about it." He shrugged. "It's not like I asked to be there. I don't want to *hang* out. I just want out."

"Of course you do. Like every convicted felon." She held up her hand. "Don't tell me, you're innocent."

"Is anyone completely innocent?"

She couldn't decide if he were being deliberately obtuse to deflect her insult, or if he were asking a serious question.

"Get out," she said. "I don't want to talk about this tonight."

"You can't throw me out. I'll just stay here and jabber, jabber, jabber all night until you decide to talk to me."

"You do that," she said, "and see if I ever raise a finger to help you."

He disappeared in a puff of smoke, with only the lingering scent of sulfur to prove he'd been there.

## ABOUT THE AUTHOR

Kelly A. Harmon was born on the Baltimore Beltway at 120 miles-per-hour in the front seat of a Ford Mustang. In the wee hours of the morning, with rising humidity swamping the day, she took her first breath of H&S-baked bread, the tang of salt air coming off the harbor and the scent of Old Bay wafting from McCormick's. Baltimore was in her blood then, as it is now.

In the intervening years, she's lived all over Maryland, written for local newspapers and beyond, and come home to Baltimore to write her Charm City Darkness series.

When the voices in her head leave her alone, she can be found haunting Enoch Pratt Library, roaming around Canton, or stopping by the Westminster Burying Grounds for a one-sided chat with Edgar Allan Poe.

## AUTHOR'S NOTE

Baltimore has been known as Charm City since the mid-1970s. Lovers of fable will tell you that journalist H.L. Mencken was the first to dub it so (Mencken died in 1956), but it was really the brainchild of four of the leading ad-men in Baltimore, brought together by then-mayor William Donald Schaefer to do something about Baltimore's poor image. (This was a Baltimore before Harbor Place, Oriole Park, or the Ravens.)

It took only five full-page ads in local newspapers, each with a charm bracelet depicted at the bottom, to cement the name "Charm City."

While I strived to be accurate in my description of the city, I'll admit that some of the scenery and locations of Baltimore depicted in the Charm City Darkness series come from the rosy recollections of my childhood. And some do not exist at all: I'm sorry to say that Assumpta's favorite coffee shop, The Charm City Brewery is completely fictitious.

# Novels by Kelly A. Harmon

## Charm City Darkness Series
Stoned in Charm City, #1
A Favor for a Fiend, #2
A Blue Collar Proposition, #3 - *Coming Soon*

## Blood Soup

A girl child must rule or the kingdom will fall, said the prophesy. The stubborn king commits murder to thwart it, but prophesies can be stubborn, too. Which triumphs in this bloody tale?

# Other Stories by Kelly A. Harmon

## Lies

Crippled and bitter, Beresh is ordered to save the life of his queen. But the medicine isn't working, and the magic...well, that's complicated. He needs to craft the proper lie to save her, but time is running out. Can he save the queen's life before the king takes his?

## Sky Lit Bargains

Refusing to become her new brother-in-law's plaything, Sigrid leaves home the day of her twin's wedding. In search of her mother's jewels, she finds more than she bargained for at her Uncle's keep. One set of jewels is as good as another, right, even if she has to fight a wyvern to get them?

## Selk Skin Deep

1967. Vietnam. Not just a Navy SEAL, but a selkie, too. When the bombs start to explode on deck, can Cade Owen save the aircraft carrier the USS Livingstone, and himself, as well?

## The Dragon's Clause

Each year the citizens of San Marino pay tribute to their dragon. Though a contract exists between them, no one has seen the dragon in hundreds of years. They people are certain they're throwing their money away. What happens when the residents renege on their contract with the dragon?

## On the Path

When Tan's soul engine explodes, the half-reincarnated souls flee to the nearby woods. Tan learns the hard way that honoring ancestors and walking the path sometimes conflict. Ghostly ancestors might not stink after three days, but they're a lot harder to throw out with the trash.

## By Morning's Light

Washed up on shore after her family's boat is caught in a storm, Lukia wakes to find her mother dead, and by tribal law, herself evicted from the tribe. Determined to earn her place, she finds a way to exact her revenge and become part of the tribe once more, but is that what she really wants?